PRAISE FOR *THE BLOOD ZODIAC* SERIES

"*The Twins* is a superb offering from Erica Crockett who blew me away with her debut novel, *Chemicals*. She's a rich and unique new voice in the world of fiction."

- David M. Brown, Editor-In-Chief, 5th Dimension Comics

"While Crockett's series maintains a dark and somber atmosphere in dissecting the primal aspects of the labyrinthine human mind, its essence is a vibrant, hopeful energy for those characters who know how to wield their spiritual clout. And that's what makes it special."

- Benton Rooks, author at *Disinfo.com* and *Reality Sandwich*

"The intimate moments that make up our lives are attentively reflected in Erica Crockett's novels. The slow burn of character study holds us rapt until we realize Erica has stepped away. Riley and Peach are running the show."

- Jon Keithley, *Mystery House Comics*

BOOKS BY ERICA CROCKETT

Chemicals

The Blood Zodiac Series:

The Ram
The Bull

THE TWINS

CYCLE 3 OF
THE BLOOD ZODIAC

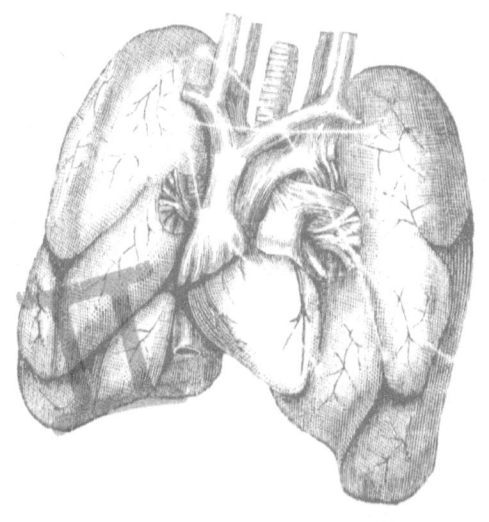

ERICA CROCKETT

Corvid Tear Media

Printed in the United States of America

ISBN 978-1-942300-08-3

First Printing, 2018

Cover Design by Jenny Flint

Published by Corvid Tear Media
Boise, Idaho
www.corvidtearmedia.com

FOR THOSE BORN UNDER THE SIGN OF GEMINI

Arguments, talks, glib conversations left vivid, lingering...so significant, communicating ancient parables.

-   Peach Barrow

FRIDAY, THE 22ND OF MAY, 2015

01   PEACH

The only thing that helps her feverish skin and the angry, pulsating rip in her throat is the flow of fresh, cool air over the tear. She's been homebound the entire week, calling in sick to work, windows flung wide. Peach claims she has the flu, but what she truly has is an infection from her wound. The one she cleaned out with hydrogen peroxide and then tattooed, lifting up the ragged flap of skin and inking the red meat of her muscle. The one she sewed up herself with a bit of fishing line and an embroidery needle. The one Lars Apitz gave her before she took his life.

And she's paying for it now. Peach refuses to see a doctor. Medical professionals always ask questions, whether or not they stop long enough to really hear the answers. Perhaps she would slip up and announce her latest work for the masters of Taurus. Maybe the doctor would be perceptive and meddling and she would be at a disadvantage.

So she relies on expired minocycline capsules she'd received to treat a mild case of rosacea years ago. There is a handful left in the medicine cabinet. She downs one now—sans water, grimacing at the pain that follows the pill as it traverses her throat—and irrationally hopes an antibiotic meant for a skin problem will keep her body from dying of a possible blood infection.

Peach knows the fever is clouding her judgment. Thoughts hop about in the depths of her mind, unbidden and unlinked. She thinks of the taste of persimmons and whether or not she likes the mellow flavor. She realizes when people call on the strength of Jesus Christ, they reference him as a man or a baby but never a prepubescent boy. She momentarily thinks that killing Lars, throwing a homemade lance through his neck, wasn't the right thing to do. If it had been, she wouldn't have been so injured herself.

But the signs had been there. The signs of the Apis Bull. And soon, she's contemplating a series of interlacing memories. She recalls the sight of monarch butterflies on stands of pale green milkweed each summer of her childhood. No matter what home she was in at the time, or who was fostering her, she could trust in seeing the orange and black of delicate wings folded like steepled hands on the bumpy pods. And when they'd take to the air, Peach would hope they would land on her hair. Her locks matched the white of the milkweed seed silk. Those wispy carriers of new life would happily mingle with her tresses. But the butterflies never did.

And now most of the milkweed is gone, a victim of Boise urbanization; summers are bereft of it, along with the monarchs. Peach reaches her arms out to her sides and imagines they are wings coated with fine dust. Floating from her bathroom out into her living room, she searches for an open pistil or the scent of milky sap. But then her arms drop and she realizes she is only a woman, one with a damaged neck. She halts her flying and the living room becomes a living room again, no longer an expanse of pasture and wildflowers in hues of red and yellow. She folds up into a ball on the carpet and shuts her eyes, playing at being a pupa instead. Her form is changing, soft matter developing crusty, translucent armor, antennae wiggling forth to mature and seek out succor.

She needs to rest in order to transform, but sleep does not claim her. She's too hot and feverish for it. Instead of waiting for the eventual descent into nightmares, she yearns to go outside. The cool air will envelop her body—whether it's in the form of a human, caterpillar, butterfly, or something else entirely.

So she opens her eyes. The veneer of metamorphosis falls away.

And she sees Riley standing next to her, where her feet tuck up next to her bottom.

"You shouldn't be here," she mumbles to him.

He smiles and offers her a hand up. Now Peach's eyes feel like leaden balls, shot for muskets, and she blinks hard to encourage them to stay in their sockets and not fall to the carpet. She takes Riley's hand and stands. He leads her outside.

On the porch, his legs brush past the coral impatiens in their sage-green pot. Peach tries to focus on Riley, but his form is shimmery; he's an undulation of condensed light, but this alone does not tell her that she is hallucinating.

"I want to give you something. I want you to get something," he says.

Riley leads Peach from her apartment out to the grassy common area. The specter of Riley walks with long strides while she lifts her chin to the sky. A breeze licks the bandage splayed across her throat. Another man stands yards away from them watching the stars, though Peach believes it to be morning and the stars should be hidden by the bold luminescence of the sun. His light hair is a halo of white under the bright moon, his shoulders firm and square, his feet anchored to the ground.

The gossamer Riley leads Peach to the man and taps him on the shoulder. He turns and Peach sees this man is also Riley. Or looks like him. Two Rileys. Twins.

This Riley is less ethereal. Peach notices once she is next to him he wears a decidedly-feminine top stretched tightly across his pectorals and high-waisted, cropped shorts. The trio is an odd spectrum of gender display, standing under the light of the Milky Way.

Air lifts the short hair on her scalp, caresses her shoulders, runs against her bare legs and tickles her nose. She closes her eyes and when she opens them, both Rileys are still at her side, their faces pointed up to the heavens. Then the Riley dressed like a woman turns his head toward Peach and speaks. His lips are shiny with gloss and a spray of yellow-gold glitter flares across his eyelids.

"You won't see it coming," the effeminate Riley says to her and then takes Peach in his arms. She sees his skin is free of hair. A white, granular coating clings there, as if he has emerged from an ocean swim and dried in the strong sunlight of noontime. He hugs her so tightly she can feel her body constrict and the surge of blood in her carotid artery lift the gauze bandage around her throat.

"Lars is trying to poison me. Take me with him. Did you see the orange and black wings, Riley? I saw those coming. You're wrong that I won't see it. I've planned for everything."

"Just relax," he tells her and stops his crushing. Peach's feet lift off the ground and her body tilts, hovers horizontally over this Riley's outstretched hands. He places a palm under her back and one under her thighs. She feels like she is learning how to float in water. A fishy, brackish odor makes her mouth salivate.

"I've got you," he says. "Just relax."

"No, me. I've got you," she insists.

Peach floats in nothing more than air. She takes in big gulps of it, unafraid of drowning.

02   RILEY

The man calling himself Aldebaran had given Riley a gift. An object that had relevance in a bygone era he knew nothing about. A handmade, ceramic statue of a bull festooned with different shapes on different body parts. He stayed awake the rest of that night post-delivery, rereading the note on the plain, white paper. The last part, the line beseeching Riley to "get in the fucking game" kept him from shutting his eyes and resting. Riley had no idea what the game could be, and while he only ever played games he felt he could win, this one had no defined rules or strategies. He didn't even know when the game started and stopped. Though he had a feeling Aldebaran and Hamal had passed the starting line long ago.

Riley must catch up.

But his desire to stay physically safe is winning out. He isn't feeling the same bravado he felt when he sought to sleep with Nell or leaned in for a kiss across Mayra's threshold. His youth and his athleticism, his health, his muscle, and his stamina, are not givens anymore. If he leaves his house and has an encounter with the man sending the strange communications, he could lose more than his toes. He feels meek so he hunkers down, takes to wrapping soft blankets around his torso even if he's not cold, drinks cocoa laced with dark rum and finishes boxes of French macarons. Except not the ones flavored like macadamia or fig. He abhors those.

When he's feeling stronger, he rereads the cards, rubs his fingers over the bull statue as if the secrets hidden there are plucked out in braille. He checks the calendar on his phone again, for the fiftieth time this week. He says the date out loud to his home of locked windows and doors and dim lights.

"May 22nd. When the next card comes, I bet it'll be from a star in the Gemini constellation. If so, I'll be right. And then maybe I'll get a notion of the rules this nut has outlined."

Then he scrolls through his call log.

Kristin's number is near the bottom of the list. Riley had called to speak with Tate a few days back and the boy had seemed confused to hear from Riley. Tate asked if it was his birthday or if Riley had seen what he was doing in the bathtub and Riley had said no, that he was just checking in. Then Kristin had snatched back the phone and whispered something about shitting or getting off the pot and how Weiser was still seventy-four miles away from Boise. She did not clarify if the locations were too close or too far apart for her liking.

Above that is Walker's number. His best friend had called to see if Riley wanted to join him and some of the other guys from the firm for a round of bar trivia. Riley was their anchor when it came to card games, actresses from the 20th century, and track and field. When Riley had declined, Walker had made a comment about contacting the police and Riley's questionable mental health, then laughed and hung up.

Double Al's number is above Walker's. He'd left a voicemail, asking if Riley wanted to get some mountain air, inviting him to come up to one of his mining claims near Idaho City. When Riley called him back and told him he wasn't ready for hiking around in the woods quite yet, Double Al had suggested he bring a walking pole and Riley could hang out by Elk Creek while Double Al ran the trommel. But Riley begged off and Double Al didn't contest it.

Next is the number to a local home security and alarm company. Even though finances are tight, the statue of the bull was a threat placed directly outside his front door. He'd called three days ago to set up an in-home consultation. He was prepared to lock his house down and make it hard for the asshole sending him unwanted gifts to get anywhere near the place without being seen.

And the last number on the list is a number he hadn't recognized. Riley let it go to voicemail, paranoid it was his stalker, emboldened enough to start calling to harass him. When Riley had heard the chime signaling a new voicemail, he took a long pull from a bottle of Jameson before listening to the message.

It was the voice of Mayra coming through the ether. She asked how Riley was. She said she was serious about Brigit. Riley assumed she was the short, elfish girlfriend with freckles riding high on her cleavage. His ex-lover did little else to explain her love life, a withholding completely in line with her personality. Riley saved the voicemail, if only to listen to the way her English had just the slight hint of an accent.

He clicks on the voicemail now, again, for the hundredth time. It is the only thing he has checked more in the last week than his phone's calendar. He can hear the slight aspiration of an E sound before the word "special" as Mayra emphatically declares her adoration for her pixie lover. He sits back on his brown leather couch, his home silent, his hand wrapped around the neck of his whiskey bottle. He imagines the way her lips moved to form the words recorded on his phone. When the message ends, he presses to start it again.

His dick grows hard, his heart threatens to break. His left foot, toeless and just beginning to mend, throbs and reminds him no matter how he hides and who he fucks and what he loves, that he will someday die.

03   PEACH

After a time, her feet tilt downward and she's subject to gravity once more. The twin Rileys flank her like overzealous bodyguards. They press in close, one under each of her outspread arms and Peach can feel their energy, their life-force seeping into the skin over her triceps, emanating out from their torsos. Her toes tangle in the long grass and the tiny hairs on her arms stand up straight in the crisp air. She places a palm to her head and understands her wig is missing, though she's sure it had been on her head when she'd curled up on her living room rug. The two men begin to shuffle her around, starting from the center of the lawn. Two partners escorting her in a cryptic dance. They move in a tight, spiraling pattern, as if they're searching for something they can't afford to miss.

The Riley that shimmers, the one that Peach thinks looks like the true Riley, masculine but wounded, keeps his eyes to the stars. He points out a ball of white in the Western sky and when Peach looks to where his finger points, the star begins to take on an orange glow. The effeminate Riley nods his head in agreement.

"Pollux for sure. Pollux it is. Who's Castor? Who's Pollux?"

Then the ghostly Riley returns his attention to Earth as well, looks into Peach's eyes and she stares back, unable to redirect her gaze. They continue to spiral around the grass as if they walk an invisible labyrinth.

The other Riley, dressed in something fashionable for a fifteen-year-old cheerleader, keeps his eyes to the ground. Peach knows this slow spiral, this pattern is meant to find something. And this twin has the job of spying out what they're all looking for.

"Have you seen it yet?" he asks Peach without looking up to her face. Her flesh is heavy and her armpits sore from where the twins put pressure on her form to move her sluggish body along. She gathers her will and breaks her gaze with the Riley made of light and forces her sight downward.

But she sees nothing more than her bare feet and what looks to be the discarded skin of a snake near her toes. And then she's passing the translucent sheath and notes the discarded chitin of a shelled prawn and then the eerie, forgotten casing of a cicada.

"Are these what we're looking for?" she asks.

They answer in tandem voices. "Stop putting those there," they say and tug her onward.

They walk in a tight spiral for ages, one twin with his face to the heavens, the other with his face to the earth, until the Riley in shorts and the yellow, knit top causes them all to stop. He points to the ground with both of his index fingers. Peach looks down and sees nothing.

"You have to open it up, Peach," he tells her. He shakes her arm from around his shoulders and pulls her down to the grass as he drops to a crouch. Her other arm slides away from the stargazing Riley. She balances on the balls of her feet and stares hard at the ground.

"I don't see it," she tells him. Then she feels the twin's hand on the back of her skull, right over her Aries tattoo. He presses her face to the grass and she presses her head against his fingers. She has no desire to kiss the soil.

"I can't open up the world. What do you want me to open?" she pleads with them both.

And then she sees a speck of something metallic. She exhales, the air from her lungs flattening the blades of grass near her mouth. She uses her fingers to pry the material out of the dirt and once she does, the pressure on the top of her neck and lower skull disappears.

The force she'd been exerting against the twin's hand now flings her backward. She lands on carpet, clocking her head sharply on the floor. She looks around. The twins are gone and she can see her body is partially in her bedroom closet, her legs flung over her dark green duffel bag. She can feel a small bump swelling with blood just under her scalp. Her wig has returned, knocked askew but present.

Her right fingers are plunged into the open mouth of a small Ziploc bag. She lifts her hand to her eyes and sees a slick of dull, soft metal near her index finger. The silver runs down her hand like a tear shed in great misery, fat and thick from an unblinking eye. It's what she gathered from the creek at the site of Lars's sacrifice.

Mercury.

SATURDAY, THE 23RD OF MAY, 2015

04 RILEY

He's fondling the statue of the bull in his hands. It's late, past eleven and he's just woken up after spending the afternoon passed out on his couch, equal parts booze and mental exhaustion lulling him into stasis. He runs his fingers over the ceramic and considers the effort it had taken for his stalker to put the animal together. The person was clearly artistic but neither practiced nor professional. The back left leg is slightly longer than the others. And there is something about the bovine's eyes that seem off. It could be their placement on the head or just the spooky lifelessness of a body part meant for sight. If they could witness things, they would see a worn-out man with ratty hair and five days' worth of stubble. He trips himself out for a moment thinking the bull can see him. That what it sees, transfers to the eyes of his stalker. He thinks to break it open, examine it for a tiny camera.

When his phone rings and it's Double Al on the line, he nearly ignores it. Until he considers the time of night. His old boss, his dad's oldest friend, has never called so late. Except for the night after Riley had learned of his parents' deaths and Double Al had finally learned of it, too.

"Double Al," he says the name and puts down the bull on a side table near the couch. He'll decide whether it ought to be smashed after another drink. He can smell the alcohol on his own breath, the stench reflected back to him when he speaks into the phone. Riley yawns wide, stretches the muscles around his mouth and thinks to enunciate to prevent slurring his words.

"Son," is all the big man with the expansive heart says.

"What's happening? Is it something about the truck? Did they find something?"

Riley conjures up the image of the smoking Dodge Ram, its tires sending plumes of black, noxious gas into the April evening air.

Double Al answers in his non sequitur fashion, but Riley notices the slight tremor in his voice. "Do you like pie?"

"Uh, yeah. I probably like cake more. Give me a good Devil's Food and you'll have me batting eyelashes at you forever. For pie, I'll eat a French Silk. Even banana cream."

"I miss apricot pie. My favorite. Though I'd take a slice of sweet potato right now. With real whipped cream. None of that canned nonsense. You know a place we could get some pie like that? Real pie?"

Riley sniffs at his own odorous funk and grins. "It's after eleven. I don't know about pie this late. Probably? But not sure I could drive. If you get my meaning."

He's more comfortable using the excuse of his drinking to explain away why he won't leave his house rather than admit his fear. Especially to Double Al. He'd rather be a lush than a coward.

And that's when his old boss gets to the heart of the matter. "I found a dead man."

"What?" Riley asks into the phone. His voice rises in volume and his eyes lock on the bull statue. "Where? Are you okay?"

"The kid was under an awful lot of rocks. Up the mine shaft on my claim. You know the claim. The one you pulled your first gold from? That one. Dead. Long dead, maybe. I didn't touch him much. I just headed back to Idaho City to get the law."

Riley's mind is foggy, his focus weak. But he can hear the confusion in his friend's voice and he wants to help.

"Do you need me? You could come to my house. I don't have pie but I could run to the gas station and get you one of those mini Hostess deals."

"No, son," Double Al stops him. "I caught some flak from the police. They're jumpy about it. No need for me to pull you into this one like I did the truck. But I had to tell someone. Not every day you find a man's corpse. I'll let you get your sleep."

"You sure? Double Al, there was a body in your mine. This isn't an everyday thing, like you say. Let me do something for you." Riley states and stands. He immediately has to sit back down, his legs wobbly from the whiskey and the shock of yet another bizarre occurrence in his life.

"Guy started out white, but being dead made him white like snow or paper. That's how I spied him from a bit off. Headlamp swiped over where he went down. Like shining the sun on a glacier. Just as cold and still."

"Boulders fell and crushed him? You think that's how he died?"

Double Al dodges the question. "My little foreign dune buggy could barely clear the rocks on the dirt road up to Elk Creek. You believe that? I need a new truck soon. So, son, any suggestions on where I can get some pie? I like my crust flaky, made with Crisco instead of butter."

Riley scours his brain for diners that stay open late and serve desserts. But then he realizes his late-night forays are to seedier places: pubs, strip clubs, the occasional gathering for a game of poker.

"Sorry, no," he finally responds and Double Al huffs, a sound of exhaustion and stress causing the connection to crackle.

"What's a man got to do for a piece of pie at night?"

SUNDAY,
THE 24TH OF MAY,
2015

05   PEACH

The first true warmth of late spring arrives. Peach opens the window in her kitchen and lets the air from outside into her musty apartment. The smell of the lamb still permeates all the furniture and rugs. It's a strong mix of sour milk, musk and dried vegetation. She looks to a small, moveable cart tucked in the corner. The wood is blond, raw and light where Roman worked at it with his molars. The indents remind her of how much she misses the presence of the young beast.

She takes an ice pack from her freezer and presses it against her neck. Her fever broke after the strange hallucination two nights back, and the swelling around her torn throat had subsided to a sliver of puffiness. The coolness on her skin coupled with the warm air makes her body relax a bit. But the wound protests, tender at first, until it goes numb from the ice. She'll be back to counseling on Tuesday, after Memorial Day, so she utilizes the time she has on this Sunday afternoon for her real work.

The baggie of mercury sits on her kitchen table. She plucks it up and squishes the malleable bead of metal around in the Ziploc, keeping her fingers on the outside of the film. She has an idea of why her fever vision led her to the mercury, but she's not completely on board with the developing theory yet. She understands the two Rileys could have been pointing out something about her last kill.

And then she thinks of Lars. The way he found her funny, how he pulled down his pants to show her the moon tattoo on his ass. She had genuinely liked him. And she had killed him and taken his energy all the same. She might have also taken something else from him. But she wasn't sure yet. That was another untested theory.

Peach realizes, as she holds up the bag of mercury to her eyes, she is only partially aware of the grander scheme at play here. While she courses toward the pinnacle of Perfect Peach, she notes she is of service to each zodiac cycle and the masters controlling each span of time. There is a discernable amount of faith at work; she pushes onward without knowing the true extent of future effort and sacrifice between now and the end of things.

"All in due time," she tells herself out loud. "The more I do, the more faith I have in my path, the more I'll understand."

She moves into her bedroom and sits down on the edge of her bed. The burner flip phone she'd used to contact Lars sits tucked behind her lamp. She knows she has to discard it soon, her fever and sickness keeping her from doing so many important things. And then she looks to her bloodstone pendant and her pink sapphire ring also sitting on her bedside table. She picks them up, one in each palm, and laments the time lost in finding the next stone.

"My friends," she speaks to them and then swings her legs onto her unmade bed. She places the jewelry on her belly, right above the place where she can gather and concentrate all her energy. Peach reaches over and opens up the drawer of her nightstand and produces her teal, Moleskine notebook. The tip of the vivid pink feather peeks out from between the pages and she plucks it up, twirls it between her fingers and sets it on her belly as well before thumbing through her book.

She has several names to choose from. But after what happened with Lars, both in terms of her closeness to the sacrifice and physical harm to herself, Peach needs an easier mark this time around. None of the names speak to her. She flips through the pages and tries to clear her mind. Still no inkling.

Then a small whisper of wind lifts a page corner. The paper peels up for an instant and then falls back. If Peach hadn't been watching, she would have missed it entirely. She considers the temperate breeze moving in from the kitchen window, finding her supine in her bed, and she knows there is intelligence behind it. There is no trajectory carrying it to her room except for a course it has set itself. She does not feel it caressing her skin or swishing her drapes. It only touches the book, once, and then it is gone.

Peach focuses on the page the little gust lifted and she runs a finger over the name she finds inked on the paper.

"Wouldn't have guessed it, but then, I've already admitted my ignorance," she says. "Thank you, Air. I value your undoubtedly wise vote."

06   RILEY

The first time he leaves his house in nearly a week is to
purchase flowers. He decides on two giant chrysanthemums. One
is orange with flares of red near the tips of the petals and the
other sports layered bursts of pale lavender with yellow centers.
Both pots are lined with silver foil and both plants are as big
around as his encircling arms. He snuggles them close to his
chest as if they are toddlers recovered from a bit of play in the
middle of a busy street.

In the Home Depot checkout line he spies a woman he
recognizes but cannot place. He's always been bad with faces
and names, needing several experiences with the same person to
leave a real indelible memory. He also does better with
recollections if he's sober when he stores them away in the
rumpled creases of his brain. Meetings with people at just the
right frequency and with clear mindedness have been rare over
the last year and a half.

He's fairly certain he hasn't slept with her. Her dress is wrinkled, her appearance firmly in the no-fucks-given camp of fashion. She has dark, short hair and she's in her mid-fifties. Her lips are pursed and her skin free from makeup. She holds a large chrysanthemum in her arms as well. She balances it on her knee brought up to the height of her pelvis in order to reach around and scratch at the back of her leg.

The woman notices Riley and feigns a smile before letting her lips tremble slightly. Then her gaze traces the length of the conveyor belt. A few customers standing in front of her wait to pay for their saw blades and air filters. Riley shuffles his weight around on his legs, the flowers growing more unwieldy solely because of his frustration at the slow-moving line. He wonders why he didn't get a cart.

The woman he can't place eyes Riley again. She gives him a little nod with her chin and he can see water well up in her eyes. They shine with moisture and her sadness makes her more attractive to Riley. Fresher, too, as if the eyes belong to a healthy fawn.

"Hello," she says to him, talking over a man standing between them with a screwdriver and a set of leather gloves in his basket.

"Hi," Riley echoes back and waits for her to either blush and clam up or blurt out whatever she feels compelled to share. He can see the restraint on her face, the worry in the line above her eyebrows. She cuts off the waterworks for a moment.

And then he recognizes where she's from. He's used to seeing her in a sitting position, offering up drinks of water, coffee, or the new option of a cranberry-apple juice. Gemstone earrings on, a crisp, ironed blouse buttoned up high over the divot in her neck.

She parts her lips, the potted mum obscuring her torso and the musky petals brushing her chin. "I shouldn't be telling anyone. Not yet. I just…it's so sad."

"Okay," Riley says and motions for the woman to move closer to him. She tells the man with the basket to take her place in line and then steps next to Riley. The tears begin to flow steadily down her cheeks and drip onto the lobed leaves of the large potted plant. He has become a refuge for her emotional display and he instantly regrets paying her any attention. He smiles at the man with the gloves and screwdriver. The man returns a hesitant grin and slips his goods onto the moving belt.

"He was so young!" she says, a bit of a shriek slipping from her mouth. "And with the holiday tomorrow, we'll have to wait until the end of the week to have his memorial. His wife is just beside herself with preparations and grief. He was so young!"

And though Riley knows the financial advising firm he uses has many employees, his gut tells him this secretary in front of him is speaking to him, divulging information, because they both have a relationship with the same person.

"How did Lars die?" he asks.

The woman doesn't answer. She shakes her head and steps in even closer to Riley, her potted mum of creamy white tangling stems with the two in his arms. The woman drops her gaze and stares at the palette of clashing colors until all the people in front of them have long since left and the cashier, a young woman with horn-rimmed glasses, calls for the next customer to come forward and check out. The employee speaks without vim, picks at her nails. The offer of help to whoever needs it a quiet accompaniment to the sobs which seem to originate out of the chrysanthemum blooms and spread out over the hardware store aisles. All the way up to the exposed rafters overhead, flowing over the nests of house sparrows tucked against junctures in the steel struts.

MONDAY, THE 25TH OF MAY, 2015

07 PEACH

There is a tomb for a shoe salesman in the Morris Hill cemetery. It's one of the largest private granite mausoleums standing on the sprawling acreage of Boise's once premier resting place. Peach walks around it twice, touching the rock where the walls come together, the jointing worn smooth by time and weather. The man must have been a Boisean through and through. No Italian marble for his resting place, though he could have afforded it.

Peach tugs at the yellow chiffon scarf at her throat and smiles at Linx.

"All for selling shoes. Mr. Kinney gets an above ground tomb for sliding mules on fat women. With those cold, metal shoe horns. Remember those things?"

Linx shakes his head and shuffles a cellophane-wrapped bouquet of white roses from one elbow bend to the other. "At least he was successful at what he did. Simplot has a less awesome display down in the newer part of the cemetery. Past the groundskeeper's house where the trees are still thin and short. And that man sold potatoes. Lots of them, but they were still just tubers. What's a mule, by the way?"

Peach cringes a bit as her wound acts up, the rubbing of the gauzy fabric enough to irritate the stitches she put in herself. She stares at the name, Kinney, etched into the lintel over the family's tomb and then thinks to seek out the Simplot monument and see it herself. She recalls her time on Simplot Hill, how she gave tribute to the symbol of Taurus, killing off grass with distilled white vinegar to set its shape in the hillside. It was as big as a sizable swimming pool. Now, the grass begins to grow again. She's driven by it lately. The curve of the circle has verdant indents in it, bits of new life leading forays into the dead perimeter. Taurus, intimately connected to Earth, probably doesn't mind.

"A type of shoe. I thought it was obvious from context? They're not made of mule leather, in case you're about to ask that question. Can you imagine us with mausoleums like this? Forever remembered for such…commonness," Peach says and pulls her gaze away from the tomb and smoothes out her dress. It's made of lace the color of Meyer lemon curd.

"I knew it was a shoe. What kind, I'm asking?"

"Ugly?"

Linx laughs. "Instead, we won't be remembered at all. Well, whichever one of us is alive the longest will remember, but other people? Me a restaurant manager, you a LCSW? We'll just go right into the ground. No magnificent tombs for us."

"Yeah?" Peach questions and steps over to Linx to slip an arm in the crook absent flowers. "I don't know if that's true. You feed people really decent spring rolls. And I've got clients who would grieve. What if we do become memorable? What if we even become infamous?"

They walk deeper into the old cemetery, away from the iron gating around the perimeter of the grounds. The pair strolls toward a tight duo of blue spruce trees and a smattering of rose-colored grave markers tipped slightly to their sides, the only headstones to suffer the effects of a mild earthquake all the other memorials withstood without effect.

"Infamy is the bad one, right?" Linx asks as he lifts the store-bought blooms to his nose and takes a long draw of their scent. "Like we've got to turn into assholes with lots of money or marry porn stars and then murder them with knives. Stab them straight through their fake boobs."

Peach lifts an eyebrow and laughs. "Okay, that was vivid. And odd. You're not very good at coming off as hardcore, Linx. Best stick to your meditation cushion. And wait, why do I have to marry a woman?"

"No one would want to marry a dude used to getting paid to have sex. Now who's clueless, Peach?"

"Infamy gets a bad rap. I mean, what about Bonnie and Clyde?"

"Who?"

"Hell," Peach says and explains as they move toward their destination. "You know. Lovers back in the Depression Era. Robbed banks. Ended their affair and their time on earth via a hail of bullets from law enforcement?"

Linx shakes his head, not recognizing the description. "So you want to become a couple and start robbing banks?"

And then the tombstone Linx has been leading them to rests directly in front of them. It's one of the pink granite rectangles. It tilts forward, the names hard to read due to the slant of the etching and the angle of its face to the earth. Linx kneels down and runs his fingers over the names he finds there. He picks a piece of orange lichen from the stone and breaks it apart in his hand before scattering it to the breeze. Peach watches the wind carry away the rust-colored bit of simple life.

No longer focused on infamy, Peach watches Linx tuck the white roses up against the base of the tombstone. He's pouting.

"I didn't meet them. Not even once. And it wasn't that they were already dead when I was growing up. It's just that they were racists."

"Excuse me?" Peach asks and then crouches down to get a look at the names. James Davis. Mavis Davis. Linx's paternal grandparents.

She tries not to laugh. "Mavis Davis? Seriously? Maybe that's why she was racist? I bet she had a healthy amount of anger over her matrimonial name. Good thing you brought them white roses. Otherwise they might come back from the dead and make fun of your eyes."

"Very clever," Linx says and smiles weakly at Peach.

She stands back up and raises her hands in mock defense. He clears his throat and lets loose a smear of phlegm, angling its trajectory away from the tombstone. The spitting isn't done out of disrespect. Just habit.

"These people were the reason my dad wasn't around when I was growing up. They didn't approve. They thought he'd betrayed his race. They thought I'd grow up to be gay. Because I'm small-boned. Crazies."

"So why are we here?" Peach questions and offers Linx a hand up off the sod. He wipes his palms on his slacks and shrugs.

"Because they're the only family I have in town."

"Your last name is Lincoln, not Davis."

"Mom changed her surname when she immigrated to California. Abraham Lincoln was her favorite president to study when she was all about the citizenship test flashcards. When dad shoved off, she had my name changed, too. Good thing I don't look like him."

"Your dad?"

"Nah, tall Mr. Abe. I think he had elftitis."

"He didn't and it's elephantiasis," Peach says.

Her neck begins to burn, more than it has in the past few days, since her hallucinations and the end of her fever. She resists raising a hand to her scarf, having already come this far with Linx without him questioning her accessory choice. Soon the energy center in the depths of her pelvis starts to throb in syncopation to the angry pulsations in her neck.

She looks around the graveyard, spies other families and couples walking the grounds, cleaning graves and pausing under the expansive maple trees to hug and talk. And then she sees him, small in the distance, stepping through the newer part of the cemetery. He wears white trousers and a blue polo and his hair is smoothed back close to his scalp. He carries two plants in his arms and his face is obscured by a set of reflective sunglasses.

But she knows it's him, because her body tells her so.

Riley.

08   RILEY

He does his best not to conjure images of a dead Lars. But the very idea of what he ought not do seeds the idea in his mind. The visuals arrive. The unmarred body of Lars left after a brain aneurism or carbon monoxide poisoning. Struck by a drunk driver, his knees bent back just like a flamingo's legs. Blue from choking on a chunk of stew meat. White from very violent exsanguination.

He never got the story out of the receptionist at the hardware store. She merely sobbed her way through checkout and when he escorted her to her Mini Cooper and opened the door for her—waiting patiently for more information—she wiped the tears from her eyes with a hand smeared with black potting soil and kept silent for five minutes. They stood that way until she mentioned to Riley he should watch the paper for the obituary and memorial information and then she shut herself in the car and peeled away from him, the hem of her long dress trapped in the door, smacking against the plum paint job.

Riley guesses the man was only a few years older than him. He was fit enough to bring down the boar hanging over his door. He had a successful, well-paying job. He doubted it had been suicide. But then, Riley knew enough of status and happiness and how the two states rarely coincided.

He winds his way between the tombstones in Morris Hill Cemetery, careful not to walk directly over the grass in front of or behind the markers. He's always been superstitious about treading over graves and with his luck lately, he doesn't want to tempt Life, the bitch, to torment him more than she already does. He's in the new part of the cemetery, thinly dotted with skinny trees. He walks across the wide, open yards of empty ground between new plots. The area is flanked by a park with plastic swings and brightly-colored equipment, a dog park full of energetic Labradors and dainty Chihuahuas, and the antiquated architecture of Boise's only synagogue. It's the oldest one west of the Mississippi River, moved up to the Bench from downtown when its original location got crowded out by the YMCA and a Subway franchise.

Under a spindly maple he stops and sets down the chrysanthemums next to a smooth, water-etched limestone marker. He recalls the day he put his parents in the earth. It was less than two years prior. It had been freezing and the grave-side service had been cut short by a gale of snow pellets that drove into the collars of coats and the uncovered ears of mourners. Riley and Double Al had been the only ones to stick it out, accompanied by the groundskeeper, a man of fifty-some years and a padded work suit to keep out the bite of cold. The man had apologized to Riley for the weather and Riley, in his sorrowful mire over their death, couldn't fathom why someone would take responsibility for an act of nature. The chaotic, powerful display of the elements weren't under any human's control. He merely stared at the twin coffins in the ground and mumbled what he mumbles now.

"They fell from the sky."

But now, with the warming weather and roughly seventeen months between the packing of soil over their bodies and the inheriting and spending of a good fortune, Riley has little to offer to them aside from flowers and an occasional visit. He wishes his father were alive to help him find his stalker and sue the bastard for harassment and loss of income. He wishes his mother were alive to push him to go back to work, get Mayra in his arms, regain his sense of manhood.

"So many lost chances at communication," he says to their gravestone. He runs a hand over the top of the rock shaped like a large slice of loaf bread. It still gleams except for a spot of bird poop near one of the corners. He spits on the white glob, mumbles "sorry" to the bodies of his parents, and wipes the rock clean with his bare wrist. He puts the lavender mum to the side where his mother is buried and the orange and red one next to his father.

He stands there, pushes his sunglasses off his face and onto his head and thinks of something to say in memory of Will and Claudette Wanner. But all that stews about in his mind is frustration and feelings of abandonment. And though he was a full-grown man when they perished, he's still angry they left him to fly around in that Cessna in western Oregon. High on whatever retirement does to a pair of rich white people, they weren't content to just see the world from the ground, like the rest of humanity. Now, they were grounded for good.

And that's when the ringing reappears in his ear. But this time, unlike after the bomb blast which left him in a world of high-pitched white noise, the ringing is only in his left ear. His right ear is operational so he shakes his head and brings up a hand to cup over his bad ear, pressing in and out with his fleshy palm to suction at the air in the canal.

A couple with two little girls in sundresses walks past Riley. The father lets his gaze linger on Riley while the mother hushes the loud questions pouring from her daughters like the incessant cawing of troublesome crows. Then they move away and Riley does his best to act normal. Until his chest begins to tighten, his breath growing shallow. He feels as if his torso is being covered up by shovelfuls of earth or crushed by rocks. His throat constricts and he considers he might be having an allergic reaction to something, but he recalls no stings, bites and he hasn't eaten anything all day.

When the world starts spinning, when the tombstones look like strange stalactites sent down by the clouds and the blue sky becomes the lawn at his feet, he crumples into a ball and covers his head, pushes on his ringing left ear and gulps for air.

Then the family returns. And the groundskeeper he hasn't seen in over a year is with them. He can hear them assessing the situation as the father tries to pull Riley back to his feet. The little girls have quit their claptrap and stare at Riley in somber quietness.

"I think you're having a panic attack," the man shouts through Riley's covered ears.

And Riley responds, his voice strangely tinny and small when heard through his one good ear.

"But I have nothing to panic about," he lies, sweat now coursing down his spine. "I'm completely fine."

TUESDAY,
THE 26TH OF MAY,
2015

09   PEACH

She finds a potted violet on her desk when she gets back to work. There is no card accompanying it, but she assumes Camille is responsible for the gesture. The morning is young and Peach intends to get caught up on some of the work she's neglected due to her infection and injury. She slides the violet to the corner of her desk and tugs at the neck of her jonquil-colored turtleneck. She's happy, for once, that her office building is kept as cold as a walk-in freezer. Until the heat of summer arrives and the AC unit on the roof will inevitably conk out from overuse in the many office suites throughout the building. But for now, the chilliness makes the knitted collar at her throat bearable.

Her laptop comes alive and she scans her work emails, memos about meetings and suggestions about break room spring cleanings. She shuffles the files on her desk and moans out loud at all the case notes she has yet to write.

Then she clicks open an internet browser and pops up tabs for each of the most popular social media sites. Peach calls to mind the name she had written long ago in her teal notebook, the name Air had chosen to be the next sacrifice.

She types in the person's full name into the four different sites. There is nothing on three of the four and on the fourth, there isn't a perfect match. Instead, another name appears. The woman is located in Boise. But her first name is replaced by two initials. The last name is the one Peach had penned in her book. She clicks on the name and smiles when she sees the woman's profile is public. The name doesn't dissuade her. Many people alter their names on social media. They use nicknames and abbreviations. Or at least that's what Peach has come to expect via her research. She doesn't have her own genuine online presence and she's happy for it. Instead she stalks via fake profiles, all with stock photos of the same woman of murky ethnicity and straight, dark hair smiling grandly out into the world.

Peach scrolls through the latest postings on the woman's page and notices there are several people hoping for the woman's speedy recovery and regained health. There is a flower icon and a sweet missive from someone claiming to be the woman's "bestie." There is another friend mentioning a hospital stay and suggesting to other visitors on her page that physical visits, to the hospital room residing in real physical space, would be much appreciated. Peach marvels in gratitude at the open communication about the woman's health for anyone to see.

"So trusting," she says to the computer screen and then checks out the woman's pictures. She's riding a wave behind a boat on two thin water skis. She's lifting a cocktail, bright yellow, up to a camera-wielding friend in some generic-looking nightclub. Her hands are entangled with a bride dressed in stark white, crinkly taffeta.

And then a picture in the album stops Peach's clicking. She enlarges the photo and stares at it for a time. If Peach is right, if the theory burgeoning in her mind is correct—a theory she's building based on her experiences with sacrificing Roman and Lars— then this woman may supply her with more than just the specific energy she's seeking. The woman's pose in the picture, the hands up under her chin, the sports bra, the calf guards on her legs: these things make Peach hopeful.

Because if the woman is hospitalized, it doesn't matter how tough she used to be. In her current form, she is vulnerable. The intelligent breeze which lifted the page containing this woman's name must agree with Peach; she needs a more docile sacrifice during the cycle of Gemini.

But if her new hypothesis is correct, it must test true with this woman. It now matters to Peach that the woman has skills, something she hadn't considered or *known* to consider with Roman and Lars. Skills Peach has some use for. If Peach can claim the woman's life for Gemini and her own machinations, she might absorb more than the energetic bond between this woman and Riley Wanner. There could be a bonus to her repertoire, a cherry on top of the experience.

Suddenly, she is hungry for strawberry ice cream.

10   RILEY

He buys a local newspaper, something he's never done before, and pulls out the section on obituaries. There is nothing about his deceased financial advisor. He folds up the rest of the paper and tosses it in the recycling bin on the way inside his house, forgetting the conversation he'd had with the librarian named Amelia when he promised to pay more attention to local news. He realizes he could have just checked the internet instead as he locks his front door behind him. Riley rests his body against it for a moment before considering what he'd like to forage from his fridge for breakfast.

Yesterday had been embarrassing to him. Once the father with his family had convinced Riley he was having a panic attack, Riley forced his mind to accept that nothing was happening to him. He was physically sound and soon after, the ringing in his left ear diminished, his ribs relaxed, and his breathing leveled out. The man helped him get off the ground and awkwardly brushed some errant grass and dirt off the front of Riley's trousers. Streaky stains had stayed behind. And his ego had suffered a smack of shame.

Riley had never had a panic attack before. As he presses his body against his front door, he tells himself he'll never have another. He tells himself he's in control of his life and his body. Fear will not break him. This stalker will not come close to taking what remains of his scant happiness.

After dry toast and mushy blueberries, Riley pulls his one remaining work boot out of his coat closet. Its pair is missing, having been cut open and pried off his injured left foot in the emergency room. He spins the boot around in his hands and thinks of buying another pair. They aren't cheap. And after he wrote that three hundred dollar check to Sev, the poet, the protective boyfriend of Nell, he didn't have much in the way of fluid cash. But if he was considering going back to work for Double Al, he'd need boots. Even if he was working in the office or the showroom floor.

He doesn't make a decision. He drapes his lazy form about his living room couches and armchairs like he's a solo participant in a game of musical chairs and takes fitful, quick naps. He watches a golf tournament on ESPN. He picks up his phone and decides there is no one who would want to receive a phone call from him. Mayra comes to mind, but then he decides she might be eating out her girlfriend, unable and unwilling to chat over the phone, and the notion makes him more livid than horny.

In the late afternoon, he opens up his door to pick up his mail tucked under the welcome mat. A card is among the pizza coupons and offers of yard landscaping. Riley doesn't feel dread, just a resigned annoyance. There is no longer the sinking feeling he used to get in his stomach every time a new communication was sent to him.

"At least this one doesn't have a gift from the Pottery Barn of Gaudy Bovines attached to it," he says as he shuts his door and deadbolts it. He takes the card into his den and perches on the edge of his messy desk. The pile of other cards rests next to his thigh.

He checks the front of the card. The handwriting is different from that of Hamal or Aldebaran. The lines are wispy and the ink disappears only to reappear further into a pen stroke. The wax on the back of the card is yellowish-gold. But this time it is simply a blob of wax. There is no imprint in its brittle surface. No return address, as usual, but he does note that the inked cancelation across the stamp has an origination point of Boise. Riley hadn't paid attention to this information before, dumbly chucking the envelopes and stashing the cards instead. This time he keeps the envelope after ripping open the side and sliding the card from its wrapping.

"What am I in for now?" he murmurs and he scans the scene of billowing clouds, cumulus, in shades of white and gray. The front type reads: On the passing of a loved one…

The inside of the card finishes: May their life be remembered by their friends and family. Condolences for your loss and warm wishes to see you through your mourning.

"Thank you," Riley replies to the text and then runs his eyes over the handwritten message at the bottom. The words are written in all lower-case except for the signature. All punctuation appears as light slashes on the paper.

on memorial day, we recall those we've lost. who have you lost, riley? poor boy. lives might be remembered by you if you decide they matter. but wouldn't it be better to be immortal? i think so. just remember, we all lose someone. some of us just keep on losing people. you're one of them, i think.

in sympathy,
Pollux

He closes it and cups his hands around the cardstock. Riley stares at the picture of the clouds through the chinks of his fingers. The slivers he can see are of their faux-bulk pierced by rays of light. It's an approximation of heaven, he thinks. And he wonders if his parents are there. And then he wonders if he believes in heaven at all. He places the new card on top of his growing pile of communications. Riley leaves the room, shuts the door and walks to his bedroom. He pulls the blinds closed and lies on his belly in the darkened room, focusing on his breathing. The expansion of his chest presses the mattress down slightly.

"Pollux," he says. "I recognize your name from somewhere. But you're no doubt a star in some far off solar system. I'll check on it. But keep in mind the clouds aren't your friends. They obscure your light."

11   PEACH

While she waits for her client to show, she does her best to push out of her mind what she has learned of the woman chosen by Air, her convalescence in the hospital, and her employment before falling ill. She pushes it all away and digs out her paperwork on her next client: the man she had a hard time naming, the one who makes her uncomfortable with his dead-on observations.

"Chacham Brunner," she repeats to herself, until a meek knock sounds at her office door and she stands to open it.

But instead of Chacham, she stares into the goateed face of Michel. His chestnut hair begs for a comb. He sucks in at the sides of his cheeks and the solitary dimple on his right rides the motion like a surfer.

"Your appointment is in an hour, Michel."

The man doesn't move into the room, keeping his position in the hallway. He has something pressed up against the small of his back and he holds it there with both his hands. Peach notices the way his eyes sparkle, mirth and mischievousness present in his mind, playing out on the surface of those dark orbs.

"*Ma chérie*, I know I'm early. But I brought you something. Since you've been ill."

When he produces the item from behind his back, Peach does her best to keep a straight face. It's a small stuffed animal. A frog: its webbed toes splayed wide, with red skin and a smattering of dark dots. It has black glass eyes. It's a fabric farce of an amphibian from some steamy tropical forest. It's a frog that if real, would kill with the poison on its skin.

She considers asking if the gift is to raise her spirit out of the doldrums of sickness. She wonders if he spent his formative years giving baubles to women to ease their troubles. In the past Michel has vocalized his belief that women are fragile, unsuited for the harsh realities of life, of fevers, and of unchivalrous men. But instead of pressing, she puts out her hand and Michel lays the palm-sized frog in her grasp. It's full of beans or plastic beads instead of fishy-smelling innards.

"The frog. You know, the frog, outside the office building? The one you hear when you leave each evening when the weather is warm? The sound you love? I thought you'd like a frog of your own."

Peach wants to ask him how he knows she adores the throaty percussion of the lone frog, but she doesn't get a chance. Her timely client, the one with the strange name, appears behind Michel and stands only inches away from the man's back. He wears a sweater vest despite the temperate weather and his thick-framed glasses sit perched on the end of his nose.

"Michel," Peach says, "my appointment is behind you. He's up now. Why don't you take a seat out in the waiting room or leave and come back? Whatever." Then she holds up the toy to Michel's gaze and smiles. "And thank you for the frog."

Chacham, who was waiting patiently, takes Peach's verbal statement as a cue to enter and pushes past Michel, not bothering to beg pardon. Michel's shoulders inch up and his lips scramble into a sneer.

"Can't wait to get in there, can you?" Michel says as Chacham moves toward the upholstered chair across from Peach's desk.

He turns and levels Michel with a calm countenance. Then he speaks.

"She's not interested in you. And she thinks the animal is a creepy gesture."

Chacham takes a seat. He pulls a toothpick from a tiny metal tube in his pants pocket and places it to the side of his front teeth. Folding his hands, he puts them in his lap and stares at nothing, waiting for Peach to join him for his session.

She can feel the anger radiating off of Michel, her skin prickling in reply. Her admirer maintains his scowl and looks down to where the frog sits in Peach's hand, her fingers open as if she's offering the faux amphibian back to him.

"You like it, don't you?" he asks her, keeping his eyes on Chacham.

"Of course," she says. "Don't let other people's perspectives make you doubt your own, Michel. It was a very nice gesture."

She ultimately has to shut the door to signal that it's time for Michel to leave. Still, she can hear him shuffling around on the other side. His breath is heavy and labored, as if he's just run a race and lost. Eventually his clamor disappears and Peach sits down opposite her client so they can get to work.

Chacham Brunner is just as detail-oriented, just as perceptive as he was the last time they met. They talk about his relationship with his mother, her abuse of him and the effect it had on his schooling and social aptitude. All he shares are generalities, avoiding the kernel of his mother's abuse, staying away from any verbiage associated with feelings or emotions.

His bluntness doesn't apply to statements of past wounds, disappointments or sadness.

"Call me Cham," he says, near the end of their session. "People prefer it. I've learned to accept that."

"Okay, Cham, but you don't need to go by what other people decide to call you," Peach says.

"You didn't have much of a relationship with your mother, did you?" the man ventures and Peach notes another feather, like the one she pulled from his clothing the last time, near the neckline of his vest. This feather is dull green and fluffy near the bottom of the quill.

Peach never knew her mother. Many women throughout the years had encouraged her to call them Mother. Or Mom. Ma. Mommy. She only gave one woman that title, long before Patti came along. Patti had received it as well, but that'd only been because the woman was adamant about the moniker, just not the work involved with the job.

"Let's keep talking about you," she tries to redirect.

"I'm right. Adopted, I'm guessing. Time in the foster system?"

Peach wants to ask him how he knows, but she figures that will just encourage his snooping into her life. So she smiles and asks him about his birds.

"So, parakeets. Or pardon, budgies. Why do you like them so much?"

He switches gears, not clinging to his questioning of Peach. The sliver of wood rolls around the flesh of his lips but his face doesn't betray an emotional connection to his pets. It's a mask of natural aloofness.

"I like the way they preen their feathers and chatter at one another. And their colors: neon green and heather gray and periwinkle blue. Some bright yellow. They're all so individualistic but at the same time a happy collective. The flock is healthy and content when together, whether sleeping on wooden rods or breaking seeds from shells. Simple. Predictable. But fascinating."

Peach nods, blinks heavily. "Do you like how they all get along with one another? How they act like family and are okay with so little?"

"No," he says and leaves it at that.

Her instincts tell her not to press the man. And as much as she believes he yearns to find a group of his own, to not stand out as an eccentric tattle tale, she doesn't care to push him. Her gut, or rather the energetic center in her pelvis tells her he might be a problem.

So when their session is finished and Cham leaves the office, Peach watches him go and spies Michel sprawled across a waiting room chair, giving the man a dirty look as he pushes through the glass office suite door. Peach takes a moment to walk over to Camille's office before dealing with Michel. She knocks, aware her colleague has scheduled paperwork hours and won't be talking with a client.

"Camille," Peach whispers through the door and then puts on a grin when her coworker opens it. Her red hair is curlier than usual, the humidity of a coming thunderstorm making it fluff out in a halo around her scalp.

"You won't believe what one of my clients said this morning," Camille says, launching into a bit of gossip. "She said she had massive ankles when she was pregnant. That they looked like her thighs had slipped down and landed on her feet. And then she says, 'but they really got bad about twelve months into my pregnancy!'"

Camille shakes her head and waits for Peach to comment on the absurdity of the client's statement, but Peach launches into her own agenda instead.

"So I have this client," she starts, "and we aren't really a great fit. I was wondering if you'd consider taking him? We've only had two sessions. We've made little headway. And I'm sure you have an opening, right?"

Peach does her best to look earnest, even a bit desperate. But her coworker isn't biting.

"Did you hear what the lady said? Twelve months! And this woman is raising that poor child. Wow."

"Camille..."

"Can't, girlie," Camille finally says. "Besides, each person we counsel and have a hard time with just makes us better mental health providers. If you can be present, you're halfway there. Those clients help point out our own weaknesses. Just keep your mind objective. Let this person make you a better listener, but don't take the fact you don't click with him personally."

"Right," Peach says, letting her grin disappear. "I'll turn it into a learning experience."

"That's why you come to me, Peach. I'm a sage. Been doing this for eons."

"Or two years longer than me."

Peach hears a noise behind her, a clearing of a throat. She turns to see Michel batting his long lashes at her.

"Are you ready for me?" he asks.

"Not yet," she answers, meaning it, but cloaking her words in a singsong tease. Cham has her shaken but Michel makes her feel safe. A hunch seeds down in her mind. It's an inkling she'll think on, a link between the men.

"But yes," she smiles. "Let's get to work."

12   RILEY

He can't call it a dream. It's not a vision. He feels awake in terms of awareness, but not awake in terms of control over his physical form. His body feels small and weak. And there is no vision except for the vision of deep, encompassing blackness. It's as if his eyelids are shut in a darkened room. His awareness is of nothing more than blackness, stillness, smallness.

And though he'd like to call what he experiences some sort of void, he cannot. Because those sensations of helplessness and enveloping night are there. So there is something. But it isn't the something that encourages or soothes. It eats away at Riley's energy, until he feels like he is part of the darkness, that which hovers very close to the nothingness. Just deep dark watching itself.

He thinks of an obscure philosopher he read about in a college philosophy class. Fridugisus of Tours. He wrote about nothingness being something. He wrote about shadows. Riley wonders if this obscure deacon traveled to a similar world of blackness over a thousand years ago.

The longer he stays in this state, the sharper his awareness of the state becomes. He feels as though he's had his eyelashes superglued to the skin underneath his eyes. Try as he might, the eyelids will not open to let in any sort of light or decipherable sight. So he tells himself that he must be in some sort of sleeping state. One where he cannot force himself back to a world of five senses.

That, or he's dead.

He thinks that when he laid down on his bed, flat on his stomach after receiving the card from Pollux, something could have happened. Perhaps he'd fallen asleep and then had a brain aneurysm? Or Pollux, or Aldebaran, or Hamal snuck in his room, getting past his locked windows and doors and slipped a knife into the back of his neck?

If he is dead, then he doesn't know what comes next. Unless this state *is* what is next. Riley wonders if he could be stuck in a perpetual state of shadows with the inability to sense anything but the black for the rest of eternity.

But even eternity is losing its effect on him, especially since he is starting to lose his concept of time. He can't remember when he entered into this odd sensory stasis, but he doesn't want to focus on when it might end or what might come of it all. Those tendencies toward control, that worry, only make him wonder if time has halted for him or if it will be knowable, traceable once more. It's an exercise in anxiety while he is still in the dark.

If time doesn't return, but the panic grows, then he'll know he's gone to hell.

He does his best to conjure up images of his mother with her wide, round glasses or Mayra in a one-piece bathing suit, the leg-holes cut high, arching over her pelvic bones. But while daydreaming or real dreaming produce some sort of sensations with thought, he still stays in the deep shade. He can try for visualizations, but all he gets are the thoughts accompanied by a black canvas.

Upon relaxing into it, Riley gets rewarded with a sensation of something other than visual darkness. Though his awareness still seems to be one with the gloom, he now feels as though his body stretches infinitely, filling all the space that the darkness fills with its absence of light. Then, this feeling of expansiveness begins to rapidly contract. Riley is a balloon losing air and surface area, until Riley feels as if he is nothing more than a small dot, a prick of black in the wideness of his previous awareness.

And he stays here until he garners another sensation. This one of hearing.

"Open your eyes," a voice commands him. It's feminine, encouraging. The voice sounds like melted butter pours.

So Riley opens his eyes. And he finds his gaze fixed on his white cotton blanket strewn over his down-filled comforter.

He finds himself still alive.

WEDNESDAY, THE 27TH OF MAY, 2015

13   PEACH

She tells herself that she's not looking for his picture. But
she is. The pulpy paper smells of ink as she runs her fingers over
the portrait of Lars accompanying his obituary. She doesn't
come away with any black on her fingers, not like the old ink on
the papers Patti would get delivered to her door every day when
Peach was a teenager. She'd read the comics only, taking in the
lines of the characters and their reset lives. Each series of panels
would put the same characters back in the same situations,
wherein they would behave the same, as always, to comic effect.
Garfield was always grumpy and Odie an imbecile. The children
of *Family Circus* never aged, their precious, precocious
statements on childhood and God predictable and rote. Yet Peach
liked to witness their perpetual rerun. She was never sure what
the comic creators were trying to communicate. Perhaps their job
was merely to entertain by pointing out the replay of life
experiences and the replay of entrenched reactions.

She didn't know then, still doesn't know now. She doesn't read the information about his life. And while she never checked the paper or watched the news spots about Roman's death, Lars had been different. He'd been a person that Old Peach, before the impending metamorphosis, would have been thrilled to date. But to Perfect Peach, he'd been a means to an end.

Peach notes the sharp widow's peak dipping down his forehead and she's suddenly back in the mine shaft with Lars dying, the lance through his neck. The last thing he'd communicated to her was his fear that she'd hurt his wife. That Peach would kill his partner like she had killed him.

His last words were a plea for another life to be spared.

Peach is glad she didn't have to lie to him. His wife would be safe.

The one piece of information she takes note of is the date of the memorial service and wake. This coming Friday. She wonders if the wife will be standing at a pulpit, dabbing at her eyes with a Kleenex while making a speech about Lars. Maybe she'll wear a pantsuit in somber colors. Or maybe she'll decide to commemorate her husband's life with a sexy wrap dress in an explosion of neon-colored floral print.

She folds up the paper and sets it to one side of her old, well-worn writing desk in her living room. Then she cradles her face in her hands, pressing her palms into the bone around her eyes, willing away an unexpected twinge of emotion at seeing her latest sacrifice's picture. Her lips quiver and the muscles in her legs contract. But she can't name it pain, anger, or sadness. Instead she rides out the physicality of the moment until it passes. Then she lifts up her head and looks around her room.

Suddenly, her perception seems altered. Her brain interprets her surroundings differently than usual. It's nothing to cause her dismay; this has been happening since she took steps toward becoming Perfect Peach.

Her couch, a hand-me-down from Linx, is a construct of cracked wicker and flattened pads. But all she can make of it right now is the artistic lines of the fabric and woven wood and how they flow from one texture to another. Before, it had merely been practical and unremarkable.

Then she notes her frugality in keeping the couch. A potted money tree plant in the corner of the room catches her eye. She likes the long, oblong whorls of leaves and the superstition attached to the houseplant for bringing wealth to its owner.

Design, money, art, and her finances: these are not things Old Peach cared for at all. Yet they are notions that support a developing theory. If proven correct, it will be wildly beneficial to Perfect Peach.

Peach sighs and draws her attention back to her desk. She pulls open a little drawer near her thigh, wiggling it to get it unstuck from its track. Shuffling around old Post-it note reminders and rarely-used erasers and highlighters, she seeks out a folded paper map of Idaho.

She opens up the map, pulling it out like an accordion. Then she stands up from her desk so that she can fit the entire map on its surface, smoothing out the stiff wrinkles in the paper. She eyes the areas around Idaho City, wishing that she could travel back up to the claim where she panned for gold with Lars. But she can't risk revisiting a place of sacrifice.

So her eye turns to other places surrounding Boise which might be of benefit. She recalls a trip she took with one of her foster families when she was nearly too young to store away memories. She does recall the smell of some piquant conifer, perhaps cedar, and a building with what she remembers as a box without solid walls perched on its roof.

She scans the map for the location of these memories. Her hand hovers over a county west of Boise: Owyhee County. She knows it to be one of the least inhabited areas of the lower forty-eight states. Yet it's practically overrun with sagebrush and open range. She finds the little dot that represents the town that once thrived there and she puts her pinkie finger on the map, covering it.

"This could be a twofer," she tells herself. "I could kill two birds with one stone."

Then she smiles at the map and takes a yellow highlighter from the drawer. Peach circles her destination.

"Or, rather, use two stones to kill one bird."

FRIDAY, THE 29TH OF MAY, 2015

14 RILEY

The last time he wore a suit was either at his parents'
funeral or his last day at the law firm. He can't remember which
instance it was, but he'd been elated at the prospect of rarely, if
ever, wearing a suit again.

Not even for his maybe-in-the-future wedding. He thinks
now, if he were to ever marry, he'd do it on an island somewhere,
white sand between his toes, all five of them. He fantasizes about
Mayra being the bride, the clause in his parents' will being
waived upon presentation of a marriage license to the estate
lawyers. And then he'd skip off into a happy life. Or stumble,
rather. On account of those missing toes.

But there is a reason such thoughts are fantasies. Today he
wears a suit for Lars's memorial. He looks around the funeral
parlor of a squat building, its walls constructed of various colors
of bricks: maroon, russet, and cream. The parlor is an Art Deco
inspired relic from the late 1920s or 1930s and sits on a corner of
west downtown Boise, near surface parking and hipster bars and

a behemoth corporate building with an atrium of tropical plants buffered by glass, thriving in defiance of Idaho's four seasons.

The parlor is like he remembers it. A wide, square space with small windows near the top of the walls, letting in scant light. Ratty, low-pile carpet and wood-paneled columns occupy the chamber. This isn't the first time he's attended a service in this particular funeral home. When he'd been dating Mayra, her coworker had perished in the field. A brush fire got him, started by his own habit of dangling an American Spirit from his lips while taking soil samples. Dry grass, dropped embers. Then the wind turned against him and whipped the flames his way, setting him alight. An alfalfa farmer had seen the man trying to outrace the combustion of his clothing, the biologist a streak of wildfire against a background of drab brown.

But this time the deceased is someone Riley knew, liked. This time he doesn't have Mayra's hand to hold, the gap between their folding chairs bridged by their entangled fingers.

He checks his phone and notes the service starts in twenty minutes. Then he scans the room for a friendly face, figuring he must know another friend or client of Lars's. But most people are already seated, faces turned away from where Riley stands in the back of the room. He spies the people he assumes are Lars's immediate family. There is a tall woman in her sixties with feathery hair cropped close to her scalp. Her spouse, a man with a dark suit, shirt, and tie, coughs into a white handkerchief so thin Riley can see light filtering through the weave.

There is no coffin in the room, but at the front of the gathering area stands a small, oak podium as rigid and cold as a deacon before a hard sermon. A spray of white lilies arranged around a free-standing, circular form catches the downward current from a ceiling duct and shimmies a bit from the piped in air. The ring of flowers is big enough for a small dog to jump through in some sort of morbid circus act. A square board is propped up on an easel, its contents covered by a velvet cloth in deep burgundy.

Riley is about to take a seat at the back of the room when he feels a hand on his shoulder. He turns toward the pressure, back toward the wide double door entrance into the front room. People cluster in the foyer, as if going into the parlor is something they must resist until they cannot put it off any longer. The mourners are shuffling off light sweaters and shaking hands and exchanging pecks on cheeks.

Double Al's giant hand is as wide as the paw of a wild cat, the meat on his palms calloused and fat.

"Why are you here, son?" Double Al asks Riley, his lips downturned, his eyes red. "I told you to stay away."

"Stay away from what?" Riley asks and shuffles out from underneath the weight of the man's touch. It reminds him too much of the crushing sensation he had during the panic attack at the cemetery. Riley hopes there won't be a repeat today in the funeral home.

"From me," Double Al says, his lips in a slight pout of confusion.

Riley shakes his head and pulls down on his suit jacket. "I don't know what you're talking about, boss. And I didn't know you were one of Lars's clients. Boise's such a small world. Like we're living in some European village and share the same well. Things don't change. They just get...bigger?"

Double Al frowns again, this time the lines across his chin crinkling deeper, longer.

"I don't know him, son. But I told you I don't want you involved in this, not when you were involved with my truck."

And then the realization, the impossible coincidence hits Riley, just as the words leave Double Al's mouth.

"This was the man I found up on the claim buried under all that rock. This boy is the dead boy."

15   PEACH

She wakes at five a.m., before the world is alight with dawn, and gathers all the supplies she'll need for her trip. She packs them away in her dark green duffel, the one with the handle she's become so accustomed to, the grip of the bag molding effortlessly to her fingers. It's her helper, of sorts, insentient but willing to be used. And while Peach understands carrying around the same bag could cause a problem for her in the future, she is nothing if not systematic in her rituals. She considers the fact that repeated systems are what make rituals ritualistic. The duffel is just as important as a warlock's athame or the swinging censer of an orthodox priest.

Once she has all she needs, she heads to complete her paid work. She's surprised at her level of focus, putting aside the idea of the trip to crank out her case notes. The idea of checking Facebook for updates on the hospitalized woman enters her mind, but she pushes it away.

"First things first. Work then play," she tells herself. Peach leaves her office after four hours of concentrated effort to escape into the desert.

The drive puts her west of Boise, outside the encroachment of the city, to the parcels of farmland and rural life the urban beast seeks to consume in its incessant sprawl. She passes dairies, their Holsteins stepping about in dirt and manure, white sections of their hides stained brown. She takes in a deep breath and recalls the way she felt when her bomb went off and she showered Riley with manure. She hadn't even been sure the detonation would work. But it had. Her efforts at research paid off. And now she was here, driving, moving forward. The fact that Riley had been downtown, on the right street at the right moment, that she hadn't known he would be there, made it all the sweeter. It was just another gift from the stars, their backing of her work strong and clear. She was their prize fighter, their ribbon-festooned darling.

She cruises through Kuna, a small bedroom community offering access to great Mexican food and cowgirl-themed bars. At least this is all Peach knows of the place. After this small town, she's passing fields of onions and potatoes. Then she crests a rise and can see the Snake River before her, the Owyhee Mountains a close promise in the background.

She passes through a designated birds of prey conservation area and notes small hawks or falcons perched on many of the telephone poles dotted along the back highway. She's not certain what differentiates a hawk from a falcon or if they are one and the same. A small specimen, young judging by the downy fluff of its belly feathers, rips into a songbird as it turns an eye to assess her passing car. She looks in the rearview mirror and sees something fall from its talons. A mangled wing, perhaps. Or the stripped skull of a being that once crooned and preened.

Murphy—the administrative seat of Owyhee County—is little more than a state office building and a small convenience store. She needs to pee, but she doesn't dare stop and risk being seen. The fewer people aware of her movements the better. So she holds it in and watches the highway slip deeper into steppe populated with the green silver of sagebrush and the white silver of bitterbrush.

Once she reaches a historical marker noting the importance of the area for precious metals, she knows she's found her turnoff. She exits the highway and cruises onto a road leading to the summits of the Owyhees. It's a paved two-lane road until it begins to climb in elevation. Then the road turns to dirt and gravel and her Honda chugs along, the front left tire sinking in a deep puddle before spinning free again. Her car makes a wheezing sound like an untreated asthmatic as it works up the incline.

All the while Peach keeps her eyes vigilant, checking the turns and blind corners of the road, scanning the rock faces she passes. A grouse shoots out of the sagebrush near the road, a bunny hops away from her approaching vehicle. A small flock of chukars glide dangerously close to the Honda's front grille. But it's not until she sees a particular texture to the rock running alongside her car that she stops.

Peach pulls her Honda off to the side of the road. She hasn't passed another soul in miles, certain her decision to come up before the weekend to avoid the ATVers and backpackers was a wise one. She pushes open her door and is greeted with a stiff gust of dust to her face. She coughs but smiles, pulls down her ragged, paint-stained baggy jeans and squats next to her open car door to urinate. She creates a muddy pond which threatens to drown a line of ants she didn't see before she let loose. She begs their pardon as she yanks up her drawers.

When she's buttoned up, she lifts her duffel from her car and eyes the scatter of dark rock. A skiff of volcanic stones dribbles down the side of one of the hills, starkly different than the solid rock reigning on the true peaks of the Owyhees off in the distance. She can access where the ancient lava flow meets the road and she walks over to the rocks, hacking to produce some phlegm in her throat. She spits and sends mucous to the gravel at her feet. She wonders what Patti would think if she could see Peach now, in the desert, spitting like a cowboy or a manual worker or Linx.

The rumble of an approaching vehicle makes Peach stiffen and turn away from her exploration, put her hands on her lumbar and stretch. She is nothing more than a daytripper, taking a break from hours in her car. A gray Ford truck creeps around the bend and a man reminding Peach of an elderly Paul Bunyan tosses a salute her way. She smiles and nods and then drops her gaze down and waits for him to pass. When she looks up at his retreating rig, she notes the back window on his cab has several decals. One stylized head of a buck with many points on his antlers, a stick figure family made of a father and three children, and a golden conifer as tall as a real sapling.

Upon closer inspection of the surrounding geology, she sees that the flow is capping a more solid, quartz-like bank of rock that's been cut through to make way for the road. She runs her fingers along the rock face and doesn't see anything particularly promising—no striations of stone matching what she learned about in a book on Idaho rock hounding. But she decides she must try anyway.

Pulling open her duffel bag, she roots around until she finds a miner's pick. She turns the faux-leather of the handle's grip around in her hands. This pick is new, but it reminds her of her second-hand store find. That other pick had been undoubtedly well-used by some miner or laborer. But Peach determined its final utility when she pressed into the gaping wound in Lars's neck.

"That's enough of him," she admonishes herself, eyeing the rock. "You didn't mope over Roman. Why do it with Lars?"

And she knows the reasoning is because Lars was different. Different because they had a relationship. He meant something to her. And then she feels somewhat embarrassed by the fact that since he meant something to *her,* his life was somehow more difficult to take than that of the tattooist's.

But this is the way of things, not just for her, but for most. In fact, it is a foundational truth upon which her sacred work operates. Relationships have power. They are conduits of energy exchange and transfer. And that flow can be disrupted, rerouted, absconded with.

She shakes her head, clenches her teeth and reminds herself that part of the beauty of sacrifices is that they are, indeed, a sacrifice to take and a sacrifice to give.

Peach swings the pick with a stiff wrist; the first rap of the pick on the rock produces little more than falling dirt and a light scratch on the firm surface. She hits harder the next time, turning her head away from the impact, aware that protective eyeglasses should have been stuffed in her bag and worn to keep her from catching a shard of rock in the eye. She says a prayer to Pollux, her star, and then begs pardon of Earth.

"I know it isn't your time," she says to the stones, soil, and swirling dust. She turns her head to land another blow to the tan rock. "But you helped me last, helped me with Lars. Please help me see my way through what I do now."

The final strike with the pick ends up hitting a weak point in the rock face and a chunk of stone as big as her torso slides away from the hillside, sending a hail of volcanic rocks, pocked and red-hued to land at her feet. Peach looks at the chunk of stone on the ground but does not investigate. Instead she puts her hand into the depression left in the bank and feels around to determine where to hit next.

When she's certain she has the sweet spot, she strikes again. This time, a smaller piece, the size of her closed fist comes away from the vein. She crouches down and plucks it up. The coloring looks promising, the broken face of the rock smoother to her fingertips than what she's been hitting.

To be sure, she spits again, producing saliva just behind her front teeth before releasing it into her hand and onto the chiseled-out piece of stone. Then she rubs the saliva around, cleaning the surface dust, bringing its true nature to light. She sees banding in a creamy yellow and streaks of brown and white.

Her hands are caked in moist mud from her saliva and the dirt, but she smiles at her find and holds the agate up to the sky. She doesn't try to catch its colors with the light. Instead, she holds it up for the currents to caress. She holds it high for the wind to bite it, the air to swirl around its mass.

Unlike her other stones, this one won't be worn. This one will rest in her pocket. She puts it there now, the ancient birthstone for Gemini found, and promises to buy a rock tumbler if she has the time, and see it smoothed and worked to reveal its somber coloring. The frugality of her find strikes her, as does the beautiful swirls of the banana-colored ribs in the rock. Art and finance, beauty and value are once again invading her consciousness, but she pushes them away to focus on a single thought that brings her immense relief.

"No more wax seals going without their imprints for Gemini," she says.

Peach fondles the agate in the pocket of her roughly-worn jeans and walks back to her car, so she can climb higher into the mountains and find what she well and truly needs.

16   RILEY

"You're telling me Lars Apitz was the man you found dead on your mining claim, in the mine shaft?" Riley asks again, for the third time, hoping he's misunderstanding the assertions Double Al continues to make. He feels a bit lightheaded but pinches his eyes shut for a moment before refocusing them on his old boss.

"Son, I wish you hadn't known the man. But yes, he's the kid I found under the rocks and you pretending it ain't so won't change things. That's why I'm here. To pay my respects. I figure if I found him, then I should see him through to the end, so to speak."

Riley motions for Double Al to follow him to a pair of unoccupied chairs at the back of the parlor. A speaker kicks off overhead and Riley only now notices there had been quiet, instrumental music playing all along. With its absence, the room is left to the frequent whispers and an occasional choked-back sob from one of the attendees.

The men sit, Double Al exhaling and wincing as he squats down. He grabs his arm and rubs it before turning his body inward to Riley's.

"You okay?" Riley asks him, trying to focus on what's happening around him to keep away the anxiety brought on by his boss's news. He notes the chill air on the back of his hands, slipping in through the ducts and the outside door that's slightly propped open. There is a small pinch in his intestines, food bunching up before moving through. He watches the way Double Al works his flesh like it's bread dough. Anything to keep him from giving attention to his own chest squeezing in, constricting his lungs.

Double Al winces again and then straightens up in his chair. "It's nothing. Think I just tweaked something when I was lifting those rocks off the man. Had a piece of granite over his spine as big as my belly."

Riley does his best not to think of Lars buried by tons of falling stone. Then he considers his recent panic attack and the way his body felt, as if it were being crushed by mounds of earth or as if all the air was being forcibly removed from his lungs. Could one be starting again, here, in the funeral home? He licks his lips and stares ahead. He tells himself to stay present. There is no danger here. Lars's family is amassing near the front row. A red-headed woman wearing a purple dress and a wide-brimmed, black hat shuffles a set of index cards from one hand to another.

So he tries to switch the topic of conversation for a moment. Riley aims to gain some relief from his impending sense of panic before the bereaved woman launches into anecdotes about life and memories about Lars.

"Any word on your truck?"

Double Al shakes his head and looks to the molding around the ceiling, skirting the line where brick becomes plaster.

"Not on that front. Lab results still a week or two out. But that didn't give me any trouble with the police. Even if the police weren't from Boise."

Riley isn't sure he understands what Double Al is saying, but the man continues. "They were county guys, and could tell I wasn't native Idahoan. Not that you are either, excepting your birth at St. Al's, but white seems to be everywhere now. Hell, my skin color gives me away pretty well. You know, I've only met a handful of black guys and gals born in Boise who don't have refugee parents from Somalia or Congo or some other bit of Africa?"

Double Al's tale continues to bounce around. "But one of the police looked up who I was when I went in to the ranger station on Highway 21, while one of the other men dialed up a Boise coroner to come gather up Mr. Apitz's body. And they gave me the stink eye, son. They might think I had something to do with the truck fire and this man dying. Weird to have double devastation surrounding one person, they no doubt think. Least I'd think it. I was thinking it when I told you not to get your nose in this."

"But you didn't do anything. Lars was buried by rock from a cave in, right? He shouldn't have been in the mine shaft alone."

Double Al grabs at his arm again, near the bicep, and rubs at the muscle. "Thing is, the police are ruling it an accident. They say they found a flake of gold in the man's water bottle. They think he was up there, panning and tinkering, and he hit some loose rock and got himself killed."

Then Double Al gets quiet and leans into Riley. When he speaks again, his volume is low, his eyes shifting around the room, cautious of others hearing what he tells Riley.

"Except I can't figure how his pick got knocked into his neck."

"His what?" Riley says with a start and then checks his own volume. "There was a pick, like a mining pick in his neck?"

"Yep. And those rocks? I didn't see evidence of a cave in. And from what I remember the last time I was up poking around the hard rock, I left a pile of granite back in that long tunnel. My memory is going on me, but if they were there, those boulders could have been stacked up on that man. After he was dead."

Then Double Al turns away from Riley, leans back in his chair until the flimsy metal backing creaks under his weight. He closes his eyes for a moment but keeps kneading at his arm.

Riley watches the woman sidle near the podium, the funeral home director or some other glum man of authority adjusting the microphone jutting up from the wooden surface. It stands erect like a metallic cobra entranced by a reed instrument. The woman is in her late thirties, attractive even without makeup on her face. Her under-eyes are puffy, her nose red and raw from the rubbing of countless tissues. He stares at her and thinks of her sorrow. If Lars's death could be considered murder, Riley thinks, it could mean something to Riley. All the letters and gifts, all the events piling around him like embers in a spent fire. These occurrences were fuel, are fuel or will be fuel. But he doesn't yet understand what's making the whole thing burn.

Then, to avoid thinking of Lars, he imagines the field biologist he and Mayra came to memorialize years ago in the same building. How he must have been a fast, bright bit of fire.

"That pick in his neck. It just seems funny to me," Double Al says up to the ceiling, his eyes still closed. Then he smacks his lips and clears his throat.

"Should have brought my cinnamon bears. I could use something sweet right about now."

17   PEACH

With the agate in her jeans pocket, Peach drives farther into the Owyhee Mountains. She passes free range cattle leading vastly different lives than their milk-heavy relatives back on the dairies. They look up from their foraging on elderberry bushes as she drives by, standing stock still with their nostrils gummed up with snot, their eyes wide and alert. She would have loved to see the bulls a few weeks ago. But her focus has changed, and as she pushes deeper into the mountains, she can feel the element of Earth swallowing her up. She hopes to find what she's looking for and then escape back out to the wide open steppe that seems more sky than earth and take in the power of Air. The element of Gemini.

The road curves and climbs. As she progresses forward, the sagebrush gives way to cedar and pine and spotty stands of white-barked aspen. She passes a turnoff that crosses over a small culvert. Buried in the dry ground are the rusting remains of an old Volkswagen Beetle. Then she cruises by the remains of a wooden building, rot and time pulling it down to the soil like a recumbent lover drawing his partner down for an embrace.

Soon she's near Silver City, the other mining town that made Idaho famous. Except unlike Idaho City, Peach knows nearly nothing about this relic pioneer community. She can see the building she remembers from her youth in the distance. It's a church; the box she recalled being perched on the roof is the belfry. And as much as she would like to drive through the town and see the ghostly ruins of part of America's past, she reminds herself she has precious little time to waste. She makes a promise to herself that she can visit the town again, in the future, once her work is done and she's become what she's always longed to be.

So she hugs another curve in the road and heads along what she believes is Jordan Creek. She spends ten more minutes on the road, driving toward Idaho's border with Oregon, keeping the water on her left. No cars pass her and she hopes for continued isolation. When she sees an obvious bend in the water, she pulls her Honda off the shoulder and parks it next to a massive boulder of granite flecked with silver bits of mica.

Instead of taking her duffel out of the car, she unzips it and pulls the two gold pans from its main compartment. She also removes a set of leather gloves and a pair of fishing waders she found at a thrift shop. Then she moves around to her hatchback and produces a long shovel. Gathering up her tools, she steps her way over brambly, low-growing shrubs to get to the bank of the creek.

Before starting her work, she thinks of the technique Lars taught her over a week ago. She thinks of how it felt to swirl the sand and rock around in the plastic pan. She remembers how to tip out the water while retaining the heavier materials. Then she thinks of Lars's smile and decides she'll have to rely on her scant muscle memory instead of dredging up the past.

She folds her hands together and looks to the sky. It's well past midday and Peach has no idea how many hours or even days her work will take. But she prays all the same to Pollux and thinks of Hamal and Aldebaran for extra fortification, although their times have passed.

"Guide my hands, Pollux. See that our work is done swiftly and well. Let me be you, rather than your twin. Let me be the brightest star, rather than the second in brilliance."

With her prayer complete, Peach wades a few feet into the creek and bends at the waist to shovel rock and silt into one of the pans she's left on the bank. A bit of water splashes on her breasts and she shivers at the icy impact, smells a rank odor akin to fish with some sort of chemical scent underlying it all. Once both pans are full, she wades back to the bank and keeps hold of one of the pans, leaving the other on a soft mound of grass. She crouches and swirls around the contents at the plane where water meets air.

Peach thinks of twins as she pans. She considers the intimate sharing of one mother and one womb and the joint experiences of sounds and sensations coming in from a foreign, outside realm. These experiences must bind twins together, conjoined memories beginning well before birth. She wonders at the undoubtedly surreal experience of looking at another person and seeing oneself, not only in form, but to some extent in personality and in mind. She thinks of her vision, the one with the two Rileys, and recalls how one looked to heaven and the other to earth. As she recollects her experience, she watches the water race by, bolstered by the late spring runoff from the snow pack up near the summit mining pits.

"Twins," she murmurs. "Like nesting dolls doubled up in a larger vessel. Yet one must be bigger, one smaller. One must take more than the other. Nothing is equal or fair when biology rules."

After a time, she notices the pan in her hand has grown lighter. She comes back to the present and notices there is little more than black sand and rough garnet in the bottom of her green plastic device. All the large rocks and waterlogged sticks coated with mud are gone, washed down the stream without any concentrated effort on her part. She's left with the heaviest materials only.

She focuses then, dumping the water carefully from the bottom of the bowl and allowing the smallest bit of fresh water back in. Moving the pan like she would move a small skillet of beaten eggs, waiting for them to set, she causes the sand and garnets to spin away from the heaviest metal in the pan. It's gold, coated in a casing of another heavy metal, this one fluid and lithe. And then she knows she was right to come here.

Mercury.

Peach puts the pan down, making sure it sits level on a mess of pebbles, and shields her eyes to look upward, in the direction of the sun. The other friend she searches for is absent now, just like Pollux, but she feels its pull, its influence just as heavily.

"I guess I understand that saying now. Or perhaps it has new meaning, just for me."

She speaks to the planet nearest the sun. She speaks to the one that shares its namesake with the precious contents in her pan.

"When the planets align..."

18   RILEY

The instrumental music, a lone piano number in a solemn, evocative melody returns over the loudspeakers. The director of the funeral home lords over the front of the large room and clears his throat. People wandering around the rows of chairs hurry to find a seat. The woman sitting directly in front of Riley produces a little plastic baggie stuffed full of pink tissues and as she pulls them from the bag and drops them on her lap, the light scent of a floral talc wafts to Riley's nose. The director waits until all mourners have taken their seats and then he clears his throat again and pulls the velveteen fabric from off the easel.

A portrait of Lars Apitz rests under the fabric. The photo is recent and Lars smiles widely, displaying the gap between his front teeth. Riley doesn't look too long at the photo. His head is a mess, a twisting thing of thoughts about Lars's demise now that Double Al has revealed his own take on whether the man's death was accidental or not.

With a short introduction, the director turns over the slender, bendable mic on the podium to the red-haired woman Riley noted earlier. She smoothes out the wrinkles her dress has gathered from all her sitting and standing and hugging mourners. Then the lady peels the wide-brimmed black hat from her head and places it, a seat-saver, on the folding chair in the front row. Her hair is slicked back into a bun that sits at the nape of her neck. She sniffs, thanks the director and grabs the microphone with one of her hands, causing piercing feedback to rip through the room.

"Sorry," she says, then pulls back her hands and leans awkwardly into the microphone. "I've never been a public speaker. But for Lars, I'll give it my best."

Double Al keeps rubbing at his arm and Riley notices he has a hard time looking at the woman standing behind the podium. Instead, he stares at the floor, at his new Lehigh steel-toe work boots worn underneath a nice pair of navy blue slacks.

The woman goes on, her stack of index cards in front of her on the podium. Her cheeks are a deeper red than her sleek hair.

"Lars was a man of action and passion. I remember one time, when we were first dating, he took me to a shooting range. I'd never touched a gun in my life, but with his wit and that persuasiveness he had I couldn't help but agree to pulling the trigger. And when I ended up putting all my shots in the chest of that shadow of a man on the paper...wow. He was impressed. I thought he'd ask me to marry him on the spot!"

Her retelling gets a small bit of laughter out of the audience and she reaches up and rubs the meat over her cheekbones for a second before moving on. Riley notices the way the ring finger on her left hand looks atrophied between the knuckle and middle joint. He suspects there was a ring there once, but now no longer.

"And as some of you know, Lars didn't just care about his career and financial esteem, which is a rare thing among men in his line of work. He had hobbies and friends. I could rarely pry him away from his ultimate Frisbee tournaments and his autumn hunts. The world for an elk tag, he'd say. And he was always willing to talk with others, to help them become better, to be a supportive part of our community. It all made him a whole man. Whatever I mean by that. I don't know what I mean by it, truly. But it feels right to say."

As much as Riley wants to hear all the woman wants to say, he can't bring himself to focus on her voice. The thought of Lars with a pick in his neck keeps entering his mind. And then his hearing gets fuzzy and all he can see is the man lying still on some cold, gravely mineshaft floor, his blood seeping out of his neck. Could he smell the iron in his blood before losing all his senses? Did he think of scavenging raccoons licking his fingertips or of mutual funds or the sexiest pair of panties this redhead had in her lingerie chest? He wonders if he went to that place of paralyzing blackness after his body sensations were null and his thoughts arrested, to where Riley was stuck for an interminable amount of time the other day.

He forces his mind away from the ghastly image by choosing instead to focus on the positive visual of Lars represented on the easel. He looks over the man more purposefully, another tactic to stay in the moment, and gets a feeling that he's really seeing Lars for the first time. When they had their meetings, Riley was always trying to get something out of Lars, be it financial information, tips on how to gain access to the remaining half of his parents' estate, even small talk about women. But he never really looked at the man's visage.

Not until now. Not until he wasn't physically present. Not until he was dead.

A discernable tremble in the woman's voice causes Riley to hear her again, to tune his ears toward listening, toward accepting new information. His eyes shift back to her, to see her shuffle around the index cards like she's searching for a specific recipe before abandoning them completely. He can tell by the way her eyes tear up that she's off-script, speaking in the moment and from her heart.

"The twenty-sixth of April. Claire, you know it," and she points down with a manicured index finger to the tall woman with the white, cropped hair. "That was his birthday. He had just turned thirty-seven and I jokingly told him that by thirty-eight, he'd have a new girlfriend."

The room is entombed in silence. People look away from the podium, scoot their bottoms around in their chairs.

"Because he was so young still," she says to the room, her hands lifted and cupped, like she's ready to catch a deluge of water and drink from her palms. "And I never wanted anything for him but happiness. That's what we want for our loved ones. Maybe that and a long enough life to find it."

Riley swallows hard, returns his eyes to the picture. There's something about Lars's portrait that bothers him but he can't identify his sense of unease quite yet. He looks directly at the man's eyes, memorialized forever, their light and vivaciousness evident even printed on foam core board.

Then it hits him. He looks at the man's hairline, how it dips down toward the middle of his eyebrows. He's beset with a significant widow's peak, a name made ironic to Riley as he listens to Lars's bereaved spouse flounder with her speech at the podium, overwhelmed with grief.

She says something more about fairness and mortality, but Riley does not hear it. His breath leaves him when his mind locates the source of his apprehension over the portrait. Two disparate images clink together within the folds of his brain and he thinks of the little bull statue, a gift from Aldebaran. He thinks of the strange markings on the ceramic but especially of the one on the head: a white triangle, upturned, the point a sharp arrow down the bovine's elongated face.

19 PEACH

Her hands are numb again, so she pauses to take them out of the frigid water of Jordan Creek. She stands up and stretches at the waist and smells cedar on the air. She looks down to her feet; a small cottage cheese container sits propped against a rock, its inside bottom now silver instead of white. The planet that shares the name of a god and a metal has been good to her. She'll be heading home with what she had hoped she'd find.

The light is dimming, the sun dipping behind War Eagle Mountain. Peach hasn't seen another soul since she set up her worksite on the river. She thought she'd heard a diesel truck heading her direction mid-afternoon, but it must have swerved off somewhere because it never passed her car or left her choking on dust from the spin of its back tires. But as she gathers up her tools now—deciding to call it a successful day and walk back to her car—her ears pick up the sound of an engine in the distance once again.

This time, the sound grows closer until she sees a Chevy truck, white except for a caked spray of mud up the bottom third of the doors. There is black text on one of the doors but she can't read it until the driver slips his vehicle into park and turns off the engine. A man emerges from the truck, a bushy white moustache perched over chapped lips. His skin is weathered and tan from countless days in the field. He wears aviator-style sunglasses and a ball cap on top of scraggly, white hair pulled back into a ponytail. The hat is embroidered with the same letters riding around on his vehicle: BLM.

Peach hopes someone hasn't seen her from a ridge somewhere and called in her mining activities to the authorities. She's about to make up a story on the spot but the ranger speaks first.

"You having car problems or just enjoying the scenery?"

She looks down at the fishing waders still on her legs. They're encrusted with sand and a black stick flush with new spring buds looks to be sprouting out of one of the gaps near her upper thigh. She knows she can't bullshit the official so she doesn't try.

"I was actually playing around in the river. I thought I'd see what the miners working around here had to do all day long. So I bought a pan to put in the water. No luck on gold, though. It's too hard for me. I won't quit my day job," Peach smiles and acts causal as dusk settles around them.

"You're lucky one of the crazy old bastards who have claims up in this area didn't find you. Good thing you're a pretty lady, but they'd likely show you a sidearm if you didn't hustle off the creek when they said to get going. But if you didn't take any gold, they don't have any right to tell you where to be. You're on public land first and foremost."

Peach nods and looks to her car, anxious to cut the conversation short. She's not sure if the ranger just wants to scare her or if she really had been in danger of being approached by some backwoods throwback with gold fever.

"Used to be this area was open to dredges. People would come out here and use motors and hoses to suck up the creek bottom in hopes of finding gold. Good thing about it was they'd get up all the mercury in the water, too. Old timers used it to clean up their fine gold. Gold and mercury," and then he crosses his fingers in an X, "they're best friends. You get a glob of mercury, there's gold inside. I learned that a long time ago. Back when I supervised a mining operation in Africa. Had some gold fever myself."

Then the ranger kicks at a rock at his feet and bends down to pick up a flake of delicate mineral as big as his hand. It looks like it could be a piece of metallic phyllo dough and suddenly Peach is hungry for a piece of baklava. He holds it up and she can see its silver sheen in the last of the day's light.

"This is mica. People who know nothing about precious metals come up here and see it sparkling in the water and think they've found a mother lode. Maybe they have, if they want to make cosmetics."

Then he crushes the mica in his hand. She notices his skin is smooth and unmarred, unusual for a man spending his days patrolling the rangelands. The delicate mineral crumbles into wispy flakes that the wind catches and sends tumbling away to the flowing creek.

"So many different shiny things up here," Peach says because she has nothing else to say.

"Yes, but it's all about understanding what's what. If you don't really know what you're doing, how can you understand how to go about your business? This applies to more than mica and gold. But you're a smart girl. You get it. "

"You have a point there," Peach says and follows with, "and I should be heading back home. Don't want to navigate those bends down out of the mountains in the pitch black."

He opens the door to his truck cab and looks over Peach from head to toe. It's not a leering glance, more of an objective assessing. It makes Peach feel like she is a horse at a livestock auction.

"Make it back safely," he says, his voice taking on a slightly different timbre and quality than before. The tone is no nonsense, bold. "You have work to do."

"I do," she says, not sure why she says it. Even if it is true.

The ranger nods and rubs at his moustache. "I'm gonna shave this thing tonight. I don't care if it's trending or not," he announces, his voice back to the more jovial tempo it held before.

"Last tip. If you see one of those half-feral miners, you keep your distance. Especially from the big fella with the gray Ford. Got a pine tree decal on the window. He talks all kinds of nonsense. Funny guy, but can scare the mercury off of gold when he wants to."

He climbs back up in the driver's seat and gives Peach a half-hearted wave in farewell. Then Peach herself is turning over her engine and heading out of the hills, back toward the wide-open steppe.

Since she's the only car on the road sloping back down to the highway, she rolls down her windows and catches the scent of an impending storm, unafraid to get a face full of whipped up dust or exhaust. The sky is too dark to see the rainclouds. She puts a hand out the window to see if she can feel some drops of water but she comes away dry, her windshield faring a bit better at catching grand plunks of sporadic drops. By the time she's clear of the dominion of the Owyhees, thunder booms loud enough that her driver-side mirror visibly shakes and the sky grows brighter with laces of lightning shooting across the giant expanse.

The meandering herd of cattle has decided to seek the open range as well. While she spent her day on the river, they'd hoofed down the dirt road to the sagebrush sea. She passes by one slow-moving cow, her front bumper coming within ten feet of the animal's flank before she sees it. Now cautious, she slows her car and keeps her eyes wide for the others she can't yet make out. A few hundred yards down the road, she hits her brakes and idles her car.

There, in the hundreds, are a milling, mooing group of cows and steers. Most keep their heads down in the stormy conditions, though rain still doesn't fall in sheets or with any sort of power. But there are one or two brazen bulls, their horns lifted high to the tumultuous air. She can see the herd of bulky and numerous forms undulating like one living mass in front of her.

Peach reaches over to her glove box and pulls it open. Behind her eyes is a tight squeezing, a deep pressure and she knows she needs to get back home before a migraine hits. She wonders if it has to do with the quickly changing air pressure and pinches the bridge of her nose. Then she returns to task, pulling out her teal notebook from the glove box and running her fingers around the edges of the pages, feeling for the feather she's kept there. When she locates it, she pulls it free and can see the pink of its tip, darker in the weak aura of her car's dome light.

She keeps her car running but pushes open her door and steps out into the atmosphere, the ozone so thick she can open her mouth and feel as though she's possessed by the air. She walks a few yards away from her Honda and keeps her chin tilted upward, a raindrop smacking her hard between the eyebrows. The cattle don't spook at her presence. She lifts the feather she took from Cham's sweater weeks ago and holds it up high, its definition lost against the spread of dark charcoal sky punctuated with white fire.

"Gathered during Earth, I now turn it over to you, Air, as an offering of my devotion to you this cycle."

As then she releases the feather, she doesn't see it go, its movement on the wind so swift, the color of night so encompassing. She turns to get back in her car and nudge her way through the herd of cattle which has filled in the space between her and the door with surprising alacrity when a luminescence catches her eye. She stares out over the mass of cows, but sees nothing. Until there, ahead of her a few hundred feet is the upraised head of one of the bulls. Peach notes a bluish-white flame zipping from horn to horn on the bull's head. Then it disappears, only to reappear dancing between the horns of another bull, this one perhaps a quarter of a mile away from her, deep in the sagebrush and dry grass.

"Ah," Peach says to the cattle and to the air. "Castor and Pollux, I never thought I'd see such a sight as you two." And then she pats the rough agate in her pocket and stands for awhile longer, hoping for more of St. Elmo's Fire, known as Castor and Pollux to the civilizations of the ancient Mediterranean. But the two sightings are her only blessings.

20   RILEY

Though he knows no one in Lars's family, he attends the wake in a little Victorian house in Boise's North End. Deviled eggs dusted with paprika are one of the hors d'oeuvres served; a tiny, elderly woman telling all in the house they were Lars's favorite. Riley does his best to stay out of the way until he gets his bearings and can clearly identify which mourners are family or close friends. Because Riley is not at the wake to mourn Lars. He's there to figure out what he looked like undressed.

When he finally gets up enough gumption to speak with a woman he assumes is one of Lars's sisters, he turns up the charm but does his best not to come off as a creep, trying to pick someone up at an event centered around death. He makes small talk with the woman who has the same deep widow's peak as Lars until he can bring himself to segue into more delicate topics.

"So Lars, didn't he have that, uh, thing on his back?"

The sister pops a deviled egg into her mouth and frowns, a bit of crumbly yolk at the corners of her lips. "What, like his birthmark?"

"Yes," and then Riley tests out the theory he hopes is wrong. "Don't you think it looked a little like a bird's wing?"

She stuffs another egg past her front teeth and nods. And that's all Riley needs. He turns white, physically aware of the blood draining from his face and when the sister asks why he's bringing up her deceased brother's skin markings, he retreats from the conversation, begging off to find the nearest bathroom.

In the small water closet, a heater of scented wax makes the darkened bathroom smell like oatmeal cookies. Riley puts the lid down on the toilet and closes his eyes, tells himself it could still be a coincidence. Fifteen minutes later, when a sharp, insistent knock occurs at the door, he turns on the faucet, wets his hands and his forehead and exits the bathroom to the frown of a teenage boy with an eyebrow ring.

Riley tells himself he has to be sure. So he talks to others. A best friend from Lars's college years. His great-uncle, wheelchair-bound. And he gathers information from all the chatting and reminiscing and when he can take no more, he leaves, glad that Double Al had chosen to skip the wake. Riley doesn't want to explain to anyone why he feels nauseated, why sweat beads around his hairline.

When he gets home, he ditches his suit jacket and rushes to the den, where the missives from his stalker are kept. And there, on top of the stack, weighing them all down is the handmade statue of what Aldebaran called the Apis Bull.

He confirms three of the symbols on the piece of ceramic. The deep, white triangle on the bull's head calls to mind the picture of Lars and his graying widow's peak. The bird's wing on the back of the bull matches what he learned of a birthmark on Lars. And lastly, the moon on the animal's flank corresponds with a tattoo Lars's college friend pressed for him to get he was in his early twenties.

The beetle and the hairs he doesn't yet understand.

But Riley decides three out of five is more than coincidence. Three out of five at the very least means correlation. Three out of five might mean that Lars Apitz, financial advisor, husband, outdoorsman, stands in the stead of the Apis Bull.

"And the Apis Bull was sacrificed," Riley whispers and rubs his fingers over the gift.

SATURDAY, THE 30TH OF MAY, 2015

21   PEACH

Though she's exhausted from her time in the Owyhees,
Peach rouses at 3 a.m. and hops on the bike she keeps in a small
closet inside her carport. As she pedals—a new, deep yellow
hoodie on her body, yoga pants on her legs—she enjoys the
silence of the unoccupied night. She passes a few cars but no one
walks about as she cruises through downtown. She lets her
thighs pull and push quickly and then she glides for a bit,
relishing the momentum brought on by her hard work.

When she reaches her destination, she leans her white
cruiser against a hedge of yews taller than a one-story building
and takes quick, light steps up a stairwell, looking around for any
early morning joggers or the unexpected security guard. Sure of
her solitude, she checks her hood. It's still firmly against her
scalp, sans wig, her blond hair nearly an inch long now and in
need of air and time away from her wig cap.

She eyes her canvas, walking around the structure before
beginning her work. She's compelled to do something artistic;

once again the feeling of finding beauty in form and creation rises within her, a new urging that she's beginning to like.

Stuffing her hands in the kangaroo pocket of her new hoodie, she thinks of her old, gray hoodie made of wool. But after she'd pulled strips from the bottom of it, it was unwearable. It's wadded in a ball and tucked behind her dresser in her bedroom and she considers doing something with it soon. Perhaps she will give it to Fire, since it was used for Fire's work.

Out comes a small box of chalk from her pocket. She runs a fingernail under the cardboard flap. Peach produces a thin stick of neon yellow chalk. The kind she remembers from grade school was a mellow hue of butter, unsuitable for her current task. She pauses to recall the feel of those moments she'd be asked to the green-hued blackboard to spell out vocabulary words. Back then, she was far from talkative. She preferred to write, even if it was in front of a classroom full of new pupils each time she was moved from foster home to foster home.

A smear of chalky dust coats her hands. Raising the chalk to the white, smooth surface, she begins to color. Her canvas is old and solid and she hums a three-note melody as she works. When she's used up the entire stick of chalk, she pulls another from the box and continues her coloring, changing white to yellow.

Standing on tiptoes, she can only reach a small portion of her canvas and moves to another section of white when she's spent seven pieces of chalk in one location. But she's diligent in her artistic endeavor, quickly moving through all fifteen sticks of chalk then clapping her hands together to smell the basic, bitter plume of chalk dust as it flows upward, rides her breath, cakes the hairs in her nose.

The only illumination of her work comes from a street light and a pendulous light fixture on the building itself. She skips down the stairs and looks back, trusts that her work is good, if only temporary, and then picks up her bike and begins the journey back home. Dawn is still far off, the air crisp and dry, the thunderstorm she met on the steppes never having made it into Boise proper. She pedals, smiles, has no concern for exerting energy all the way home, uphill.

22 RILEY

The pressure on his chest causes him to wake before the sun
is up, his legs tangled in his cotton sheets, his bandaged foot
throbbing. He bolts upright and places his hands over his lungs.
He does his best to take deep, measured breaths, but his chest
feels like it's bound by straps of leather, pulled tighter with each
exhale and then buckled into place. An impending sense of death
pervades his being. He's convinced of his mortality, convinced
that he's currently dying. He doesn't dare close his eyes. He
thinks that if he does, he'll travel to the same place he was before.
The place of deep black.

He thinks of his mother, then, her hands placed over his
own, willing him to settle his nerves and calm himself. He
imagines that she tells him he's fine, there's nothing wrong with
him other than a bit of anxiety. And drumming up his mother's
visage actually helps. Minutes later, the vice across his chest
loosens and he feels less like he's buried under pounds and
pounds of rocks.

When he's regained his mind and body, he tosses the covers off the bed and thinks of Lars, the man who was actually buried under rocks. Then he thinks of the bull statue, resting in his den. Since he knows he's done with sleep for a good while, he lets himself consider the facts.

This person or people, Hamal, Aldebaran, and now Pollux, might be responsible for Lars's death. The symbols on the bull, Lars's physical traits: the similarities are uncanny. Riley decides that if this person, this degenerate stalker could be capable of setting off a bomb packed with manure or defacing property with astrological signs, could he also be capable of murder?

Then he lets his brain accept it all. He decides to link together all the events that have happened to him over the past three months. He treats them like puzzle pieces: the truck bombing, the sheep with numbers and pictures around their necks, the graffiti on the streets. Could they all belong in the same puzzle box? For now, Riley puts them all in the same pile but refuses to start messing around to see if the curving edges and indents click together. This refusal is fueled by fear, pure and strong.

Then the tattooist comes into his mind, the man's buttoned up collar, his gruff response to Riley's drunken behavior. The man was murdered. That was widely accepted by both the community and the authorities. But until now, Riley had never seriously considered there might be a link between the strange greeting cards and the death of a tattoo artist he'd met only once in his life.

Riley gets out of bed and retrieves his laptop from the den, not wanting to look at it in the same room the cards occupy. They are like rotting fish, moth balls, pictures of ex lovers with propensities to break hearts. So he takes it to his living room and hits the power button. Then he peruses Facebook, typing the man's full name, Roman Saucedo, into the search bar.

The man's profile comes up, a picture of him flashing what looks to be a gang sign at the camera, though Riley allows he's not an expert on hand gestures and crime. But there are other pictures, of concerts with friends and a child's birthday party. Riley scrolls through postings on the man's wall. They are mostly posthumous. People talk about missing his jokes. Others make speculations on whether or not Roman is in heaven or hell in an angry, hurt-and-mourning sort of way. Some simply will him to rest in peace.

Scrolling further down the page, Riley notes people have left birthday messages as well. These were posted before Roman's demise. One message promises an outing to a local brew pub. Another jokes about his march toward his thirties and away from twenties. Then there is picture of a cat in a conical party hat, frown under its whiskers.

It's the birthday wishes that hit Riley the hardest. He checks the age of the man. Twenty-nine. And then he considers the shortened lives of both Roman and Lars. And then he remembers what Lars's wife had brought up during her eulogy. Lars had also just had a birthday.

A thought strikes Riley and he checks the exact date of Roman's birthday: March 30th. He knows that Lars's birthday had been in late April. He tabs open a new browser and types in a search for horoscope parameters. He notes the dates that bookend each cycle of the zodiac.

Roman had been an Aries. Lars had been a Tauran. His past as a lawyer kicks in and he's immediately running through scenarios in his head. Riley wonders if this could be a pattern. Aries comes first in the zodiac procession, then Taurus. Could these men having birthdays close to their dates of death be circumstantial or significant?

Riley calls to mind the last note Aldebaran sent. If he is correct in the connection between the Apis Bull and Lars, then his crazy stalker has effectively laid claim on taking Lars's life.

Someone else surely could have killed the man or it could have truly been an accident. But the letter exists as some sort of evidence to Riley, however weak. Evidence that the man was not merely looking for gold in a mine shaft alone when he was the victim of a cave-in.

Then again, the police have ruled Lars's death an accident and Riley trusts they would have suspected foul play if they had any evidence to assume so. They'd seen the body and the scene and Riley had not. So despite his sense of paranoia concerning Lars and the odd connection between the way the man supposedly died and Riley's new panic attacks, he had to give credence to the idea that Lars's death could have sincerely been an accident.

On the other hand, Roman's death was clearly homicide, but none of the cards had made mention of Roman at all, nor alluded to a planned murder. If the two deaths were in fact linked, the evidence was not there to support it.

But his gut tells him differently. His gut tells him there is significance in the birthdays, one following another. Aries and Taurus. And if his gut is right, Riley knows he can't afford to ignore his two data points. Because though he doesn't have a pattern, he does have instinct.

And instinct coupled with knowledge alerts him to the fact that Gemini is currently happening, number three out of twelve signs. And if there is a developing pattern of birthday boys getting slain, then someone with a birthday in the Gemini cycle is in line for the next bout of slaughter.

Riley holds the laptop in his lap, the heat of the computer causing his thighs to become uncomfortably warm. He closes his eyes and shuts out the brightness of the screen and considers what he should do, how he should proceed.

He hopes he's not right. He hopes the dying won't continue. But then, he'd hoped the cards and notes and gifts would stop. But they had continued, like he suspected they would. Riley's gut screams at him to pay attention, to ferret out more information, to build on these bits of knowledge until they are a web, then a map, and finally a sturdy foundation. Some part of him knows more deaths will be as certain as the communications from his stalker, as certain as his toes never growing back.

SPRING, 2000

23   PEACH

It's the third government building she's tried and the effort has taken up her entire Friday. It's the first time she's ever skipped school and she did her best to mimic a phone call in Patti's voice for the admin office at Boise High School, but even if she fooled the secretary, she would pay in a backlog of homework. And since Patti wouldn't allow Peach to learn to drive, she was dependent on the bus getting her around town. With the spotty transportation schedule, she'd waited an hour and twenty minutes for one transfer, slipping into a frozen yogurt store and getting a kiddie cone, blackberry and vanilla swirl, to keep her occupied.

But this time, this building proves to be the right one. She reads the sign on the door into the office: Child Welfare. She enters, eyes the people reading magazines in pleather-cushioned chairs. The room smells like Clorox and a radio at the front desk pumps out hits from the eighties behind a glass window keeping the masses out and the receptionist in.

Peach considers filing a complaint about her adoptive mother, but she's not here for that. Besides, she's not sure what she would say. Patti's self-absorption, her negligence, her inability to show affection, even if these aspects are provable, they'd likely tell her that she's luckier than most. She has a home and besides, as a sixteen-year-old girl, she is capable of matching Patti's weaknesses point to point.

Instead, Peach has sought out the building for another reason. She's spurred on by the icy reception she receives from Patti each night the woman comes home from her corporate job. She's tired of her situation and she seeks to remedy it.

So Peach decides to find her biological mother.

"I'm Peach Barrow," she tells the receptionist, doing her best not to look the woman seated behind the glass directly in the eyes. "I have an appointment. I'm here to talk to someone about my biological mom. My real mom."

The woman flips through a mess of files scattered across her desk, a bismark donut hanging out of one side of her mouth. She locates Peach's file and waves at her to have a seat. Peach sits, waits, doesn't read and doesn't talk to any of the other people in the room.

When she's called, she pops up and follows a person she assumes is some sort of case worker into an office the size of Patti's walk-in closet. The woman shuts the door once Peach is inside and Peach stands, mute, until the lady urges her to sit.

"I don't bite the friendly ones," the woman tells Peach, but it fails to produce a smile. Peach slides into a folding chair across from a beaten up, metal-framed desk and agonizes over what she'll say to the woman.

"Are you nervous? Because there is nothing for you to be nervous about. You're in a safe environment. That's priority number one for us," the woman smiles, showing stubby little teeth. She has large hoop earrings and a mole above her right eye the size, shape and color of a number two pencil eraser.

"So what can I help you with today, Peach Barrow?"

The woman looks down at the file and her eyebrows lift. "Or rather, wait, Barrow isn't the last name listed here."

Peach finds her voice. "I know. But that's the last name I want to go by."

The caseworker grins and shrugs. "Fair enough for now. Please, what do you need?"

"I was wondering if you could tell me who my mom is. I mean my real mother. Not Patti."

The woman scoots Peach's file away from her and folds her arms, though her face stays placid.

"I can't tell you that information. You're not eighteen yet."

Peach pushes, showing more aggression than she typically displays. "But would you even tell me if I were eighteen? Or are you just trying to put me off?"

Flipping on a small fan clipped to the desk, the woman lifts her brown, shoulder-length hair off her neck and waves a hand, trying to get air across her upper back.

"Hot flashes," she says and Peach doesn't comment because she's not sure she knows what hot flashes are. Patti complains of them constantly, but when Peach asks her questions, she snaps, gets sullen and complains about Peach's youth.

"Here's the thing, Peach Barrow," says the woman. "Sometimes, when women must give up their children for adoption, it's not in the interest of the children or the parents or the state for that matter, to reconnect the biological families. Sometimes files get marked as closed and off-limits, and I'm sorry to say that your mother's file is just that. Shuttered."

Peach finds honesty in her confusion. "Well I wasn't *children*, I was a *child*. And I don't understand what you mean? So my mother didn't want me to find her?"

"I'm not saying that necessarily," the woman hedges and directs the current from the fan onto her face. A long eyebrow hair flicks wildly and Peach stares at its dance. "There are other reasons we don't give out information. Sometimes the woman is, I suppose you could say, not mentally capable of dealing with the stress of a reunion with a child she gave up for adoption."

"So, what, my mom might be crazy?"

The woman lets out a nervous laugh and shakes her head. "I'm not saying that, Peach. I'm just saying that sometimes that's a consideration."

"But you don't know for certain she's not crazy?"

"No," the woman answers, "I don't. But I do know that sometimes people get lost for a good reason. And even if someone, like yourself, comes along and wants to find them, even for the best of reasons, they still don't want to make a connection. I'm sorry to be so honest with you, but there it is."

Peach considers forcing out some tears to help her case. She feels sad, frustrated, but nothing happens in her eyes, no trickle of water or reddening of the whites.

"Then that's what it says in my record? That she doesn't want to ever meet me?"

"Not at all," the woman replies. "It doesn't say that."

"Then what does it say?" Peach huffs.

"I can't tell you that either," the woman says, turns to catch the fan's breeze at the back of her head and lets out a weighty sigh.

FALL, 2011

24   RILEY

"So tell me what got you interested in contract law?"

Riley tells himself not to reach up and pull at the tie around his neck, but his Adam's apple rubs on it roughly when he swallows. As many times as he's rehearsed his answer to this question, and as many times as the bullshit has flown easily past his lips, this time he has a hard time finding the words that will impress, or at the very least placate the partners of Johnses, Mikelson and Rhodes.

He smiles at the two men and one woman, all in their late forties, all staring at Riley, waiting for an answer. The woman, Rhodes, pours herself a glass of water from a delicate glass carafe situated in the middle of the conference table and takes little sips, her other hand on her stomach. Johnses, a lanky man with a foreign accent Riley can't place, flicks the metal lip of a paperclip between his fingers. Mikelson smiles placidly at Riley, his eyes the color of watered-down pea soup.

"Well, I suppose it was in my second year of law school at the University of Idaho. I was helping one of my classmates with her work in the law library. She'd referenced a case I was unfamiliar with, Dawn v. Heinlein, and the nuance of that case, the way Heinlein's lawyer called into question the diction of a sub-paragraph in a real estate contract and winning the case, I was intrigued then and there."

"Wasn't Heinlein a writer?" Rhodes asks, the water in her glass slowing draining away with each small drink.

"Yes, but not this one. This was a house-flipper from Omaha."

"Ah," Johnses nods and asks another question. "You think you would be happy doing this kind of litigation? As you know, it isn't flashy. We don't get airtime on television defending high-profile criminals. Rarely will you be strutting around, proving your case in front of a judge, let alone a jury. Your face will be in books. All day. For a bare minimum of sixty hours a week. What are your thoughts on that?"

He thinks about days spent in a darkened room, NPR on the radio while he digs through cases to find examples of precedent that benefit his firm's clients. Nothing could be more agonizing to Riley. When he was younger, he considered going into law as a way to fund the excesses of life. But then, after spending three years in law school, he knew that even if he could fund the drunken nights, poker games and fun with women, he'd be constrained by his image and his responsibilities. And as much as his father wanted him to be a lawyer, he couldn't see himself practicing law until retirement, to then putt around a golf ball and think of all the time he'd wasted in meaningless, nitpicky work.

"Actually," Riley begins and notes how his voice squeaks. He coughs and continues. "Actually it sounds horrible to me. But my father was adamant I go into law and I, of course, want to make him proud. Just like any son. Besides, I must have a career of some sort. Why not contract law? At least I'll make a decent living."

The partners level him with stares, Rhodes putting down her water glass and pursing her lips.

"Are you saying you don't have a passion for the work? Do you even want this job?" Mikelson pushes.

"Honestly, no." Riley says and then reaches up and loosens the tie around his throat. His muscles relax and he thinks of getting out of the interview, going back to his apartment, lacing up his running shoes and hitting the Foothills trails, his feet slapping against the hilly terrain.

"Okay, well," Johnses says and looks at his partners. They're all seated on the same side of the long, surfboard-shaped table. The other partners nod at Johnses and Riley waits to hear how they'll beg off, tell him that they'll be in touch and then scoot him out of the office with a pat on the shoulder and a wry set of smiles.

He reaches down for his briefcase, a new bag of polished, nutmeg-colored leather. It was a gift from his father. He clutches the handle, ready to leave the room.

"Okay," Johnses repeats. "We'd like to offer you the position."

Riley's fingers fall away from the handle and he shakes his head. "Did you hear what I said to you? About not caring, having no desire for this line of work?"

It's Rhodes who speaks. She has her glass back up to her lips, two fingers of water left in the bottom of the heavy tumbler. He wishes it were vodka and that he could snatch it from her grasp and down it himself.

"We heard you, Mr. Wanner. But we've also heard your father. He very much would like to see you working at this firm. And, as friends of your father, we'd like to make that happen."

"Because of who my father is in the Boise community, I could have said anything today and you would have still hired me?" Riley says, disappointed his honesty didn't produce a pass for him to escape his father's expectations.

"Mr. Wanner," Rhodes pauses for a drink and then grins. "You could have come in here in a two-piece swimsuit, your hair dyed purple, singing the national anthem of France, and you'd still be offered the job."

Riley clutches at his briefcase and brings it up to his lap. "I could say no, still."

"But you won't," Mikelson replies. "So we'll see you bright and early Monday morning."

Riley can't even bring himself to say the "no" let alone live it. He nods slowly, looking down at the conference table. If only there were an ocean swell beneath it, a wave he could ride to another brighter and more beautiful shore.

MONDAY, THE 1ST OF JUNE, 2015

25 PEACH

The elevator doors part, delivering her to the correct hospital floor. Peach pushes past a man clutching a mylar balloon and a basket of vivid yellow roses. She asks him to excuse her and tells him his flowers are beautiful, all the while keeping her face looking downward, her lemon chiffon, gauzy scarf tied around her throat.

When the elevator doors close she walks to a window looking out over the hospital complex and adjusts her scarf. Her wound is healing nicely, but the fabric she's forced to wear each day to hide her neck from others makes her skin feel confined. Coupled with her wig, Peach feels as though her head is encased in a bubble, a shield to hide what she's not yet ready to show the world.

She looks down at the gift bag hanging from her fingers. The words *Get Well Soon* are printed in a bright blue on the green bag, the colors eye-catching and loud. She turns away from the window and walks into the respiratory health ward of St. Luke's hospital, gunning for room number 2015.

As she walks past the nursing stations and visitors there for other patients, she prays she finds the woman alone in her room. Her page on Facebook had continually implored visitations by friends and family and one person was nice enough to advertize not just the room number of the sickly woman, but the times which she was not hassled by medications or doctor rounds. Peach did her best to gauge when she could have the most time alone with the woman, undisturbed by health practitioners and other well-wishers.

No one questions where she's going or whom she's visiting. Most of the nurses are caught up checking charts and weaving in and out of the rooms grouped into clusters of threes in each little wing of the respiratory ward. Orderlies and nursing assistants push around carts laden with food or medications or clean linens.

When she locates the room, she knocks on the door, unsure of what she'll say if someone does come and pull it open. But the room is quiet and she grasps the handle and pushes her way in, closing the door behind her. The woman lies in the hospital bed, long brown hair pooling at the tops of her shoulders, clear breathing tubes up her nose. The thin sheets cling to her legs and Peach can see that she's leggy, more bottom than torso. And luckily for Peach, the woman is sleeping, her eyes sealed tight in the dimmed light of the room smelling of antiseptic and strangely, strawberries.

Peach quietly slips into the small bathroom attached to the room, shutting the door slightly but not latching it. She doesn't make any more noise than necessary. She feels around in the gift bag and pulls out a navy blue scrub top and slips it on over her golden poplin blouse. Then she smoothes down the fabric on the blue slacks she wore for the occasion, checking her pocket for her piece of agate. When she exits the bathroom, she says a quick prayer in her mind to Pollux, her friend she can see each night just after sunset in the western sky.

"Hello," Peach says, "How are you feeling?"

The woman doesn't stir and Peach moves to the bedside, the bag still in hand. She reaches out a hand and touches the woman's cheek, ready to pull back if her eyelids flicker open. But the woman is out, drugged into a state of unconsciousness.

Giddy with her luck, Peach looks around the room, especially near the ceiling, doing her best to check for cameras. She sees none and figures that with most patients hooked to machines, the readings from those monitors are the only alert system the nurses have when something goes wrong with their vitals. This system works perfectly for Peach and she decides serendipity and fate are at play so she can't afford to hesitate now.

She puts the gift bag on the bed and sits down, situating herself so that if there is a camera trained on the woman, it will be filming her back. And if said theoretical footage is silent, it will look as if Peach is carrying on an intimate conversation with the woman, huddled over her reclining form. She reaches into the bag and pulls out an X-ACTO knife in a plastic baggie, its keen edge capped with a plastic sheath. She removes the knife and the cap and presses the tip of the metal into one of the woman's fingers. Peach expects the prick to wake up the woman, but she doesn't stir. Peach watches the blood course down the blade of the knife and waits until enough blood has covered the blade completely. Then she caps the metal and plops the knife back into the bag, sealing it closed.

Peach reaches for a box of tissues near the bed and presses on the tiny cut with one of the rough sheets until the bleeding stops. She notes the calluses on the woman's hands and tiny, white scars on her knuckles, years of lacerations and scrapes building scar-tissue, causing the woman's knuckles to look bigger than they really are. They remind her of aerial pictures of dry, ancient canals found in South America.

Her theory comes to mind but she pushes it away, not willing to waste time on thinking about what might be possible when she has important work to do. She pulls three other items from the bag: a glass jar, a plastic breathing apparatus, and a crème brûlée torch.

This last item had been a wedding gift from one of Adam's relatives, a cousin, and Peach had never used the tiny butane torch. She turns it over in her hands before clicking it on. A blue flame brightens the room.

"I guess I've found its use," she says.

26   RILEY

Riley cannot fathom what makes him so special that he might be connected to two deaths over the last two months. He's spent the past day arguing with himself—telling himself that he's delusional and self-absorbed, more than he ever thought possible—and the deaths of Roman Saucedo and Lars Apitz have nothing to do with him. There is no intimate tie outside of casual acquaintance. He reminds himself, though the city has grown substantially from the time he was child, most longtime residents were interlinked and connected to other Boiseans on a scale both eerie and synchronistic. Riley had drummed up the memories of several odd connections he'd had with other residents of the community in the recent past. The wife of his third-grade teacher walked the same stretch of Greenbelt he used to run when he had all his toes. He'd had sex with more than one set of sisters, unbeknownst to him until after the individual trysts. In this way, he'd almost talked himself out of his potential link to the two deaths as anything past common, mid-sized town interconnectivity.

Until he saw the statue of the bull in his den.

He'd been avoiding the room since his last panic attack. It had made him unable to sleep the rest of that night. But he has to pay his bills, and they're in the den. As he grabs them and his checkbook, thinking briefly of his dwindling fluid funds, the little ceramic statue catches his eye. His gaze lingers over the sharp, white triangle on the beast's forehead. He feels compelled to trace the shape with his fingertip, a bit how he traced the pattern he'd wanted tattooed onto his skin that night it came to him unbidden, over and over on the surface of his guestroom comforter. But instead he leaves it where it sits, weighing down the cards.

After he writes his checks—always a fan of hands-on payment of his debts instead of leaving them to automation—he escapes his house. His fear of going out begins to dissipate under the pressure of an overwhelming need to flee from his incessant, negative thoughts. This is enough: outweighing his fears of panic attacks or his stalker. His first stop takes him somewhere to deal with the roiling in his gut. He gets himself a fresh raspberry shake at a drive-in and sits in his car, downing the thick ice cream and gingerly chewing on the fruit so he doesn't get the teardrop-shaped seeds stuck in his molars.

Then he drives past Mayra's house. He doesn't stop, doesn't consider how he might pry her away from her new girlfriend. He decides he must deal with one mental tumult at a time. He drives by Blaze Lounge and wonders if he'll ever go back into the strip club. He stops at a grocery store on Front Street and buys a bag of salted almonds and ibuprofen and wishes as he swipes his debit card that liquor was sold in Idaho grocery stores.

And when he gets back home, he knows the bull is waiting in the room. And he knows the bull is the link he cannot escape. His outing hasn't caused any new revelations or ways of thinking about the deaths of Roman and Lars. If it weren't for the ceramic gift, he could let it all slide. But the bull is a keening, cutting siren ringing loudly in his mind.

Riley admits to himself he is linked to these deaths, but he doesn't understand how quite yet.

He goes into his den and eyes the elliptical machine. His body tells him to get some exercise, but instead he takes a seat at his desk and digs around for a ream of lined paper in a drawer near his thigh. When he finds it, he pulls a few sheets free from the plastic wrapping and sharpens a pencil.

He allows himself to look at the bull, keeping one hand palm down on the desk, the other with the pencil raised, ready. The creation is odd, ugly. And he feels a wave of revulsion cascade along his spine and nestle in his belly. He thinks to pick it up and smash it against the edge of the wooden desk. Why he doesn't reduce the thing to shards, he can't say. A force seems to keep his anger in check, his mind on a more important task than destruction.

Salvation.

His eyes drop to the white spaces between the blue lines on the paper. He could fill them with anything, any story, any emotional bit of written communication. But what needs to go there, what's *right* for the pages, is ready to seep out of him and take the form of words.

It's time to face his fear by giving it not one name, but many. Riley takes a deep breath and touches the graphite to the blank page, ready to write down the names of everyone he's ever known.

TUESDAY, THE 2ND OF JUNE, 2015

27   PEACH

She has a bottle of Chardonnay in her hands and a sleeve of bright orange carrots tucked under her arm. She knocks again at the door and Linx finally answers, Peach shifting her weight from foot to foot under the uncomfortable glare of Linx's gearhead neighbors. Though it's early in the morning, before most people are making their way to work, the three men are outside, working on their racecars, eyeing Peach.

"Let me inside. I feel like I'm about to star as the victim in an urban *Deliverance*," she jokes as she gives Linx an awkward hug with her laden arms. She slinks past him and slips her shoes off in his little foyer.

"What's *Deliverance?*" Linx asks, demonstrating his gaps concerning pop cultural references. Peach can't imagine his tiny, California-based Thai mother letting him watch a man get raped in the backwoods of Georgia, Hollywood-created or no. She wonders if it would be right to expose him. At least he'd be old enough to compartmentalize the disturbing scene.

He forgets his question. "Baba is outside. I finally got that stake tethered in the grass just right so he doesn't get tangled up. Now he can wander wherever."

Peach walks into Linx's kitchen, the smell of ground coriander pungent and sweet in her nose. She can't remember a time she's entered his home without some piquant or lively spice greeting her arrival. She leaves the Chardonnay near his stovetop and waves at it.

"Another gift to thank you for lamb-sitting."

"I wish you'd share it with me," Linx says and moves to check out the label. Peach can see he's pleased, sucking his cheeks tight against his teeth. The effect makes him look even younger than he already does, roaming around in a body seemingly just shy of adolescence.

"And I wish you'd share a cheeseburger with me," Peach says and smiles. "But we can't always get what we want."

Linx takes his gaze away from the bottle and steps close to Peach. He flicks the high-buttoned collar of her lemon-yellow blouse. "Don't you want to undo some of those buttons?"

"No, I'm trying out a new style," she explains and pulls away. "So Baba is grazing?"

Peach nearly calls the lamb Roman, having to constantly remind herself that Linx was given the responsibility of naming the lamb. Or at least naming the animal something they could both speak out loud.

Grabbing her hand, Linx leads Peach to a set of sliding glass doors looking out over his rectangular-shaped backyard. The patchy, pitted lawn is kept in constant shade by a gigantic elm tree. It's a sweet, bucolic scene and she knows it's vastly better than her apartment for the growing animal.

Peach opens the door and calls out to the lamb, her voice soft, her cadence a singsong cooing. The little ram trots over to her immediately, abandoning a patch of grass that he'd been munching on in a bit of dappled sun. He butts his head against her thighs and bleats. His forehead leaves a smear of mashed grass on her jeans.

"I've brought you carrots," she tells the little beast and pats his head.

"You know, with the lamb and you here, my house almost feels like it's occupied by a little family. The offer still stands, about you moving into my spare room. Cheap rent. No funny business except when you want funny business. I'd take that deal if you were offering."

Peach's fingers come away soft with lanolin and she smiles at Linx. "I appreciate the offer, but I'll be okay. I think I've got some ideas on how to get my finances under control."

"Oh yeah," he laughs, "since when? Are you staying awake at night watching reruns of Suze Orman?"

"No," Peach says and doesn't quite know how to explain her new understanding of budgeting and investments. All she knows is when she thinks of money, she no longer sees it as intimidating. Instead, it's manageable and even a bit titillating.

"You're just a financial whiz now? No problems paying rent? Did you win the lottery and not tell me?"

"Stop," she says and presses on his chest. She bends down and rips open the bag of carrots and offers a fat stick to Roman. He takes it and feeds its length into his mouth. Peach can see two points on the top of his head that bulge a bit. She wonders when his horns will break skin and begin to grow.

"What are you going to make me for breakfast?" she says and looks up at Linx.

"Why should I make you anything? I'm not your little house bitch," he says with a smile and then his lips turn downward. His eyes follow suit and Peach can sense the change in his focus and all levity that had been there vanishes.

"By the way, how was your date?"

Roman chomps away on his carrot, the vertical slits of his eyes glossy, his yellow irises bright.

She thinks of the top of Lar's ass, inked with a moon. She thinks of his hands in the water of the mountain creek, swirling the contents of the green pan. She thinks of how he spit blood, at the end.

"I never went," Peach quips, her voice tight and choppy. "It just didn't feel right."

Linx's lips curve upward but he forces them back into a line and she watches them rise and settle and is glad he cannot tell when she lies. Peach knows his affection for her blinds him, totally and staggeringly.

"I think you like me, Peach Barrow."

"Meh," she responds, shrugging her shoulders.

Linx bends down and tickles her sides, making the lamb jump away nervously. He continues the assault, taking the battle to the backsides of her knees. Peach collapses into a fetal position, hands slapping him off. Her lungs, they're breathless.

28   RILEY

The list of names is written over the course of twenty-six hours. Riley does not stop to sleep. He eats uncooked Ramen noodles, folding the plastic wrapper away from the tan, crunchy block and munching on it. Bits fall onto his pieces of lined paper and they remind him of maggots. He wipes them to the floor and continues with his dredging up of personalities and faces and monikers.

The first hundred had come easily. These were people who Riley had friendships with; some were intimate connections, others old coworkers. It was after this group where the going got difficult. If he was right to consider Roman a victim of his stalker's bizarre game, then he would quite literally need to remember everyone with whom he'd ever had a dealing, an acquaintance, even a friendly exchange of greeting from time to time. It's not an impossible task, but improbable to carry out with one hundred percent accuracy.

Riley is aware he'd only seen Roman once. He'd been insistent the artist was the only one he wanted to ink the tattoo on his mangled foot. The design was simple, just as Roman had said. It was creatable by any tattooist. But if Riley had picked another, that person could have met their demise instead. He doesn't pause to think about the simple line of black ink in his dermis. He can worry about what he'll do with the stalled progress of his tattoo later on.

He holds to the list. The list becomes everything for twenty-six hours. The second hundred people are harder to dredge from the depths of his memory. He squeezes them out, listing cousins he knows exist but has never met. He gets out his high school yearbook which helps him log another hundred or so names.

When he gets to the four hundreds, he must face the fact he's had intimate relationships with many women. His personal count extends well past one hundred and fifty, but this is just a number he's added to each year. Most of those integers do not carry names. Many of his conquests have become nothing more than scraps of sensation: the braided hair a hippie used to tickle his nipples, the girl with her pubic hair shaved into the shape of an arrow pointing down. If he can't drum up a name, he simply writes down the memory. He lists them this way and will worry later about how he might contact them. Because if Roman was killed because of him, he is sure anyone who's had his penis inside of them could be slated for execution.

The last run of names or descriptive placeholders has him thinking of favorite grocery store cashiers and the neighborhood girl, the one he thought was gay, who used to mow his lawn two years back. He thinks of all his neighbors as placeholders on a game board. Something vaguely reminiscent of Candy Land. For now, he writes down *Neighbors +/- 13*. Then he lists physical descriptors of the man Riley would always nod to when they crisscrossed paths on their running circuits. Lastly, he jots down the name of his first babysitter.

And when his brain feels wrung out and useless, he finally gets away from his den and the list and the bull and the cards and uses the bathroom. Pissing feels like a sacred bliss, his urine running fast and copious from him though he's had little water or booze to drink. He fills his bathtub up with warm water and nabs his phone. He soaks his right foot while un-bandaging his left and checking his stitches. The wound looks clean; the flesh puckers and reminds him of meat on the rack of a dehydrator. He cleans the scabbing gently with a bar of soap and thinks he'll be able to get the stitches out soon. They would have been out for good long ago if he hadn't kicked Sev while he was prone on the ground.

At least his toeless foot is one thing he can't blame on his stalker. That was his doing. He had some help from his coworker Newt, but Riley knows it was he who didn't check the chain.

He thumbs through his call log and sees he's missed a call from Detective Mallory, the lead detective on the Roman Saucedo case with the odd sense of humor. He doesn't remember hearing his phone ring. He checks to make sure it's not silenced, the button firmly indicating it is not. She didn't leave a message so Riley decides not to call back. He's tired and consumed with his list. If he talks to her now, he'll likely come off brain-addled and weird. And he has no desire for another trip down to the station.

He texts Walker, tells him to come over after he gets off work and he gets a one word answer back in the affirmative. The warmth feels good on his feet, though he can't keep the left foot in the water long. He thinks about what it will be like come summer and swimming. He'll be able to forgo the one rule he remembers from his swim lessons as a five-year-old: point the toes.

Riley doesn't dare lie down before Walker arrives so he makes a pot of coffee and drinks from the carafe. He gets through four cups by the time his best friend arrives just past seven in the evening.

"Don't tell me it's another card," Walker says. He's brought Chinese again. The smell makes Riley's stomach turn.

"Yeah, but that's not what I want to tell you about. I got a statue!"

He feigns a look of delight on his face, eyes wide and his mouth open, a touch maniacal. Then Riley moves away from the takeout and makes for his den. Walker leaves dinner in the foyer and follows Riley, his finger in the air, ready to address a problem.

"Wait, a statue? What the hell, Rye? When are you going to take this seriously instead of acting like an overzealous kid at show and tell?"

"I'll tell you about it in a minute. Even show it. The whole shebang."

Riley plucks up his papers. He runs his fingers over his list. Walker Kauffman is written near the top of the page.

"But first, let me check again. You're Pisces too, right?"

Walker eyes the stack of cards and the bull statue but doesn't reach out for it. "Yeah, February 20th. Why?"

"Okay," Riley exhales, "I won't need to worry about you for a good while."

Walker snatches the sheets of paper away from Riley and frowns. "Brother, what are you talking about? You never get me a gift anyway. Why does my birthday matter? And this list of names? You taking stock of people or weeding out the naughty from the nice?"

Riley reaches over and flicks the pages with his finger. "All the people I know or have known. Well, most of them. I'm sure I've missed people; I can't possibly think of everyone. It's hard to compile something like this. But I think the bulk of them are in there."

Walker hands the papers back and shakes his head. "Why?"

"Because I have a theory. And if I'm right, two people I've had connections to have been murdered in the last two months."

"Two people? What, there's someone else besides the tattooist?"

"Yeah, my financial advisor."

Walker takes the pages again and looks over the names slowly, his nostrils flaring slightly as he reads. "So your financial advisor is dead? I haven't heard about another murder."

Riley's skin tingles. The coffee plays in his veins, caffeine more bountiful than platelets. He blinks rapidly.

"They're calling it an accident. But if it isn't an accident, then it has something to do with me."

"With you?"

"Yes," Riley says. He knuckles his eyes, nods his head five times. "But getting down all these names was the easy part. Now comes the real work."

His friend puts the list down on the desk and looks back at the bull. Riley watches how his eyes skim over the little statue, narrowing to flattened slits. He keeps his attention on the bull but Riley can hear the tone of disbelief in his friend's voice. Only then Riley considers he might sound paranoid, even insane to Walker.

"And what work do you need to complete?" his friend asks, head turned toward the statue with the odd markings. It's the same stoic fixation Riley remembers of Walker, when he'd get lost in some heavy law tome at the firm.

"I've got to figure out birthdays. For all of them."

Walker looks at Riley then and gives him a weak smile. "And you want me to help you?"

"Please," Riley says. "I'm forgetting what sleep is."

WEDNESDAY, THE 3RD OF JUNE, 2015

29   PEACH

The best time to arrive at the discount thrift bins is just as they open on a weekday morning. She slips into the fenced junk yard outside the warehouse of soiled toys and broken vinyl records and clothing both outdated and peculiar. But she has a feeling what she needs is somewhere in the mounded messes of discarded vanity lights and rickety lawn chairs made of brittle plastic that litter the asphalt just outside the main doors.

She considers the other shoppers around her. She knows many of them might be hunting for a particular bargain but that others are sincerely destitute enough to not be able to afford the prices at regular thrift stores. These people remind her of stories of poverty she's heard from other licensed clinical social workers decades deep into their work. Most of her clients can at least afford second-hand clothing which isn't musky with mold.

She takes a moment to acknowledge her fortune. And as she does, her newfound talent of financial acumen hits her once more. Here for a bargain instead of concern over masking some of her purchases from receipts and records, she lets her frugality drive home the decision to come to this particular place. She pushes away her thoughts on finance and calls to mind the other motivating factor that made her drive here and wade through other people's castoffs before heading to work: artistic impulse.

Peach gazes at the corners of the junk lot, thinking her object of interest might be pushed up against a length of fence or a concrete wall. Instead she finds ratty, old golf bags with broken handles and a stunning number of bent plastic boat oars. They don't resonate necessity to Peach. A garish red, rickety coat rack tempts her, but it's not what she's hunting.

Changing tactics, she heads inside. The warehouse is already warm though it's still early morning. Peach is grateful for the high ceilings so the air isn't too tainted with the smells of items previously well-used by humanity. A woman works the register, more interested in picking her teeth than watching the people mill about. There are several families with shopping carts stacked full of dusty stuffed animals and kitchenware.

She stares out over the expanse of material goods, overwhelmed at the sprawl of items. Peach leans against a table stacked high with worn shoes, her eyes flicking about, searching. Then she sees it. From where she stands, it looks about perfect.

Walking to her intended, she passes another family, this one clearly from some Western African country. The mother has a vividly colored piece of cloth wrapped around her head. And in the fold-down cart seat are two babies, twins, propped upright and no more than a few months old. Their heads loll on their weak necks as they look around, eyes wide and bulging.

She sends a little prayer of luck to the twins and takes their presence as a good sign. When she moves to her desire, standing in front of the object she so covets, an air conditioning unit high above her in the rafters kicks on. The fan sends an icy draft down on the tops of her shoulders, her wig shielding her head from the cool gust. Summer is on its way. But Peach isn't ready to see the last weeks of spring and of Gemini slip away just yet.

Peach nods her chin at the object. It feels right to greet it with a physical gesture. She runs her hand up and down its height. It seems intact. She smiles and moves in even closer to it.

"You're perfect," she whispers.

A man she hadn't noticed, who'd seen her pat down the thing before talking to it, sidles up next to Peach and smirks. He smells of peppermint and carries a toaster from the seventies tucked under one arm.

"Don't think it has vocal cords, sweetie," he laughs.

"It might surprise us both."

"If it does and I'm around, stand back. I'll clock it good with this toaster."

"Don't break it. You'll go without toast tomorrow morning."

He looks to the pea-green sides of the kitchen appliance and nods his head.

"I bet it still works. They made everything to last back then. Even the people were sturdier."

"All started falling apart in the eighties," she jokes.

"Yes, I think you're right," he says and then leaves her be.

30 RILEY

Walker had promised to help Riley, but when he got deeper
through the list and saw the vague descriptors for some of the
people, he'd thrown his hands in the air and let loose a stream of
swear words. He said he couldn't find birthdays for women
described by nicknames only or by the size and shape of their
breasts. Then he had begged Riley to go to the cops, to get out of
his house and to get some sleep. He'd left the Chinese food
behind and after Riley watched his friend leave, he pitched the
breaded, saucy chicken in the garbage can. It was best if he
didn't have reminders of his stalker's gift of deep-fried flesh sent
via mail.

Today he keeps at the list. He slept last night. Fitfully,
waking briefly, convinced he was a blackbird with an injured
wing, but it was better than no sleep at all. And when he roused
around noon, he took some time to masturbate, doing his best to
think of anyone but Mayra. But her supple form, nutmeg skin
and dark locks of hair materialized immediately. Her image

brought along the scent of gardenia, and he spent himself with surprising alacrity.

He uses two factors to narrow down potential victims on the list. The first is physical proximity. Because he has no evidence to make him think otherwise, he assumes the people in danger are the ones who live in Boise. This assumption whittles down the list significantly. He does not think about what it means for the people on the list if the assumption proves false. He uses social media, plunking the names of his old high school friends into the browser and finding a majority of their locations with a quick scroll of the keypad, getting discernable joy out of the voyeurism. It feels like the research he used to do in contract law. He puts checkmarks next to the ones he can't find. These souls will require more time on his part. He will need to roll up his sleeves and dig for their information. But his current pace has him hopeful he can get his list to a manageable number.

The second factor is based on Riley's relationship with the people on the list. While Riley and Roman were little more than acquaintances, Riley figures he can't feasibly contact every person on the list. Hell, he can't even *name* everyone on the list. There is nothing to be done for all the women that are little more than sexualized descriptions. Besides coming off as a complete nutter, he's not sure he wants to destroy his reputation so soundly across the expanse of the Boise community with bizarre phone calls and ominous warnings. If the deaths stop, he'll be known as the paranoid guy who tells liquor store workers they might be murdered because they regularly sell him Jameson.

What he doesn't want to admit to himself—though the knowledge of it is there and real and heavy in his gut—is while he doesn't want anyone to be murdered, he especially does not want the people closest to him to die. This selfish, ego-laden drive is paramount; Riley doesn't strive to have better ethics than the average human being. He tells himself he can only care so much, that his heart is not so large, and his psyche not so hearty.

These cutting tactics leave him with many of the original hundred or so people he was able to think of and easily add to the list. He reads the list out loud, checking off the names he still needs birthdays for. Some he already has down.

Tate Marchesi: January 29th.

Kristin Marchesi: April 5th.

Mayra Pena: October 22nd.

He reviews Kristin's birthday, happy the date has already passed, though it's not due to any reserves of sentimentality for his ex. He figures it will save him an awkward call and the responsibility of talking to her any more than he needs to in order to speak with Tate. He's also pleased the birthdays for both Tate and Mayra are far off and can be tucked out of mind.

But for each person's birthday he does know, there are five more he's ignorant about. Riley takes the time to draft a new list, just with the names of the individuals he's singled out in importance. Suddenly his task seems manageable, his stalker someone he shall inevitably thwart.

He holds the list out in front of his chest and spins around in his office chair. This makes him the sun. Planets made of rock or water or gas or flame, dependent on his glorious form, arrayed before him. He is the most precious of all bodies in the galaxy. And these folks are his subjects. The sun means to protect his friends. For they are locked in his orbit and he owes them.

They are what make the sun, the sun.

31 PEACH

She leaves her thrift store purchase in her car when she goes in to work. When Camille leaves for lunch and comes back just after 1pm, a wrapped BLT in hand and an extra Coke for Peach, she wears a smirk. Her coworker hands her the fountain drink and points out Peach's office window, the glass looking out over a sliver of newly-mown grass and the parking lot.

"When I saw what was sitting in your passenger seat, I thought you might like some caffeine. You know, wake you up a bit, snap you back to reality," Camille says.

Peach doesn't bother to look out the window. She knows what Camille has seen and doesn't feel like defending herself.

"It's nothing. Part of an art project," Peach shrugs.

She waves at Camille to sit down and eat her meal at the desk. The woman pulls up the client chair and unwraps her sandwich, pieces of shredded iceberg lettuce falling to the carpet.

"You sure it won't drive off in your Honda?" Camille pries. "We haven't had one of our let's-pretend-I'm-counseling-you-just-for-fun-but-not-really sessions in quite a long while. Is there something you want to talk about, girlie? I don't have a session for another hour."

Peach watches as Camille rips off parts of the end of the French bread laden with mayonnaise and places them on her tongue. Not that she could, but if Peach had the desire to confide in someone, share the details of her ego's maturation in the past two months, she wouldn't trust Camille to understand. While the woman was astute and well-educated, she was also moralistic to a fault. And what Peach was becoming had no validity existing in Camille's vision of an ethical world.

"I'm feeling great," she tells her. "I actually took your advice the last time we talked. You came up with that nice little tip about using my fear of not reaching my full potential to propel me forward. I've felt a little like I'm both the predator and the prey, but it's been working. Old me and new me trying to do this give and take. For some reason it makes me think of the *Growing Pains* theme song."

Camille mumbles something through the bread in her mouth and then takes a sip of soda to wash it down. "Interesting you put it that way. Predator and prey. Why do you think you see yourself in both positions? Both pursuing and being pursued. Does it add a little thrill to what you're doing?"

A flash plays out across her mind: an image of a tattoo needle in her hand wielded deftly and deeply into the left ear of Roman Saucedo. The memory of violence fades. It's replaced with an image of an idolized Saint Roman in sumptuous robes, backlit with his chin held high.

"I think it's thrilling enough. I find myself engaging fully in the process. It's definitely colored by the predator and prey relationship. Old Peach needs to die in order for New Peach to survive. Predator assumes the energy, the life-force of its prey. That exchange is necessary and powerful."

Taking another bite of her BLT, Camille looks out the window again to the parking lot. Peach can tell she's weighing her words because she squints her eyes when she's contemplative. Peach waits for her to speak, doodling looping circles on the back of a ripped-open envelope.

"I'm not sure it needs to be as impassioned as all that," Camille cautions. "You might be setting yourself up for failure if you don't attain this new state you seem to be chugging toward. The lion doesn't always take down the gazelle. Sometimes the one hunted gets away. What if Old Peach, as you call that part of your personality, wins out in the end?"

Suddenly Peach is back in the waiting room outside Lars's office. Her eyes had slipped over the cover of a magazine before she checked out the artwork on the walls. What had the picture been? A photo of a cheetah and zebra nose to nose, eyes locked? She wonders if Camille actually read that issue or if the metaphor was serendipitous. Either way, with the quest to let loose Perfect Peach, the idea that her old, meek, weak self might stick around and put up a fight and even win said fight is something Peach isn't ready to accept as an option.

She's not sure what's most diplomatic to say to Camille, so she goes with what pops into her mind.

"It's not a question of passion. Or even ethics. It's just an exchange of energy. Moving it from one being to another. Or one self to another self. Completely natural."

"Hmm," Camille muses verbally through her last mouthful.

She finishes her sandwich, wads up the wrapper, and tosses it in the trash can under Peach's desk. She gets up from the chair, wiping crumbs from the corners of her mouth and stares out the window. She points again at Peach's car and smirks.

"All right, Peach. Another question, though. Are you still having sex with your best friend, that small Asian guy?"

"Why?" Peach asks.

Camille smoothes down her curly hair and cocks her head at Peach. One of her earrings made of lengths of blue and black beads rests on her cheek.

"Because if you're not, I'd like to posit a dirty guess as to why you have that thing in your car."

32 RILEY

After he calls his maternal aunt he hasn't spoken to since the funeral of his parents, and written down the birthdays of his cousins who live in Boise, he decides to escape his house. But it's for a purpose. He's stalled out. Zero progress has been made on ferreting out birthdays for the remainder of his list. He's discovered dates for most of them, but some of the names and the people associated with them are too difficult to find via the internet. He needs an expert on research.

So he goes to the library.

When Amelia sees Riley striding towards her desk, he notes how she sits up a bit straighter and her eyes flick from him to the computer, back and forth as if they're trying to decide what's more entertaining. Finally her gaze settles on Riley as he sits down in front of her, scooting the oak-framed chair close in to her desk. She smiles and deep divots punctuate her cheeks. Riley is pleased she seems to have forgotten their weird exchange right after the bomb went off downtown. He does his best to look non-threatening, sane. He trots out a sly little smile he usually reserves for women he intends to fuck.

"Did those astrology books come in for you?" she asks.

"Haven't been contacted yet," Riley says. "Too many of us conspiracy freaks in Boise, I suppose. I actually came for your help with something else."

"Oh," she asks and her dimples disappear. "What's that?"

"Birthdays," he says. "I need to learn a good method for researching birthdays of individuals inactive on the internet. You know, the holdouts, the Luddites."

He tries a smile and Amelia reciprocates. She shimmies around in her chair just a bit, enough to send the polyester blouse that billows out over her wide form into subtle vibration.

"Well, birth certificates are public records. You can't get a copy of one unless it's your own, but you can look at them. Are you sure there isn't a database on the internet where you can find this information?"

Amelia clicks her computer monitor to life and nods at the screen while she does her perusal. Riley cracks his neck and eyes the airplane curio on her desk. His sleep-deprivation is catching up with his body. Coupled with his decrease in physical activity thanks to his amputation, his body feels like it's atrophying muscle and blossoming new aches at the same time. He eyes the other library patrons, less paranoid than he was the last time he was in the building. Now he fears his own body's new-found anxiety, brought on in a swift and crippling manner. Fears it more than the derelicts, college kids, and stay-at-home mothers who frequent the Boise Public Library. His dedication to the list keeps him focused, away from thoughts of Mayra or money or work or sex or more greeting cards.

"Here," she says and turns the screen so Riley can see. "A simple search produced this site. Looks like you can enter a full name into the database and get a birthday for the person. Pulls from government records."

Riley slaps his palm against his forehead. "Shit," he says. "I think I've just been out of it lately. Missing things and making assumptions. One big one being if you're not on social media, you're a ghost. Staying awake for too long can be dangerous."

Amelia giggles her high-pitched squeal at his response. Riley decides not to ask what she finds so funny about his inability to find a simple website with a basic internet search.

"Put your own name in there," he tells Amelia. "Let's see if it actually works."

She stops her chuckling and swings the screen back around and types in her full name. She clicks her mouse and a few seconds later she's nodding her head again.

"Sure, it works," is all she says.

Riley realizes she's not on his list and should be. Then he thinks to ask for her birthday but he doesn't want to come off any creepier than he already has. He's only interacted with the research librarian a few times and one of those times he was making odd comments about explosives. Riley tells himself there is very little chance she would be a target of his stalker, if indeed his stalker is also a murderer. He does not consider his weak connection to Roman now. It's all too confusing and muddled and twisted to constantly reassess. Instead, he focuses on the prospect of getting the rest of the birthdays of the people on his list. For good measure, he'll look her up on the site later. He'll figure out her last name and add her. She's just one of the ones he's missed. But she'll be the first he rectifies.

Amelia looks at Riley and smiles again. "Sleep deprived, eh? Too many long nights thinking about the astrological glyphs around Boise?"

"Something like that," Riley says. He's ready to gather up his body, and his slightly-wounded ego for missing such an obvious tool on the internet, and head back home to finish his list.

"Well you aren't the only one. As I said before, other people are in here asking questions. Even some city officials, especially the mayor, are starting to get a bit antsy over the symbols. You know how he wants Boise to become 'The Most Liveable City in America'?" Amelia raises her fingers to concoct some energetic air quoting. "With strange symbols popping up around town, it's something to concern those who want Boise to be spic and span for new immigrants."

"Maybe the trailblazers who came West all gung ho on Manifest Destiny got the idea from an old news rag's horoscope column?" Riley kids, his mind slipping toward images of Americans moving *en masse*.

Amelia graces him with a slower nod of her head, but doesn't share a giggle. There is something about her jovial attitude and willingness to talk that endears her to Riley. It's this and the fact he doesn't desire her sexually which defines her value. She's a nice girl. He reminds himself again to put her name and birthday on the list.

She goes on. "It's almost like whoever is doing this, putting up these symbols, it's like they're trying to communicate something to us. Maybe start up a type of dialogue?"

"Sounds like I'm not the only paranoid one in close proximity," he replies and nods, smiling in her direction. "But there hasn't been another symbol. I've been watching the news and reading the paper. Well, sort of. I've been internet browsing more than anything."

A laugh escapes Amelia's mouth. But it isn't the same gleeful twittering Riley heard before. This noise is laden with uncertainty, unease.

"Actually, I have a friend who's really into running. Jogs each morning despite the weather or her schedule for the rest of the day. As you can tell, I don't go with her," and Amelia looks down at her soft, large body.

Riley remembers the pound of the asphalt on his heels and swallows hard. He waits in silence for her continue.

"Well, my friend, she ran by Boise High School on her normal route a few mornings back. And she said in the early morning sun, she could see someone had taken yellow chalk to the pillars at the front of Old Main, the central structure of the school."

"Okay," Riley says, not certain of where she's going with her story.

"The pillars were colored with bright yellow chalk up a third of their height. Probably as far as the person could reach on tiptoe. And only two of the four columns were decorated with chalk. The ones in the middle."

"You're losing me, Amelia Pearson? Phillips? Price?"

Amelia ignores his fishing and pulls out a piece of paper, like she was prepared for his inability to envision what she currently describes. Quickly sketching long, cylindrical masses down the middle of the paper, she draws four in total. Then she turns the tip of her pencil horizontal and colors in the pillars in the middle.

"There," she says and places the paper in front of Riley. She taps the middle columns with the tip of graphite, eyes downcast on her work. "This style of column is known as Ionic, something you learn as an Art History major. See how the top and bottoms have this flaring effect with a leveling out on the ends?"

"I think I see," he says but doesn't want to agree to what Amelia is alluding to. He doesn't want to really and truly see it.

She picks up the paper and puts a fold down the page width-wise. Opening the two halves up like a book, she stops when the shaded, colored columns align next to one another. She holds it up in front of Riley's face and drops her voice to a ghost of her normal volume. They sit together in anticipation, two participants sharing a supernatural secret.

"Put them side-by-side and ignore the other pillars. See? Like the Roman numeral for the number two. Like the astrological sign for Gemini."

FRIDAY,
THE 5TH OF JUNE,
2015

33   PEACH

"Patti, I really can't talk right now. I'm in the middle of something."

Peach's adoptive mother hacks a phlegm-heavy cough into the receiver of her phone in Florida. Peach wonders if the years of smoking Pall Malls are catching up to the woman. She thinks of the woman's silver cigarette case etched with the outline of a lake. Scads of tobacco plants have rotated out of that shiny coffin.

"I wanted to remind you to pick me up from the airport on Monday. The flight is at two, the number is 784 out of Denver. Is it United? Must be United. I hate to put you out, but I can't stand the thought of taking a taxi. I don't want my luggage smelling like a curry."

Peach stands tight against a white wall, her back to people passing her. She tries not to draw attention to herself. She knows Patti doesn't mind putting Peach out. She's been doing it with aplomb since Peach was twelve. When Peach finally realized she was adopted more for the benefit of Patti's image and abhorrent neediness, coupled with loneliness, than due to any desire to mother, she had accepted their relationship for what it was. Peach gave and Patti took and the roles were seldom if ever reversed.

"I'll be there. I have it down on my calendar. But I really need to go."

Peach squeezes the rope-like handles of another gift bag. This one is printed with the command *Be Well!* over and over in tiny, white cursive. She tucks the body of the bag and its contents between herself and the wall she presses up against. The plastic crackles.

"Because I remember all those times I had to drive you around when you were a teenager. This is the least you could do for me," Patti continues.

Peach doesn't bring up the fact she wasn't allowed to drive and couldn't afford to buy a car with her own money though Patti had a well-paying desk job and could have purchased a vehicle for her adopted daughter. Instead she ends the conversation firmly, calling forth a little Perfect Peach to get the job done.

"Let's not talk about what's owed, Patti. I'll see you on Monday."

Peach hangs up the phone then and tucks it into her pocket. It's rare for her to be terse with the woman but she's determined to ignore the twinge of regret that bubbles in her gut. She uses one hand to reach up and adjust a yellow linen scarf around her throat and turns to face away from the wall, into the bustling corridor of the respiratory ward of St. Luke's.

She thanks all her helpers for seeing her job completed for the day, before Patti had called her up. She would have hated to have been interrupted. She'd had precious little time to do what needed to be done, racing, pushing herself to completion of her task in less than five minutes. The lady in the bed had been unconscious, just as last time. Peach thought she could see some payoff to her labors though it was too soon to see definite results. The woman's physical degradation might be imagined. Or it might be present, but on account of the late stage cancer instead of Peach's sinister actions.

As she walks towards the elevator, she passes an orderly, a woman who appears to be Persian or from one of the countries in western Asia, its name ending in –stan. She nods at Peach and smiles but keeps walking. In all her visits to the sickly woman, this is the first time a hospital employee has acknowledged Peach. She freezes for a moment, terrified her face will remain imprinted in the woman's mind, fodder for questions asked by police. But then she gathers up the courage to watch the woman push on with a cart of packaged, sterilized instruments. The orderly passes many people and with each person she passes, she turns her face toward them and smiles.

Peach blinks back water in her eyes and lifts up her feet, making for the elevator. The woman is friendly. There is very little likelihood she will remember Peach with the number of people she looks at, smiles at each day at work. Peach convinces herself she'll just be one of the many who visit the hospital, bereaved or elated or sick. She'll be unassuming, average, forgettable. She knows then that, for this orderly, Peach will be nothing more than an exercise in manners, a passing nicety. And those things don't have faces.

As the elevator slides smoothly down to the first floor, she's perplexed by her desire to cry. Perhaps it's because just now, in the glancing eyes of the orderly, she was Old Peach. The tears well up as they would upon spying an old friend. For the first time in a few months, Peach is glad she hasn't transitioned to Perfect Peach yet. For then she would be a glamour, an event.

34   RILEY

For someone who feels as though he has hardly anyone important in his life, Riley certainly had a number of names to type into the birthday database. He completed the task after arriving back home from the library. Unease settled in when Amelia alerted him to the two pillars potentially signifying the sign for Gemini. If it was the third symbol in the zodiac procession, then his instincts were likely correct. Not only had he received a letter addressed by Pollux—researched by Riley and confirmed to be the brightest star in the Gemini constellation—but now the symbol had been displayed in Boise. That, or it was just some chalk on old, marble pillars. But as much as he wishes it were something inane and meaningless, he can't truly believe it to be so.

Out of the hundred and four people on his condensed list, only five of the people turn out to be Geminis. He's thankful for it. He can practice his ominous warnings on a handful of people instead of scores.

He writes the five names on another piece of paper, another paring down, another subset penned so Riley can focus on the most important people for the time being. He reads the names three times. He fidgets, folding the piece of lined paper into a tight square. Then he opens it back up and flattens out the folds with his fingers. Does it five times total. The names aren't listed in a particular order. He's already played favorites; his master list of over five hundred Boise-based individuals whittled down to one hundred and four he cares to save.

His eyes glide over each first and last name. They may become mantras to him before Gemini slips to Cancer in mid-June.

Jeanne Ringel. She was Riley's neighbor the entire time his parents lived in their house in southeast Boise, bought when the land behind his backyard was little more than dry cheatgrass and grasshoppers during the summer. She had been elderly then and Riley assumes she is in her late eighties by now. He has her on the list because he's certain she is still in Boise if she's not newly deceased in the past year. No obituary has been uncovered. She attended his parents' funeral. And he remembers playing in her home when he was a child. She would give him meringues and he loved the way they would dissolve, crackle on his tongue. She was a grandmother figure to Riley, even brought a bottle of schnapps to his parents to give to Riley a few days after he turned twenty-one.

Damon Linder. A fellow law student, moving in the same cohort as Riley at the University of Idaho, they became friends during late nights of pounding coffee and Ritalin and reading texts on property law. They'd joked about starting a firm together, but Riley had been certain he'd be leaving Idaho and trying his luck in California after getting his degree. When he decided to return to Boise at his father's insistence, Damon had already gotten a position with a firm specializing in elder law. They had coffee a few times in the years since law school ended and Damon would always speak of saving money for a cabin in McCall, a resort town north of Boise, or buying a new speaker system. The man was obsessed with music and though they'd been friends through law school, their paths had swerved off in different directions since receiving their degrees.

Soo Lim. The first time she arrived to babysit Riley, he stared at her, mouth wide, until his mother swatted the back of his head. She was the first Asian woman he'd really ever seen, Boise having a small percentage of Asians compared to the past when many Chinese came to Idaho because of the gold rush. Seven years his elder, at fourteen, she was an adult in his eyes. She was always smiling, and when Riley pestered her enough, she would speak seemingly random strings of words in Korean to him and he'd listen, captivated. She was tall for her age and forced Riley to eat her mom's spicy *kimchi* whenever he had a cold. Riley hadn't seen her since he was twenty-five, running into her at the grocery store. She was still tall, willowy and ebullient in personality.

Newt Parnwell. The man partially responsible for Riley's amputated toes. Riley knew next to nothing about the man. They worked together, but as new as Riley had been to the gold equipment production shop, Newt was newer still. Riley did know he was obsessed with two disparate things: championship ballroom dancing and NASCAR. The only reason Riley included him on the pared down list at all was because he was a co-worker and because his actions, his role in dropping the anvil, made a huge impact on Riley's life. Roman Saucedo simply inked a black line on Riley's foot. Newt had been an accomplice in the loss of appendages. Whether or not Riley liked it, Newt had some significance.

Nicole Trey. This ex-lover had popped up twice in Riley's life recently. He's not keen on the idea of contacting the leggy brunette, but he certainly doesn't want to see her hurt. Of all the Geminis on his list, she's the one he's closest to, or rather, had been the most intimate with. Their last encounter, outside a house not far from his own, had been awkward. When he was around Nicole, he remembered how shitty of a person he could really be. After all, she'd been Kristin's best friend and he'd still fucked her. Around Mayra, Riley could pretend to be honorable, a man of worth. But around Nicole, he felt base. And worse yet, he didn't care once the sensation hit. He was fine to revel in his questionable morality.

He nods his head at the list and pulls his phone out of his pocket. Next to the names and birthdays are phone numbers. He eyes the digits for the woman who he lived next to growing up. Jeanne Ringel. Before he can talk himself out of it, before he even knows what will come out of his mouth, he dials her number. It rings and he can taste the vanilla fizz of meringue on his tongue.

35   PEACH

Before she heads deeper into the chain store selling dry
pasta and women's bras and charcoal grills, she stops at a row of
bins near the front doors. The company supplies recycling bins
for an array of objects. A gray bin is lettered on the side with the
words *cellular phones and ink cartridges*. She pulls from her
cream-colored purse the flip phone burner she used when
speaking with Lars. Last night, she took a hammer to it,
smashing the interior structure of the thing. She removed the
SIM card, crushing it with the hammer as well, and scattered the
remains of the data chip around the parking lot of a gas station
seven miles from her home. She wipes the battered phone's
casing with her sleeve, a bright bit of yellow cotton, and slides it
in the recycling bin.

From there, Peach walks toward the aisles full of kids' toys.
She notices several recognizable lines, largely based on
television shows she watched as a child revamped and
repackaged for a new generation: *SheRa*, the golden-haired

Princess of Power, Transformers, Teenage Mutant Ninja Turtles.
Peach figures parents her age are more than willing to buy their
children a toy that reminds them of their own youth. Or the toy
companies are out of new ideas.

She passes giant, rainbow-colored bouncy balls and an aisle
of swimming accessories. She holds a pair of pink goggles up to
her eyes and smiles at how tiny the plastic frames are. The world
is suddenly a rose-hued fog. Dropping the goggles, she walks on
until her eyes catch her intended.

There are three of the items she's seeking so she takes them
all. She holds the square boxes in her arms, her hands bearing
most of the weight of the squat, little tower. When she gets up to
the check stand, a tall, young man watches her dump the boxes
onto the conveyor belt of his station. His hair is a tangle of
intricate cornrows and he keeps his mouth shut as he works. He
moves the boxes along the price scanner and totals out the
purchase, never vocalizing how much she owes. Peach digs her
wallet out, pulls forth cash and then looks up to see a store
manager hovering next to the guy. This woman smiles at Peach
and scoots the cashier away from the boxes. She bags them
herself and then hands them to Peach.

"What a great purchase," the manager says and the young
man looks about the store, like he's waiting for something more
exciting to occur. "Do you have kids waiting on these at home?"

Peach hands over her money, accepts the change and takes
up the bag.

"No," she replies. "Just a lot of people to entertain."

36   RILEY

Riley makes three phone calls.

Jeanne Ringel doesn't pick up her phone but he's hopeful he
has the right number when her message machine kicks on, a
quiet approximation of the voice he remembers from his
childhood flowing into his ear. Except now there is a tremor to
her voice, an audible mark of advanced age. She never states her
name, only the phone number he's just dialed. When the beep
sounds on the machine, Riley pauses for a few seconds before
speaking.

"Um, yes, Mrs. Ringel? This is Riley Wanner. I was calling
because…okay, I don't know how to say this…but I'm worried
about your safety. I can't say why, but you might be in danger.
Only until the later part of June. But that's a long time from now.
Who knows what could happen to you. Because there might be a
murder happening soon. Okay, I'm sorry. I didn't want to have
to do this to you. Again, this is Riley, the boy who grew up next
door to you."

And then he hangs up the phone, his heart pumping, already unsure of what he's just said. He has no idea if the message was impactful or confusing. Plus, he has no idea how an elderly woman might protect herself from his stalker. Widowed years ago, Jeanne likely still lives alone on a long, wide flag lot. If she were attacked, the foul act might not be easily heard or seen by others. He considers making a point of driving past her home for the remainder of the Gemini cycle, but he doesn't want to come off as too strange if she catches a glimpse of his Nissan each time she goes out to get her mail.

He shakes his hands out to relieve some tension and lets the adrenaline in his blood push him to dial the next number. Damon Linder picks up after the third ring.

"Hello?"

"Hey, Damon. It's Riley Wanner. How are you?"

"Damn, Riley!" Damon's effervescence tells him he's touched Riley has called. "What are you up to? I heard you left your firm?"

"Yeah, a while back. Been a hard year and a half. We'll have to grab some coffee sometime and chat."

"For sure," Damon echoes the sentiment and then Riley hears the shrill cry of a baby over the receiver.

"Is that your kid?"

"Indeed. Three months old. I think *I* don't get any sleep but my wife practically has the little guy attached to her chest twenty-four hours a day."

"Married and a child since we've caught up last?" Riley feels uncomfortable already. Damon mumbles confirmation.

Now he considers backing out of the call. Until he thinks of Damon's wife and their child. They would be devastated if Damon were to die. Riley thinks of dirty diapers left unchanged, casseroles delivered to combat the hunger that settles in upon tragedy. He thinks of dwindling finances and a water drill slicing into granite, spelling out Damon's full name.

"Listen, Damon. I actually called because I've just had a sense lately that I should touch base with you. You know the tattooist who got murdered a month or two back? I knew him, and ever since he died, I've had a strange feeling. Like he might not be the last one. And for some reason, I guess just gut intuition, I keep thinking I need to warn you of something."

Damon doesn't speak for a moment and Riley remembers how sensible, logical the man always was. He stays silent, waits until the silence is pierced by another wail from the baby. Then his old friend replies.

"Okay. So you're just warning me to be careful, to not get murdered? This doesn't have anything to do with gambling, does it? No bookies out to destroy those you used to care about?"

"Nah. Chips and cards have nothing to do with this. But yes to you being cautious," Riley says, "as bizarre as that sounds. Really, I'm sure I'm just having some weird dreams lately. I'm not one for following my gut over my mind, but something this time around told me I needed to at least contact you."

The geniality returns to Damon's voice when he speaks. His tone relaxes and his pitch lowers.

"Thanks, Riley. At least you were brave enough to follow your hunch and call me. But you take care of yourself. You said things have been rough, right? Reduce your stress, take some yoga classes. Learn to meditate. Maybe see a counselor if you don't already?"

This last suggestion lets Riley know Damon thinks he's on the verge of a mental break. He probably won't take Riley's words into any sort of consideration. And while he knew that was a possibility before calling, he doesn't want Damon to treat the call with flippancy. But any sort of adamant warning given now would only support Damon's view that Riley is mentally fragile. So Riley decides to cut his losses.

"Good idea. You take care of that wife and son."

"Certainly," Damon replies. "And I'll call later in the week and we'll schedule in a cappuccino. You still drink those?"

"You know it," Riley says and then ends it with a farewell, knowing Damon will never call back.

Riley feels slightly queasy and takes a seat on his couch. The room is dim, his curtains pulled. He lifts up the paper and looks at the remainder of the names. He plans on dealing with Newt in person rather than over the phone. He's not sure yet what he'll do with Nicole. He dials the number he has for her, but then something doesn't feel right to him and he doesn't follow through. He hangs up before a connection is made. He decides she might also deserve a personal visit.

Riley decides he has time. Judging from the deaths of Roman and Lars, if they are indeed a trend, the murders occurred at the end of each zodiac cycle. The realization struck him while he was in his cups one night. He'd grabbed his laptop and looked up the dates that coincided with the zodiac cycles and saw how the deaths hung on the waning cusp of each period. Riley operates with the idea he has until the days before June 20th to contact the Geminis. If there is to be another murder, June 20th will likely be the date of the deed.

The last name he looks at on the list belongs to Soo Lim. He dials the number he found for her and when the phone clicks live, he trusts that he'll say the right thing to her. But a man's voice is on the other end. He answers with a huff of air instead of a simple hello.

"Is this the number for Soo Lim?"

"Yes," the man responds. "This is the number."

His voice is heavily accented and gruff. He sounds older than Soo Lim and Riley wonders if it's her father.

"Might I talk with her, please?"

"She is not here. She is in hospital."

Riley's voice catches in his throat. He's stricken by how wrong his theory might be. The stalker could kill whenever he saw fit to take a life. Had the maniac already gotten to his old babysitter? Afraid to ask, Riley presses himself to speak anyway, ready to accept whatever information comes.

"Is she okay? Was she attacked?"

"Why attacked?" the man responds, his voice lifting. "She is sick. Are you a friend? She likes people to visit her."

He presses his eyes shut for a moment and breathes deeply. She's okay. Rather, she is not okay, but her current state cannot be blamed on him.

"I'm Riley Wanner. Soo Lim used to babysit me."

"I remember you. You held onto her legs all the time when you were scared. She would come home and laugh at that. Go to see her. I will give you information."

Riley makes the man hold for a moment while he fumbles around in a drawer in his coffee table for a pen. He concentrates hard to understand the words over the receiver and he writes them on his left forearm.

When he hangs up the phone, he looks at the black ink on his skin and all he can think of is thin, jubilant Soo Lim in a hospital bed like the one he was in recently. He'd been toeless and morose. He grants she likely has more pep. He imagines her grinning through her illness, asking the nurses for hot sauce with each shitty cafeteria meal.

The smile he shows his living room comes from knowing she is safe. She is tucked away and tended. Outside, where the light is low and things may hide, she doesn't reside. No lone woman on a park bench, legs swinging, perpetrators of heinous acts crouching in the shrubbery.

37 PEACH

She finally has time to concentrate on her art project. Her find from the thrift store has lingered in her living room, untouched, for too long. She eyes the form of it and then moistens five paper towels and runs them over the plastic, cleaning away smudges of dirt and a streak of something vividly blue, perhaps the scrawling Magic Marker of a child.

Peach is sans wig, sans scarf and enjoys the way the air plays over her free scalp and her scabbing wound. All the ache and puffiness has left the muscle of her throat and when she looks in the mirror, trying to catch a glimpse of the inked Taurus symbol, she's happy to see that it's completely buried away under the crust of dried blood and the mending skin. Likely, the ink never set in the meat of her muscle. But she knew that when she put it there. Soon she'll remove the stitches and soon after that, when the wound is healed, she'll use makeup to cover up the penance she had to pay in order to make her second sacrifice.

"All part of the energetic exchange," she says to the tall item. She stands back to make sure she hasn't missed any layers of grime. She tests out the movable parts of the thing, how they spin in a circular motion and one section of plastic pops off at a slight touch. She returns it to the base and nods her head. The object will do nicely.

She retrieves a tool she's used several times in the last week. The little crème brûlée torch has spent its fuel three times over and she refills it before tucking it into the pocket of her baggy pants. In the other pocket sits her agate. Grasping the bones of her creation, she shuffles it out her front door, inspired and ready to create.

The sun is fading and the area around her apartment building is quiet. Mona, her neighbor, is nowhere in sight. Peach decides to deliver a bag of hard, herbal candies to the woman soon. Her gut tells her it is best to keep track of the woman's whereabouts.

She sets her inspiration down on her concrete patio, next to the planter of coral impatiens, and digs her small butane torch from her pocket. She clicks it to life and eyes the base of the structure. Peach cups her free hand over her nose and mouth and applies the inch-long flame to the plastic. It smokes at first, sending an acrid blackness into the air. She does her best not to breathe it in and curses the absence of a respirator. Then the plastic begins to warp and melt away, dripping in a softened wave to her patio. Its flow reminds her of quicksilver. Once she's happy with the extent of the destruction, she flips off the torch and removes her hand from her mouth to gulp in fresh oxygen. Between sips of pure air, she gets smacked with the pungent zing of burnt chemicals and her eyes sting at the odorous assault.

Peach looks down on her evolving creation and grins. There is more to do to change the form of the thing into a specific entity, something with connotations, something that can evoke.

She means to send a strong message. One maddening in its impact.

"It's just the start, but in the end, you will be perfect."

The plastic on the concrete hardens. It takes on the appearance of a globular humanoid made of flowing curves. A homunculus, even. Peach stands a giant over it, the singsong string of *fee, fi, foe, fum* at the ready, anxious to pass her lips.

SATURDAY,
THE 6TH OF JUNE,
2015

38 RILEY

Because he would rather talk to Newt Parnwell in person during a workday, he waits on checking his name off the list. And because he still can't muster up the gumption to call Nicole or go back to the house where he saw her last, Riley decides to do what Soo Lim's father told him to do. He goes to the hospital.

The hospital isn't the same one he was in, where they took his toes and left him alone in his bed, his only comfort the curvy ass of a nurse and an occasional visit from Walker. Yet he still gets shivers walking the corridors of this place, smelling the scent of ammonia and mediocre cafeteria food. It reminds him of when he opened his first card sent from Hamal. That had been the beginning of it all, though he hadn't known it at the time.

He watches as people pass by him, visitors to other patients in the hospital. Most of them have presents of some sort: mylar balloons, roses, Styrofoam takeout containers of food from the outside world. Riley wonders if he should have brought something for Soo Lim, but he only wants a moment to talk with her and warn her about the potential danger she is in. He thinks his warning will be gift enough.

When he locates her room, a male nurse is just leaving. A flattened, flexible bag that once might have contained saline or some other IV fluid rests in his hands. He has a buzz cut and thin arms sandwiching a boxy torso. He eyes Riley up and down.

"Are you here to see Ms. Lim?"

"Sure am. Is she seeing walk-ins?"

The man sniffs. "She had her eyes open earlier today. Even with what she's facing, she's a graceful lady. You know, strength of character."

He can't see into the room, to see whether or not the woman is awake or up for a visitor. His mind reels, concocting tales of why he should be granted entrance. As if he has to convince this nurse of his suitability, of his attachment. He becomes Soo Lim's younger lover, or her best friend at an imagined real estate brokerage firm, or her favorite bartender.

"Graceful like Cinderella?" He's reaching but goes with it. "I don't want to walk in on her sponge bathing. Singing some sweet tune and waiting for the mice and birds to come out and dress her."

Riley tries a laugh. The nurse shakes his head and waves him toward the door of the room.

"There aren't any vermin in this hospital. She was dozing, but might be awake now. Go right ahead. Before someone else beats you to it."

Riley kills the imagined roles of importance in Soo Lim's life. "So she gets a lot of visitors?"

"That woman," the nurse says, "has so many friends, relatives and coworkers out here each day I don't know where she finds the time to rest and heal."

Riley realizes she may not be adequately monitored in the hospital. If people come and go all the time, what's to say someone, like Hamal, Aldebaran, or Pollux can't come and go as well?

"And that's a safe thing? That anyone can come and see her?"

"We can't regulate it, if that's what you're asking," the nurse says and squeezes the empty bag in his hand. "The staff is busy enough managing pain and keeping people alive. We aren't too focused on social calendars. Certain patients get someone to sit with them twenty-four seven. People swap out every few hours. But those patients aren't like Ms. Lim."

"They aren't Korean?" he kids.

The man frowns. "I'm one quarter Laotian."

"Congratulations?"

"I mean they are people who need to be watched. For a reason not applicable to Ms. Lim."

"Right," Riley nods. "She's not a flight risk or a fall risk. She's not going to sharpen a bedpan for slitting her wrists. I hear you loud and clear. I suppose I'll just say hello to her and then let her get some sleep."

"Perhaps," the nurse mumbles as he walks away, "you'll speed up her recovery. Anything to get herself out of bed and away from you faster."

Riley lets the jab slide. He brings up his knuckles to rap on the open door before announcing his presence. But he holds back instead, walking quietly to the open door and peering inside. Soo Lim is in the hospital bed, her eyes closed with a clear, plastic respirator over her mouth and nose. Brunette hair hits just at her shoulders and her skin is softer, plumper than he recalls from his youth.

There is something about the way she rests that calms him. A bowl of untouched Jell-O rises and sinks on her chest, a muted television casts flickering variants of light and dark onto the white sheet tucked around her legs. Riley sighs and feels his old babysitter is safe in her little hospital room. And though he knows the staff can't watch every patient all the time, he also knows both Roman and Lars were in relatively secluded places at the time of their murders. A bustling, lively hospital, thriving with people very engaged with life and death at all hours of the day would likely be the last place his stalker would want to off his next victim.

So Riley decides Soo Lim will be safe within the walls of the place meant for healing and fixing. Instead of scaring her with talk of a psycho killer or killers terrorizing him and other Boiseans, he trusts she will be guarded and cared for. There are others on his list of five that he's more worried about. Specifically Nicole Trey.

"May you have all the birds and mice at your beck and call. I hear robins are great at following trends in casual wear. And dormice can do some wicked drop curls," he whispers.

He watches her sleep for a moment longer and is happy he won't have to face her, though he's come down to the hospital to do just that. He wonders if she would bring up the same memory her father had recalled if he were to wake her, warning her of some bizarre threat. Perhaps she'd mock him for hiding behind her knobby, long legs when he was seven and she was fourteen. Perhaps she'd see through his ruse, see his anxiety and self-doubt, his questionable life choices and she'd think that he was still the same pathetic, cowering child.

39   PEACH

The Saturday afternoon is warm and dry and Peach takes a
sip of pink guava juice from a tall, plastic glass. She sits on the
lawn in Linx's backyard and watches the growing ram rub his
nose in the fecund and vibrant earth. The moisture of his nose
causes blades of brown, dead grass to stick above his upper lip,
making him look like he has a tan mustache of vegetation.

Linx crouches next to Peach and offers her a bowl of
strawberries. They've been hulled, their skins crimson and
heavily-pocked with dark, teardrop seeds. Their scent mixes with
that of the sod and a smell of burning mesquite in someone's
grill, houses away.

"They're local," Linx says. Plucking a strawberry from the
bowl, he holds it out to the lamb and calls the animal toward him.
"Baba! Baba black sheep, have you any wool? Yes sir, yes sir,
three bags full!"

Peach pops a strawberry in her mouth and enjoys the
tartness of the fruit on her tongue. "Two things. First, he's white,

not black. Second, where did you hear that nursery rhyme? I can't believe your mother sang it to you."

"She didn't," he answers as the lamb ambles over to his outstretched arm. "A grown man can watch reruns of *Sesame Street* when he's sick in bed with a head cold. I have no shame about it."

"But I'm pretty sure it's baabaa, as in the sound sheep make. Not Baba. He's not a character in *Arabian Nights*. Though if he was, he might be into *Sesame Street* as well. Wasn't he the thief who figured out the magic password, 'Open Sesame'?" Peach says and laughs, pops another berry into her mouth.

"Be nice to me," Linx adopts a pout and watches the lamb munch down on the berry before he removes his hand. "I'm first-generation American. I get a pass on some things."

She runs her fingers through the blades of grass surrounding her and suddenly she's recalling her strange vision, the one with the double Rileys. She remembers the one dressed like a woman, pointing to the ground, at something for Peach to find. Peach believes she'd already found it, but she has a sudden panicky moment when she wonders if what's she's interpreted as the correct object is nothing more than a piece of the bigger picture. Might it just be a small sliver of her treasure, as each blade of grass unites to create an expanse of soft, green yard?

"Patti is coming on Monday," Peach says and directs her mind to think of something else. "Any way I might be able to talk you into having dinner with us once she's back? Might take the brunt of her passive-aggressiveness off of me when she has two people to judge and berate."

Linx pulls another strawberry out of the bowl for the lamb and tosses it at the animal's front hooves. "How can I say no to an evening of Patti's false tears and your clenched jaw?"

"Thank you," Peach says.

"You're welcome," Linx echoes. "Want to hear about a dream I just had?"

"Not really, but I doubt I can actually stop you."

Linx pouts again and starts in on his story.

"It was strange. I don't know where I was, but I was with a group of friends. Except these are people I've never met, in this life, at least. There was a building, something vaguely European but not totally. Parts of it looked like sand held together by water. You know, how it looks when you make sandcastles on a beach? And this group I was with was invited by some odd people, men and women, to eat food together.

"So we went to this big hall full of people this group had invited. It was a bunch of strangers feasting and sharing a meal together. And none of us really knew what was happening, but I wasn't too worried about it. I can't even remember the food we ate. But when we were done with the meal, they shuffled us into this giant theater. Then, these men and women put on costumes and performed a play. And the entire time I felt like the theater was under the ground.

"And at the end of the whole thing, they asked us if we'd join their cult. And if we didn't want to, then we were asked to leave. But the people who did join the cult, they were taken away to be shown something else. Some big secret like the workings of the cult explained to them. I remember one man who was in the cult. Must have been a leader. He was dressed like a giant bull, with horns on his head and everything. The other ones who had costumes, I can't remember what they looked like. It was so surreal."

Peach doesn't know how to respond to this recounting of his dream. She's shocked Linx has had such an experience. As far as she knows, her friend has no knowledge of ancient mystery cults or religions. Yet she can't help but think that his dream is a message for her. Another element of synchronicity egging her on. Though Linx can't describe the dream in much detail, she doesn't think it's a mere coincidence he's had it. Not when she's just passed out of the cycle of Taurus. Not when there were others on the stage, in different roles. Might there have been twins? A crab or a lion or a pair of silver fish?

She takes up another strawberry and licks a bit of juice from its side.

"Tell me, Linx," she asks, "did you join the cult? Did you go with them and learn about their practices and beliefs?"

Linx laughs and his chuckling spooks the lamb. Roman, temporarily known as Baba, scoots backward, away from Linx. He turns his quivering flanks and makes for a sunny spot of grass away from the staccato laughter.

"Of course not," Linx answers. "Even if it was just a dream, I'm not crazy. Enough of my logic remained even though I was asleep. Those people were strange and I got the feeling I wouldn't be management, if you know what I mean. Maybe I'd be used or worse, sacrificed. Why would I ever decide to get on board with something like that?"

Peach plops the strawberry into her mouth and follows it with a chaser of guava juice. The fruit flavors delight. She answers Linx as she licks her lips clean of sugar.

"Just checking."

MONDAY,
THE 8TH OF JUNE,
2015

40   RILEY

He heads for the back room, the workroom where the men make the trommels to uncover gold. But Double Al sees him come in the front door and grabs Riley's arm, tugging him into his office. As much as he wants to tell his old boss that he's just there to talk with Newt, he does have things to discuss with Double Al. But all the old miner wants to do, initially, is talk about Lars.

"I'm telling you it wasn't an accident, what happened with your finance man. But I don't want to tell the police that. I bet they'll try to link my truck and this death somehow if I give them hell about Mr. Apitz. Imagine me talking about how there wasn't a cave in and asking them why they think there was? They might laugh me out of their Podunk station."

"Sounds like you're dealing with a guilty conscience?" Riley asks. Even though he'd like to tell Double Al there might be a connection between the truck and Lars's death, he wants to alleviate his friend's feelings of assumed guilt, not rally them on.

The task at hand is warning the Geminis, not worrying Double Al.

"I'm dealing with poor sleep and an ulcer that's tormenting me. Thing must be as big as a baby's hand. I eat Tums more than I eat sweets. That's strange for me."

"Then what are you going to do?" Riley asks. He remains standing and watches as Double Al paces the room. The man's skin is dark, but the circles under his eyes are blacker and puffier than Riley has ever seen them. They remind him of the rubber stoppers on the bottom of chair legs.

"I guess I'm going to keep working, son. I'm going to let it go. Because even if it was some foul end for that boy up in my mineshaft, how am I going to do anything to find his murderer? Besides, who knows what the cops will do if I keep poking. They might focus more on my black skin and less on me. Who knows where that would end. No, I'll just stick to my work."

"What about the truck explosion? Those lab results must be back by now."

Double Al shuffles around the papers on his desk and pulls forth a tabbed folder marked "Truck Stuff". He hands the folder over to Riley and frowns.

"First page in there. They faxed it to me yesterday. I'd forgotten we even had a fax machine until it whirled on. Scared the shit out of me."

Riley scans the paper and quickly reads the summation of the findings. He's shocked at what he sees.

"Magnesium, lithium carbonate, potassium nitrate," Riley reads out loud and pauses to think. "Plus carbon and other materials. Fireworks? Someone set your truck on fire with fireworks?"

"Yes," Double Al says and summons the folder back to him with a wave of his hand. "They opened up the gas tank and used something to catch the firework sparks and flames and direct it into the belly of my Dodge Ram. Fire was so hot, they don't know what sort of wick was used. No trace of it. Definitely natural. Maybe some stupid kids acting out, but not going to rule out a hate crime. What if the police think my truck relates to your friend found dead up on my site?"

Riley would have never guessed fireworks would come into play in the truck bombing, but suddenly he considers there might be a way to get a lead on who torched the truck. Perhaps there is a definitive way to get a real name or even an image of the perpetrator who might be one and the same as his tormentor.

"But this is a good thing. Fireworks in the springtime? This person had to go to a shop or online to get them. Don't they need to sign a waiver to buy fireworks? Won't they have that on file?"

"That's what I asked, son. And turns out they only sign something if they buy illegal fireworks, the kind that go in the air. They sign something saying they plan on taking them and using them out of Idaho borders. If these were just fountains, sparklers, they don't get anything from their customers. Besides, could have been fireworks stored in some garage since last Fourth of July. It'd be a complete dead end."

The container of cinnamon bears Double Al is so fond of eating sits on a bookshelf behind his desk. Riley walks around to it, picks it up, and digs himself out a small handful.

"I see why you want to focus on work."

"Part of that focus is on your insurance claim. And your disability claim. You've got to make a choice about coming back to work or not, son. Because if you do, there's not going to be any temporary disability pay out. If you're fit to work, which you are, they'll give you nothing."

Riley sees stars, sparks and flames in his mind. He knows Double Al is right; looking into the fireworks would be a dead end.

"And if I'm not fit to work, what's the likelihood my claim will go through?"

"Good," Double Al says and snatches the container away from Riley. He caps it, puts it back on the shelf. "But you're not going to like the stipulations. There are consequences for going on the dole."

"Which are?"

Double Al shakes his head and pauses. Riley can see there is something he doesn't feel comfortable sharing with him at the moment. With the level of stress Double Al's under, Riley doesn't feel like pressing it.

"Okay, we can talk about it later. But push it through. I'm not coming back to work."

"You sure?" Double Al asks.

His face goes slack and Riley considers that he might be compounding the man's woes further with his refusal to come back to the business. But Riley knows if he's busy hunting down his stalker, he doesn't have time to waste pushing papers and listening to his coworkers joke about his toeless foot. He can worry about finances after this all ends. He can't envision it going on for much longer. With his attention on rooting out this nutjob, he'll be back to the mundane aspects of life in no time.

"For now I'm sure, but maybe not always. Nothing is permanent, right?" Riley replies, trying to soften the blow. "But hey, I realized this morning I haven't had a drink in a long while, at least a long while for me. So things must be looking up. I might actually be staying out of trouble for a bit. Or at least taking a break from it."

"You know what your father would say, son?"

"My father seemed to be friends with all of Boise. And people are always telling me what he'd say. So yes, I know what he'd say. And sorry, Double Al, but I don't really give a shit about the opinion of a dead man."

Double Al's eyes widen and he opens his mouth to speak but Riley stops him.

"I've got to talk to Newt real quick before I get out of here. I'll talk to you soon, okay? You call me if you learn anything else about the pyromaniac or Lars."

And then he leaves, without turning around to wave or embrace Double Al, and heads straight for the double swinging doors into the back room. He wants to address the situation with Newt in the same way he'd approach a healed wound covered with an adhesive bandage. He means to rip it off quickly without much thought or hesitation.

He's greeted with the smell of soot and the sound of power tools doing their grinding and sawing and filing. Three men are at work in the area and Riley figures the rest must be at lunch or out back testing the equipment. He's happy he won't have many witnesses to this odd exchange.

He sees Newt near a set of heavy, desk-sized bellows and does his best to gain the man's attention by waving around his arms. The ex-coworker wears a pair of earplugs and a set of plastic, protective goggles. At first he doesn't see Riley, but then he catches him out of the corner of his eye and stops his pumping of the bellows and peels off his leather gloves.

"You coming back to work?" he hollers at Riley over the din of the shop.

"No, I came to say something to you," Riley responds.

"Is this about the foot? Because the chain…"

Riley cuts him off. "This isn't about that. I just wanted to warn you I think someone is messing with me and people I know. This yahoo might be dangerous. Just keep an eye out, okay?"

"Why you telling me this? We ain't friends," the man hollers back at Riley. He pushes his goggles onto his forehead and hacks a wad of phlegm into his mouth. He sends it pinging into the furnace.

"I just have a feeling," Riley hedges. He's pleased he's direct with the man, but he doesn't want to launch into an explanation of his entire theory.

"You sure you ain't just fucking with me? Because of you losing those toes?"

Riley's anger rises so quickly he nearly rushes to close the gap between them, thinking to bring his fist up to punch the man. The last thing he needs is another trip down to the police station to talk to another cop or detective. Especially if he's right. Especially if Newt somehow ends up dead after Riley's punched him in the nose.

"Not a joke. Just protect yourself."

"I've got it covered," Newt laughs loudly, his buggy eyes growing more pronounced with his expressive chuckling. "I'm a dead shot with a rifle. And I've got a lot of rifles."

Riley feels like he's done his part for the man. Even if he doesn't like him, he's been warned. And the man does seem capable of self-defense.

"Well, that's it. I've got to go. Security guy coming to look at my place."

Newt stops his laughing and pulls the goggles back down over his eyes. "Don't be a pussy, Wanner. Get yourself a Glock. Maybe a nice Winchester. Them is all the security you'll need."

41   PEACH

He brings her a coreopsis flower the color of ripe mango
and she takes it from his fingers while telling him to have a seat.
Michel looks around the room and stretches his back by grabbing
the side of the chair meant for clients, pulling his slight form into
a sort of spiral contortion. Peach hears a pop and a mellow sigh
escapes the man's mouth.

"Aren't you going to smell the blossom, *ma chérie?*"

Peach brings the bloom up to her nose. It might have a light,
mum-like scent if any scent at all. The flower he's brought her
smells like nothing. It could be made of silk and plastic if the
delicateness of the petals and the stickiness of the stem didn't
betray its authenticity.

"It's very nice. Thank you, Michel."

"I had to bring you something. After that asshole, after what
he said."

"Who, Chacham? Don't pay attention to him, Michel. Remember what we've talked about in terms of perceptions and judgments. You aren't responsible for his."

Michel relaxes in the chair, facing Peach. He smiles.

"Do you like your stuffed frog? Have you named it?"

She'd almost forgotten he had given her the poison dart frog toy. Peach tries to think of where she put it but can't call the location to mind.

"No name, yet. But I'll think of something great."

"So," Michel starts, clapping his hands together. Peach can see the outline of the sole cigarette in the shirt pocket of his tissue-paper thin, vintage dress shirt. "I want to talk about kids."

"Excuse me?" Peach asks, startled Michel has decided to broach the subject. In the past, when she'd attempt to bring up his childhood or whether or not he had children or had designs on having children, he would change the course of the conversation, directing it towards ruminations on past violence or outlandish, flighty goals.

"Kids," Michel says, "I want them."

"Well that's a positive thought. What's made you decide you'd like to raise a family?"

"You," he responds. His smile grows wider, the skin crinkling near his eyes with the heavy lashes. His sole dimple is a fetching focal point on his cheek.

"Michel, please remember what we've discussed many times in the past. About transference. If I inspire you to have children, that's great. But don't tell me you plan on having those children with me."

He slides the cigarette from his pocket and slips it past his lips. He holds it with his teeth, careful to keep it as dry as he can, away from any saliva in his mouth.

"I've been thinking. Twins run in my family. They're usually identical. And I don't know how it works, but what if I were to get a set of fraternal twins? I could have a boy and a girl at the same time and call it good. Ready-made family, *ma chérie*. Doesn't that sound nice? One pregnancy but two kids? I'm sure you'd fall in love with them both as soon as they were out of you. You'd fall in love."

First Linx talking about bulls, now Michel talking about twins. Peach bites her lip and wonders if the universe is sending her more omens, more signs that her work is good. For now, she'll take it as validation. She deems what Linx and Michel have verbalized to her as holy communiqué. The masters of the last zodiac cycles, they must be very pleased. Linx and Michel are the mouthpieces. Both acting as Metatron.

"That's wonderful you want children, Michel. But, as we've talked about before, any sort of relationship between us would be inappropriate." Peach thinks of the client and counselor relationship, how it's a shield she uses to keep Michel away. She has yet to tell him the real reason she'd find any sort of congress between the two of them to be unnatural, abhorrent.

"Fuck rules," Michel says and bites down hard on his cigarette. He chews on the end of it, flecks of dried tobacco escaping the paper and sticking to his teeth. "You know I'd do anything for you, Perfect Peach. What other man has ever said that to you? Tell me."

Michel stands abruptly and spits his cigarette out of his mouth. It falls to the carpet, a rain of brown tobacco and soggy, translucent paper. The tips of his ears turn red and he grasps on to the edge of Peach's desk with both hands, until his fingers and nails turn rose, then white as milk from the pressure.

It takes her a moment to remember Michel has always sworn he's never harmed a woman. While she doesn't feel she is in danger, she does feel annoyed at his display of anger. She decides to control the situation. Old Peach would have cowered, perhaps picked up the phone on her desk and dialed for help. But the evolution of this Peach has given her strength.

"Mr. Rothschild," she says in an even whisper. "Take your seat. Now."

He holds the desk for a moment longer, until she can see the blood begin to flow back into his fingers. Then he lets go and falls back into the upholstered chair. He looks down at the ground and plucks up the spent cigarette, half-chewed and unraveled. He tosses it on her desk.

"Just don't doubt me," he says as he bends over from the chair to pick tobacco leaf from the low-pile carpet. "I'm working on my stuff. I come here to see you, but I come here for me, too. I'm trying to quit this rage. And I haven't done any self-harming lately."

He shows her his forearms. The skin there is unmarred. He thumps his stomach and it sounds like a thwacked watermelon.

"Eating well and no bruises or cuts. I could be the best father you've ever seen, *ma chérie*. Don't count me out yet. If I need to leave our sessions in order to make you my girl, I'm ready for it. Don't you think about doubting my devotion."

"I've never had the thought pass my mind," Peach smiles.

She casts her eyes down to the mangled mess of tobacco and wrapper. "Your poor cigarette."

"I'll take another," he says.

From where he means to take one, she does not know. It will not be bought. Of that she is certain. Just as certain she is of his unwavering attention and dedication. He could give Linx a run for his money on that account. She allows her mind to conjure an image of both men, one at each of her sides. But several steps behind her. She is the lead flyer. All others angle out in a sharp V behind her.

"Where did you go?" Michel asks with a smile. His nails have regained their normal coloring and he's sitting comfortably in the chair again.

"I'm sorry," she says. "This isn't a time for daydreaming."

"Were you dreaming of our little ones?"

"Come on, Michel," she corrects firmly.

"Come on, Perfect Peach," he urges with a mischievous smile.

42   RILEY

Though the man looks shady to Riley, with his head capped in a billed hat, his eyes red and deep-set, his lips thin and dry, he does his best to calm his nerves. He sticks out his hand for the man's identification. It hangs from a blue fabric lanyard around the man's neck.

Riley snatches it up to look over, even reading the fine print on the backside of the laminate. Then he holds up the picture on the card level with the man's face. The guy from AGT pulls his neck away, the fabric loop drawing taut. Riley looks past hair color and eye color and compares the spaces between eyes and nose, mouth and ears. This is the way software systems verify identities, or so he believes, and he tries it out himself. Perhaps there is a home version of such a system associated with modern security cameras. When he's satisfied the man is Mr. Lancaster from AGT Security, he releases the card. The man clears his throat and cracks his neck, glad to free of Riley's grasping.

"I just can't be careful enough," Riley says.

"I'm used to it. That was nothing. One guy asked for my home phone number once, then made me wait outside while he called my wife to ask her if she thought I was a moral man. Whatever that means. There are people more paranoid than you, Mr. Wanner. It's my job to help put some of those worries to rest."

"I appreciate you coming out. I won't waste your time. Come on in."

Riley opens his door wide and the man immediately asks if he should remove his shoes. Riley tells him not to worry about it. With a tablet and stylus in hand, the security appraiser takes his time, beginning with the living room. He uses his hands to feel the casings around windows, stands with his back in each corner of the room, gauging where a camera would best be placed. He asks Riley about his nightly habits: if he arrives home at odd hours, if he sleepwalks, if he leaves his bedroom at all to use the toilet or dig around in the refrigerator. Riley answers all the questions, though he's uncomfortable with the level of specificity that the man requires.

"Does it really matter that I eat Kraft Singles in the middle of the night?" he asks.

"It does to sensors and cameras," Mr. Lancaster replies and presses his stylus to his tablet to write down a note.

When he's done casing the downstairs of the house, Riley follows him upstairs, flipping on lights for the man as they climb. The man sees a smoke detector at the top of the stair landing and reaches up with his finger to depress the testing button. No loud siren emanates from the plastic disk.

"Time to replace batteries," he says and then turns around to look at Riley. "Keep in mind that security isn't just about cameras and alarms. You need to stay diligent. You'll be the person keying in codes or programming sensor sweeps. If something does trigger the system to alert our staff, you'll be responsible for calling anything off that's not a real threat."

Riley doesn't appreciate the lecture. He simply nods his head and follows the man around the upstairs of his house. He spends extra time in Riley's bedroom, looking out the window, eyeing the brittle metal drainpipe that runs up the exterior of the house, right past Riley's bedroom window.

He makes another note on his tablet and then asks Riley to take him outside so he can check the perimeter of the property and the structural integrity of any fences.

"Plus," the man says, walking down the stairs, followed by Riley, "people tend to forget about the shrubs. They'll say they hate landscaping, so they let bushes get wild and big right by the walls of their houses. You might as well be inviting thieves and degenerates to camp out underneath windowsills in those bushes. Lawn maintenance. It's a must."

"Understood," Riley says. "I had to scare off a hobo the other day. He was stewing beans under the yew hedge in the backyard. It was either swat at him with a broom, share his baked beans, or make him a pet. Go the whole nine yards and get a tag made up, name him Hobbs the Hobo."

The man doesn't crack a smile. His face remains sober and he asks Riley to lead him outside. Riley forces a smirk, determined not to let the awkward situation get to him. Even if the man the security company sent out is a bit of a tool, in the end, his house will be better protected from late-night visits by Pollux or Aldebaran or Hamal. Riley has about all the gifts he can stand from his stalker.

"This way," Riley answers and takes the lead to the glass sliding doors leading out to his backyard deck. He thinks about what he's willing to give up for a sense of security. He's willing to make an effort to protect himself, but he hopes he doesn't become a humorless, hyper-anal man like Mr. Lancaster.

Riley pauses to open the vinyl blinds and crank them away from the glass so he can open the door. He flips up the latch on the metal handle but doesn't slide open the pane of glass. Blinking heavily, he flips the latch back down, locking the door.

The security man notices Riley's bewildered look. His tablet drops to his side and he turns his attention outdoors. Mr. Lancaster walks up to the window to look out at what Riley has already seen.

There, in the deck chair where Riley drinks his whisky and ponders his life and sometimes sleeps to the hooting of an owl, is the stiff body of a blond-haired man.

43   PEACH

At a stoplight near the interstate intersection leading to the Boise Airport, Peach slows down so she's certain to hit the red light. A young man in his late teens with dreaded hair and a skinny pit bull squats on the corner. The boy doesn't have a sign. Instead, he pours a stream of murky water from a dented, stainless steel canteen into a bowl created from cutting the bottom off of a gallon milk jug. The dog laps at the water and then shakes, sending saliva all over the boy. The panhandler waves at the car nearest him at the intersection, but the driver keeps facing forward.

The young man is burdened with invisibility to most of the drivers. But Peach sees him with a vivid crispness.

She honks to get the boy's attention. When he looks around, she takes her hands off the steering wheel and beckons him over to her Honda. He stands up from his crouch and the pit bull follows without a lead. She rolls down the window on the passenger side of her car and he ducks his head down to deliver a smile. His teeth are dirty yellow, as if thousands of cups of coffee have passed his lips.

"I'll take any change. I'm not picky," he says. Peach can smell the booze mingled with sweat and filth on the boy. It causes her stomach to lurch.

"I've got a twenty for you if you're up to doing a little work. Are you interested?"

The panhandler acts to open her door. But she shakes her head and points to a parking lot in the distance.

"See that lot near the family-style restaurant that serves chicken-fried steak? About a block away? Gather up your stuff and meet me there. I'll drive over and wait for you."

The light changes from red to green. Peach rolls up the window and takes a right at the intersection, cruising into the parking lot and shutting off her engine. It's early afternoon and the bulk of the lunchtime crowd has left the restaurant long ago. She looks to the windows of the diner and can make out a waitress wiping down tables with a floppy, wet rag.

The boy moves quickly and Peach watches him lope toward her through her rearview mirror. The pit bull dodges a bicyclist, turning at the last second to nip at the passing spokes. The panhandler pulls his dreads back and ties them together with a twist tie. It's the same type of paper-covered wire found on bags of bread.

Peach opens her car door but doesn't stand up. She shakes out her arms, tells herself to relax. She's uncomfortable with soliciting help from a stranger, especially to carry out one of her rituals, but she can't risk being seen by the cameras on the lights at the airport intersection and has no idea what sorts of cameras are placed around the airport property. She looks to the sky, to her current best friend Pollux and wills the star look after the boy she is about to put in charge of her display for Air.

He waits with his dog for Peach to speak. The pit bull sniffs the soles of Peach's Oxfords and then wanders off to piss on the yellowing grass alongside the road.

"Thanks for agreeing to this."

"I haven't agreed to anything yet. What's this job?"

"Down to business. I like it," she says and looks around the parking lot. There are a few cars scattered about but none of them contain any people. Yet Peach must be certain this boy can be trusted to do the work.

"What I need you to do is simple. You'll find it weird, even. But what I need from you more than the job, is a promise. You cannot, under any circumstances, tell anyone about me."

The boy flips his dreads around and whistles for his dog but the pit bull ignores the call. "What? You someone special? All depends on what you need. And it might cost you more than a twenty."

Peach looks into the back seat of her car, where the three boxes she picked up from the retail store sit. "I'll give you forty in total. But I want you to spend twenty of it on food. Go into that restaurant in a bit and get yourself something to eat. The other twenty you can spend on whatever."

"Right, mom," the boy quips. "But you still haven't told me what you want me to do."

She doesn't know if she can trust him. Perhaps he'll just laugh and walk away, finding her request absurd. But she's running out of time. Patti's flight arrives in fifteen minutes and she's convinced that now is the time and the place for a display. Fortune favors the bold, she tells herself. Perhaps the stars favor the bold as well.

"I'll tell you. But you'll have to do it right now, as soon as I pull away. I'll know if you just take the money and fuck off. I'm going to sit and watch, out of sight. Don't let me catch you skipping out on the deal."

Then Peach reaches into the back of the car and pulls the boxes forward. They're light enough to push into the young man's hands. He looks down at the items and his lips part to show off a pierced tongue. She removes her wallet from her purse, pulling out a twenty and two tens, and tosses the bills on top of the boxes.

A light uptick in the breeze threatens to take the payment on his behalf. The wind sets Peach at ease. He clamps a palm over the cash while reading the text on the top box, eyeing the picture. He flicks his eyes in Peach's direction.

"This could be fun," he says. "If this is as wild as it gets, I'm definitely game."

44   RILEY

Riley knows standing near the sliding glass door, his fingers on the handle with the security man next to him, will do nothing to change the fact there is the body of a man on his backyard deck.

"He hasn't moved," Mr. Lancaster observes.

"I can see that," Riley says. "We'll have to go and look, don't you think?"

He flips up the latch on the sliding glass door and pulls it open. The sound of the metal base moving along a track doesn't rouse the attention of the man in the chair. Riley steps outside, not sure if he should be making noise or if he should remain quiet and attempt to sneak up on the stranger. Perhaps he sleeps, or is focused on something in the far distance. Perhaps he is drugged or stiff with rigor mortis. When his foot finds a brittle twig on the deck and it snaps with a loud crack, the man in the chair stays stock still.

Mr. Lancaster moves to the side of Riley once more and approaches the chair from a wide arc, coming from the right of the unresponsive man. Riley makes straight for the back of his deck chair, his hands tensing into fists. He expects at best a derelict high on weed. At worst, a corpse.

Riley's eyes flip from the back of the man's head to the face of the security guy. Though he's shadowed by his billed hat, Riley can see his eyes are narrowed and his lips are pressed tight together. Riley creeps forward, a mere few feet away from the stranger, and he looks again at Mr. Lancaster. The security guy has seen the man's face in the chair, coming around to the front of him before Riley. His expression changes from one of suspicion to one of confusion.

"No wonder he didn't move," the man says and Riley half-leaps, half-jogs to put himself directly in front of the sitting man. He's at the ready for a confrontation.

What he finds instead is a mannequin. Its limbs have been bent into a sitting position and a cheap wig of blond hair is perched on its head. It's held there by strips of double-sided sticky tape that poke out from behind one of the mannequin's ears.

And while it is clearly a male mannequin, complete with a flat chest and muscular arms, it has been dressed as a woman. It sports a yellow tank top and a lacy, white skirt. The hands are stiff and pointed but forced to rest in the lap of the dummy. And in the mannequin's palms is a folded piece of paper.

Mr. Lancaster walks around the odd scene, dipping his head down to peer underneath the deck chair. Then he grasps the shoulders of the mannequin and shakes it, hard, but he's only greeted with the sound of rattling plastic and the shifting metal of the chair legs.

"You definitely need us," is all he says to Riley.

The gift must be from Pollux and the note will be some mildly threatening missive. But Riley picks up the paper anyway and unfolds it, ignoring the security guy's insistence that the paper not be touched by Riley before it can be taken to a lab and dusted for fingerprints. He reads in silence:

do you believe in an evil twin and a good twin? i don't. i just believe in twins. it's always the case that one twin takes and the other is taken from. sometimes a twin can detest the other twin. sometimes a twin will sacrifice immortality for his twin. what kind of twin would you be, riley? i give this twin to you. for practice. play well.

Pollux

"Let me read it," Mr. Lancaster says and reaches for the note but Riley turns his body away and tucks it into his pocket. While he's busy shoving the paper deep into his jeans, he notices the mannequin doesn't wear any shoes.

And there, on the left foot of the dummy is a sight that makes Riley's chest constrict. His sense of balance leaves him. He puts his arms out to try and stop the world from spinning, but he pitches backward and his ass lands sharply on the deck.

A disturbing spectacle is displayed before him. Someone has taken a flame to the dummy, removing all the toes of the left foot. It ends in a charred mangle of bulbous, melted plastic.

Riley runs his fingers over the lumpy area and notices the toes on the right foot have been spared. He takes back his hand and places both palms flat on the deck to stabilize his vertigo. He hisses; a glass shard he missed when he broke the shot glass, deep into drinking with Walker, pricks his palm. He straightens up, flicks the shard hard. It skitters down the steps of his deck. The tightness around his chest increases and Riley knows he has precious moments before he's consumed by a full-on panic attack.

Mr. Lancaster hovers over Riley and offers him a hand up, but Riley motions him downward. The deck boards creak as the man crouches, all ears to Riley's whispering.

"I want it all. Cameras, motion sensors, everything. I want

to lock this fucking place down."

45   PEACH

The parking garage nearest the baggage claim is the oldest
parking structure on site at the Boise Airport. Light does its best
to pour over the high concrete sides of the multilevel structure,
but the place is still dim and smells of motor oil. Her Honda
takes up a space that's seen countless comings and goings over
the years. As often as she's come to the airport, it's always been
to retrieve others. She's rarely taken wing herself. Her ex-
husband Adam talked of taking her to Cancun to see Mayan
ruins and an ocean the color of the sky above it, but he'd never
made good on his promise.

Peach waits for Patti in the garage for a half hour before
Patti calls to confirm whether or not Peach is indeed there and
waiting for her on level three, where she specified. It gives Peach
plenty of time to debate if she did the right thing in handing over
her tribute for Air to a vagabond. Instead of stewing over it, she
gets out of the front seat and leans against the hatchback of her
car. Patti must be moving past the line of taxi drivers waiting for

new arrivals to Boise: her nose in the air, her wheeled suitcase squeaking its way after her stiff form.

And ten minutes later this is exactly what Peach sees when Patti finds her parked car.

"I told you the east side of the third level, Peach. This is the north-east side. How did you expect me to find you?"

"Hi, Patti," Peach says, letting her adoptive mother's instant criticism slide off her. "How was the flight?"

"I took more than one flight. Connection through Denver. I swear, I should just stay in Orlando. Everyone wants your money at airports now. No one will give you a meal on a plane without asking for ten dollars for a sandwich. A sandwich on white bread with wilted lettuce! And they don't accept cash. I think that's illegal. I don't know how they get away without accepting legal tender made by the United States government."

"All right," Peach says and puts out a hand to take Patti's suitcase. "Let's get you loaded up and home."

Patti moves around to the front of the car while Peach opens the hatchback and heaves the heavy suitcase up and inside. She eyes the back seat, where her three boxes used to be. Only an hour before, the items had been in her possession, waiting to be used. It's enough to fortify her on the ride from the airport to Patti's condominium near the Boise River.

Peach gets in the car and latches her seatbelt, only to notice Patti isn't wearing hers.

"Put on your seatbelt. They're fining people for not wearing one. The person without the seatbelt gets ticketed, not just the driver."

Patti huffs and pulls the seatbelt strap around her thin torso. Peach notes the extra wrinkles around her mouth and the way the skin on her neck sags lower than the last time she was in Boise. Suddenly Peach cannot remember the woman's age. She seems on par with Methuselah.

"The air here," Patti sneers, "is so dry. I forget how it is until I'm back. Thank goodness I have five humidifiers in the condo. I'll have them churning out vapor as soon as I get home."

Peach puts the car in reverse and leaves the garage. There is a line at the payment booth. When she rolls down the windows to get some relief from the stifling, stale air of the garage, Patti rolls them back up and cranks the air conditioning on full blast.

Once they're at the toll booth, Peach rolls down her window again to pay the attendant with cash. Patti does the rolling up of the window for Peach. This is typical behavior when they are together: a battle of wills staged on a mundane battleground. Then they're off, taking a gentle curve away from the airport grounds toward the interstate on-ramp.

As they pass the airport's welcome sign—a large, multi-ton sandstone boulder etched with the words Boise Airport—Peach slows the car and smiles when she's greeted with her most hopeful, best expectation. Stuck to the sides of the massive rock are three battery-powered bubble machines. They each chug away, sending delicate, soapy spheres into the bright afternoon air.

She rolls down her window again and a bubble finds its way into the car. The light ahead of them shines green and Patti snaps, commanding Peach to drive on. The bubble enchants with its iridescence. Reaching out a finger for the bubble to alight upon, it bursts, leaving a sudsy residue on the tip of her fingernail. She wonders if it's folly, trying to catch something that Air has already claimed.

"This city is getting strange," Patti says. "Let's go, Peach. Look at the light!"

And while the bubbles don't have the same impact as the truck alight with flame or the rain of steer manure on a crowded street, it's a quiet, dignified dance Peach can appreciate. She finds it lovely and peculiar and just the sort of creative respect for Air she thought necessary. She doesn't care if the entirety of

Boise hears about the bubbles at the airport or hears nothing. It's enough for her that it manifested. It had been a calculated success, trusting the young man. She sends him positive vibes, wherever he stands and begs with his pit bull at his side.

"Go, Peach, go," her adoptive mother screams. She slaps at Peach's leg until she rouses from her enchantment. The window goes up, Patti yanking at the button on her armrest. Peach's ring finger gets a little pinch before she returns both hands to the steering wheel. If there is a way to disable the button on the passenger side, she'll find it. Why it's even there, an avenue for usurping the power of the driver, she doesn't know.

For now, she returns her focus to taking Patti home. A flurry of bubbles sees them off, ephemeral and ethereal, like loved ones left on the docks, watching their matriarch cruise into the horizon.

SPRING,
2009

46 RILEY

After an hour of sitting on Kristin's couch, waiting for her to curl her hair and attach false eyelashes, Riley throws down the *Cosmopolitan* magazine he's scanned cover to cover and picks up the television remote. Now he knows his best lipstick shade, ten tricks women use to coax men into cunnilingus, and that trending summer dresses look like potato sacks. Shows don't fare much better. There is nothing of interest to him, though he leaves the channel on a golf tournament while he paces around the front room of her one-bedroom apartment. He's grown accustomed to her tardiness, but Riley considers walking out of the apartment without saying goodbye and enjoying the party on his own. This will show her there are consequences for making him wait.

There's still snow on the ground in Moscow, Idaho, even though they've already passed the spring equinox. Riley feels restless, anxious for a bit of warmth and sun. He decides to get some air out on the second-floor walkway overlooking the library at the University of Idaho. When he opens the door, he's face to face with Nicole. She pushes by him, swaddled in a body-length parka, blotting at her red nose with a tissue.

"Is she still getting ready?" Nicole asks.

"Of course," Riley answers and shuts the door, staying inside. Even though Nicole is sick, he likes her ruddy cheeks and her watery eyes. It makes her seem alive, vibrant with the actions and percolations of her body fighting off a virus.

Nicole removes her coat to display her short skirt, high boots and tight sweater she'd been hiding underneath. Riley does his best not to gawk, but he likes the way her legs seem to reach all the way up to just under her small breasts. Her brown hair cascades down her back, ending where her hips begin. She looks like a wispy, wild thing. A woman made of flowing matter.

He gets out of the narrow entryway and retreats back to the couch. Riley decides since he has something to watch now, to keep him company, he won't scuttle off to the party. It'll save him from having to explain his ditching of Kristin when she locates him later in the evening.

Nicole leaves her coat on the floor and wipes off her boots on a green runner. Then she sits on the other end of the couch from Riley and turns her head away every time she coughs.

"I'm sorry to expose you to my plague. But I'm five days into it, so I doubt I'm contagious."

"It's okay," Riley says and turns his body toward Kristin's best friend. He's never had a real conversation with the woman. Kristin has always been the buffer between them. It strikes Riley that this may be the first time they were completely alone together, without Kristin demanding attention.

"You're studying history, right? Senior year?" he asks Nicole and she nods her head, blows a bit of clear mucus into a well-used tissue. She doesn't offer up more information and neglects to ask Riley about his final year of law school.

He picks up the remote and switches the channel from golf to a mixed martial arts fight. Two men scramble to put one another in locks while they roll about on a slightly padded mat. One of them has a leaping tiger across his pectorals, plucked out in red ink.

"I'd never want to do MMA. Some dude's balls mashed up against my leg or in my face? Scrotum sweat? Shit no."

Nicole keeps her head turned away while eyeing the television. She doesn't comment or smile. Her eyes fill with water and she blinks back the tears of sickness.

Riley takes a look at her boots. They're soft, gray suede with black buttons running up the sides.

"Great heels. Are they new?"

And this finally gets a response from Nicole, but it's not the simple chitchat Riley expected.

"Look, I already have a best friend. You're dating her. Really, you don't need to get to know me for her sake. I doubt you're interested in what I have to say or think anyway. About as interested as I am in your thoughts and feelings."

"Whoa. Harsh," Riley says and scoots to the very end of the couch. "Message received and noted."

Then Nicole stands, tosses her used tissue in the kitchen trash under the sink and washes her hands. She comes back with a bit of paper towel and folds it into a triangle and keeps it palmed in her hand. She sits back down on the couch, except this time she sits next to Riley, so close that their thighs touch.

"I said I don't need another best friend. I also said I'm not interested in you. At least, not your mind."

Nicole lifts up Riley's hand and places it between her breasts. He can feel the ridges of her sternum through her sweater and skin. He leaves his hand there until she swings one of her legs onto his lap. Then he uses both hands to massage her breasts until he decides to slip a hand under her skirt while he bites at the inside of her neck. She tastes slightly of Vicks VapoRub, but it doesn't quell his vigor for her.

A rustle comes from the hallway. Kristin throws open the bathroom door and skips out to the front room where Riley sits, Nicole now back to the other side of the couch. Kristin's black hair is in tight ringlets and her eyes are shaded in an emerald green.

"I'm ready. Finally," she says.

"Finally," Riley and Nicole echo in unison.

FALL,
2008

47   PEACH

It's her favorite college class: Abnormal Human Psychology. And today, the professor with his heavily gelled hair and popped collar rips the cap off of a dry-erase pen and scrawls on the whiteboard two words that cause the students in the lecture hall to whisper and laugh: serial killer.

"From your reading last night in Goldberg and Winn, who can tell me some of the more definable traits of a serial killer? Go ahead and shout them out and I'll write them on the board."

He smiles at the class, a man in his late forties, flashing newly-bleached teeth. Peach didn't do the reading and keeps her head down, acting as though she's digging through her notebook for notes she's already written somewhere.

The characteristics materialize in voices husky or small or feminine. From all areas of the lecture hall, the words zip at the professor and he does his best to keep up with what people yell: male, white, trophies, ritual, social isolation, more than two kills, similarities between victims and/or methods of murder, trauma or problems during childhood development, obsession with fire, low I.Q., psychopathy. Then he caps the marker and turns back to the class.

"Some of these are correct, some of them are wrong," then he points to the word *white* and shakes his head. "There are killers of every ethnicity." Then he points to the word *male.* "And women kill, perhaps not as much, but there are theories that they might be as homicidal or even more so, just that they don't get caught as often."

This statement makes a number of students break into laughter and Peach slumps down in her chair. She doesn't enjoy the topic. She doesn't understand people's preoccupation with serial killers. The obsession with individuals who violently take the lives of other people seems bizarre to her. Her armpits begin to sweat and she pulls her long, blond hair away from her neck to give her skin more air.

"Low intelligence quotient might be correct for most unorganized serial killers, but many that take the time and effort to plan out their kills show above average intelligence. And psychopathy is a non-issue. Those two things might be correlated, but there is no causation."

Then the professor looks back at the board and shakes his head before addressing the lecture hall. "Did any of you do the reading? Or did you watch *CSI* instead? Folks, of all the traits listed on the board, there are only two that hold as strong descriptors for a serial killer. Now which ones are they?"

No one raises a hand. The professor looks up to the stadium-like seats in the lecture hall of Boise State University and scans the crowd. Until his eyes grow wide as they land on Peach.

He points to her with his marker and grins. "You, miss. Want to take a guess at which ones are traits that seem to span any type of serial killer in any era, any culture?"

The students near Peach turn to watch her as she stares at the board, doing her best to pick the two correct qualities. The green letters turn into meaningless blobs for a moment. As she contemplates, they signify concepts once again. She decides to pick the one trait that defines serial killing as she knows it, and the other quality that seems general enough to be likely in most, if not all, cases of a serial killer's history.

"Two or more kills and trauma or problems during childhood."

The professor puts his marker down in the metal tray underneath the white board and then digs around in his bag for a moment before pulling his hand out, closed.

"Ding ding ding," he says. Peach gives him a shy smile in return. Then he takes the stairs up the lecture hall two at a time and delivers a cherry sucker into Peach's hands. "Well done!"

She peels the wrapper off the lollipop and sticks it in her mouth, feeling like a star pupil in a fourth-grade class. But she'll take her small victory.

The professor makes his way back down to the desk and the white board in the semi-circular pit of the lecture hall. With a flourish, he takes back up his marker.

"Now, does anyone want to tell what motives are typically given by serial killers as to why they kill?"

People begin to shout out their answers once again. One girl, no more than eighteen, shoots her hand in the air. As he writes words down on the whiteboard, unable to see her hand, she finally begins to shout out his name until he spins around and nods to her.

"Dr. Whiteland, I read somewhere that some people think serial killers aren't natural born. Or maybe some of them are, but that others can learn how to kill. Is this true?"

Peach sucks away on her lollipop and waits for the professor to answer. He cocks his head to one side and speaks.

"From what modern research shows, yes, serial killers can learn their trade. They don't have to be born a certain way or be set on the path at a very young age. Just like all people in life, serial killers, just as doctors or teachers or priests, have free will. They can choose to kill and learn how to do it better, smarter, cleaner."

The girl nods and Peach watches as the professor goes back to his whiteboard and writes down more terms: financial gain, lust, mandates from gods and demons.

The zealous student shoots up her hand again and holds it in the air above her desk. She keeps it there, hovering, as she speaks.

"But some of them are just born wrong. Aren't they, Dr. Whiteland?"

Another student shouts out the phrase "voices told them to do it," and instead of writing it on the board, the professor underlines the words "mandates from gods and demons" three times.

Peach slurps away on her sucker. A canker forms on the side of her tongue.

"Sure. There are those in my field who might argue there are bad seeds amongst us. But more often than not, it's a combination of things which make a person go off the rails in such a dramatic manner. As for me, I believe there is a small percentage of individuals who cannot help themselves. Even with free will. It's as if free will is an illusion for them or they are an exception to its effects. They move through the world feeling burdened with a destiny to take lives."

The girl lowers her hand. "Have you ever talked to a serial killer? One of the ones who can't do anything but kill? Like it's their fate or something?"

Dr. Whiteland turns to the board, rubbing out a misspelling with the sleeve of his jacket. The lecture hall grows quiet, awaiting an answer which never arrives.

TUESDAY, THE 9TH OF JUNE, 2015

48   RILEY

He keeps the mannequin outside. He thought to move it off the chair, but then he decided he didn't want it in his home. The thing wasn't ticking or vibrating or giving off any sort of indication it might be a bomb. Even if it's not a physical danger, Riley has no desire to lift up the dummy of himself, or perhaps his twin dressed in drag. It can serve as a scarecrow for the starlings apt to shitting on his deck.

Watching it from his sliding glass door, he's not sure what he expects of it. It hasn't come to life. Other than the clear message sent with the missing toes and the piece of paper, there would be little about the life-sized doll to make Riley think the mannequin was supposed to mimic or resemble him in any fashion. He'd noted—when he'd fallen to the ground while struggling with the panic rising in his body—how the plastic of the dummy smelled. He couldn't put his finger on the scent. It wasn't an overtly chemical smell but something more familiar to him: a mixture of malodorous things.

With the arrival of the dummy and the note, Riley decided this morning he couldn't put off calling Nicole any longer. Now, with the afternoon drawing to a close, he forces himself to get out his phone. The oven is clean, his laundry folded. There are no more spurts of busy work to keep him from reaching out. And he knows he must, if only for his own sake and peace of mind. But still, he hesitates.

Riley forces himself to dial the number he has for her and waits in anticipation as the phone rings only to go directly to voicemail. Instead of leaving a detailed message, he asks for Nicole to call him back and then he leaves his number, in case she can't see it on her phone.

He fixes himself cream of mushroom soup and drinks it directly from the metal pan once it cools. The top of the soup congeals into a thin, gelatinous layer. He pulls his phone from his pocket over and over to check and make sure it's not on silent. But Nicole has not returned his call.

Ditching the empty pan in the sink, he calls two more times, each time getting the voicemail, each time leaving a new communiqué urging Nicole to call.

Two hours later, when she hasn't returned his call, Riley decides to take a walk down the road to the house he saw Nicole emerge from a few weeks back. He goes to put on a pair of well-worn leather sandals, their tread nearly smooth before he remembers there are no toes on his left foot to hold the sandal to the sole of his foot. Instead he puts on the heavy boot, with the Hacky Sack in the void between him and the material of the shoe. With his runner on his right foot, he heads out into the warm evening.

He takes his time, focusing on feeling the way his left foot and leg have acclimated to the missing toes. His gait is noticeably different, a slight limping then pushing upwards with each step on his left side. Riley decides one day he'll run again. While he was fitful and anxious for it to happen a few months ago, now he's fine taking the time to heal. Other, more grandiose problems plague his mind now.

After the third glance over his shoulder as he strolls, he admonishes himself for thinking an inanimate mannequin might be slinking behind him.

When he reaches the house where he had the odd exchange with Nicole, he notes her car—at least the one she was trying to get in to make an escape from Riley—is not in the driveway. He climbs the gentle incline up the walkway to the front door and depresses a lit doorbell. Electronic chimes sound throughout the house.

A man answers the door. He's in his early twenties, hair mussed and a stained t-shirt cockeyed on his torso. Boxers with an open fly hug his lower half. He squints out into the light of the evening sun and rubs his hands across his cheeks and down his neck.

"What can I do for you?" the man asks.

Riley looks around the man into the home. It's littered with clothing, cardboard boxes and what looks to be crates for small and medium-sized dogs. A waft of cooked hamburger hits Riley's nose.

"I was wondering if Nicole Trey lived here. I've been trying to get in touch with her. It's kind of important I speak with her."

The change in the man's face is so markedly abrupt it causes Riley to step back. Wonder settles in about a blunder. This man could be his stalker. Though he doesn't recognize the guy, he decides he could be in Nicole's house, just having killed her, deciding to pause and make Hamburger Helper before leaving the scene. Because this is something a sociopath might do. Or if Nicole is being held captive by this man, in one of those tight, metal cages in an upstairs bedroom, then Riley might come off the hero if he can figure out a way to save her.

The man stares at Riley with open disgust; his lips curling back to reveal his teeth, his eyes squinting deeper, into dark, little arroyos. Riley matches the man's gaze and sniffs.

"What? Does she live here or not? Do you know where she is?" Riley presses.

The man scratches his upper arm, still sneering. "What gives you the right to come here and ask those questions, asshole? What kind of prick would come here, asking me about Nicole? Is this a fucking joke?"

And then the man's face crumples into a mass of wrinkles. His chin quivers and he turns away from Riley to hide his distress.

Then Riley knows he has truly and grossly miscalculated. His imaginings might all be wrong. Something dire may have happened to Nicole. And he searches for the most tactful way to question the man. The best method to communicate he meant no harm, to get the man to speak up if Nicole is hurt, if Nicole is dead.

49   PEACH

She sits on her bed, missing Roman the Lamb, but glad of her alone time before picking up Linx and going to Patti's house for dinner. In her lap is an open book: *Rendezvous with Rama*. She reads the chapter where the Hermians, the residents of Mercury, threaten to blow the alien vessel Rama out of orbit around their planet. Though it's humanity's first encounter with an alien craft, the Hermians worry the ship will stop its trajectory between Mercury and the sun, blocking the vital energy of the light from reaching Mercury's surface. They're prepared to destroy it if it gets in the way of their source of power and life. Regardless of its rare and great nature.

Peach closes her eyes and thinks of the Hermians' position. She wonders what she would do if anything came between her and her goal, her focus, her sun. She knows what she would do. She would take it out, shatter it, and eradicate its very existence. Peach notes she is already doing this, on a small scale, but there has been little to threaten her own trajectory thus far. She

reminds herself she can't get too comfortable, though.
Something could always come, darken her skies and blot out her
light.

She decides to forgo a scarf around her neck for dinner at
Patti's and instead puts a wide bandage over the healing wound.
When she picks up Linx, he immediately asks how she hurt
herself. She says she was clumsy at work, forgetting she had a
pair of scissors in her hand, using the blades to scratch at her
throat. She tells him it's a minor cut. It looks worse than it really
is. Still she has to put up with Linx leaning over to the driver's
seat and planting a kiss just to the side of the tan-colored
bandage.

Patti, however, does not ask what happened to Peach's
throat. She waves both Linx and Peach inside her condo near the
banks of the Boise River. She hasn't changed the décor since the
late eighties and the walls are slightly yellowed, permeated by
Patti's cigarette smoke.

"I'm making us American tacos," Patti says and then bustles
back to the kitchen.

Linx smiles at Peach. "At least they aren't Mexican tacos.
You think she's got some made out of fake meat for me?"

"Unlikely," Peach whispers. "I guess it's corn shells and
toppings for you."

They walk into the kitchen and Peach recalls the way she
felt spending her teenage years in the condominium. Her days
and nights were spent largely alone, since Patti was a workaholic.
Peach would take a box of crackers from the kitchen and eat
them out by the river, watching twigs and ducks float by. In the
late spring, the cottonwoods would release a snow of seeds
coated in fluffy silk. She'd spend hours outside, her clothing
turning white as she was coated in arboreal fur.

"Can we help with something?" Peach asks as she watches
Patti dump a packet of taco seasoning into a pan of ground

turkey. She flips the meat around with a wooden spoon and turns to Peach.

"You're not a cook, Peach. Just have a seat at the counter."

Peach looks at Linx and smirks. They both pull out dark maple stools to perch upon. Before Patti can say something offensive to Linx, Peach decides to stymie her adoptive mother with a conversation she'd never expect.

"So I've been thinking about the money I owe you," Peach says. Patti immediately drops the wooden spoon and fumbles to pick it back up out of the pan.

"Yes," Patti says, not looking at Peach. "Go on."

"The way I figure, with the interest rate you're charging me, 3.7 percent and the money I have left to pay you, that if I up my payments to three hundred dollars a month, you should have all your money back, plus interest, in four years. How does that sound to you?"

"When did you get so good at finances?" Patti asks and plucks a piece of meat from the pan, sticking it in her mouth to taste. She frowns and picks up the salt shaker.

Peach ignores her comment and presses Patti for acknowledgement of what she's said. "That's a full two years sooner than we talked about. I'd like to get that money back to you and be done with it."

In traditional Patti fashion, she opens her mouth to say one thing, then she notices Linx, someone outside the family and thus worthy of a charade. She looks at him like he's just come into her home and she walks over to the counter and smiles at Peach.

"Don't worry about the money, dear. You'll pay me back when you have the funds. I trust you'll do the right thing," she says, her voice sweeter, higher than usual.

Then Patti reaches across the tiled kitchen counter and takes Peach's hands in her own. "It means so much to me that you're paying me back. You know you don't even have to give me the money. I have enough to get by on. Even if I pay two mortgages on two different houses. But I guess that's my choice so it's my burden to bear."

She releases Peach and goes back to her simmering meat. Linx kicks Peach's leg, hidden by the wooden paneling up the sides of the counter. Peach smiles at him and shakes her head. She's accustomed to Patti's false displays of selflessness and motherly love when other people are around. For most of Peach's adolescence, the few friends she did invite over to the condominium believed Patti was nice and welcoming and supportive. But Peach knew better. And she knew if she didn't pay back the money she borrowed from Patti when she had exhausted all other possibilities of finding the money elsewhere, she would be belittled, vilified and harped upon until every borrowed cent was back in Patti's possession.

"What would you like to drink?" Patti asks and then offers them a selection of soda pop, juice and an unopened bottle of Shiraz. Peach takes some juice and Linx opts for the wine, but Patti takes her glass to the tap and gets water, tepid, and sets it on the counter.

"I need to get to the store and get my Diet Cokes. No sugars for today. Trying to watch my figure," she quips. Her fishing for compliments about how thin she is, how she doesn't need to worry about calories does not catch results. When neither Peach nor Linx oblige her with flattery, she takes a sip of the water, purses her lips.

"Water is the only thing that doesn't make me feel fat or weigh me down. It's the purest of things on God's earth."

Linx sips his wine in response and Peach stands up, stretches, and offers to grate the cheddar cheese.

50   RILEY

Talking with the disheveled man reveals he probably isn't keeping Nicole in one of the dog crates upstairs, nor has he suffered because of some sort of danger to or the demise of Nicole. Instead, Riley learns that Nicole has dumped him, broken his heart, moved out and blocked his number from her phone.

The man sobs openly, wiping his dripping nose. He rubs the mucus into the fabric of his boxers.

"I know she was too old for me. But I would just tell my friends she didn't look older and that her ass was one of the nicest I'd ever seen. Who cares how old an ass is, am I right, man? As long as it's firm. Listen to me. No one knows she dumped me. You gotta keep your mouth shut about this."

As if Riley knows this man's friends. Or this lovesick fool is well-known in Boise and there is some danger of telling the wrong person about a breakup Riley doesn't care about. Still, Riley does his best to comfort the man but doesn't dare reach out and touch him. When his weeping begins to subside, Riley excuses his intrusion and tells the guy that he'll get over it soon enough. As he walks toward the driveway, he hears the guy holler for him to stop. Riley cranes his head around to see the narrowed eyes and teeth-baring sneer the man had presented when he'd opened the door to Riley.

"You never said why you're looking for Nicole. Are you fucking her? Is that it?"

Riley doesn't feel like lying, nor does he feel like backing down from the emotional man. He imagines the snot growing crusty on the man's underwear. Annoyance and disgust flood his mind.

"No, I'm not fucking her. What's the use in riding a horse you've already broken? Unless you like your mounts boring and tame. I'm interested in wilder things now, kid. Don't worry about it."

"What the hell does that mean? She isn't a Palomino. She was, no, *is* my girl. No touching, douchebag," the man calls after him.

Riley lopes away, his left foot stiffer than when he started out from his home a half hour before. The young man doesn't object further, just shuts the door. Then Riley can hear a loud sobbing coming from inside followed by the cranking of metal music from speakers adjusted for maximum volume.

Riley pulls his phone from his pocket and dials Nicole's number again. He gets her voicemail but he's fortified each time he hears her recorded voice. At least he has the right number. If she chooses to ignore him for the remaining weeks of the Gemini cycle, it won't be on him if she gets hurt.

He notes how he's building a stiff, hard wall around his heart and his mind. But he thinks of it as a fortification, complete with ramparts and boiling oil and crenellations to hide behind. He's at war with an unknown enemy. And if he wants to win, which he does, he figures he'll have to control his emotions when it comes to the casualties. That is, if he can't stop the casualties from occurring in the first place.

He leaves her a message, again saying his name and number. Except this time he says he needs to talk to her within the next forty-eight hours, for her own safety. If he needs to scare her into responding, he will.

Passing by the house of the divorced man with a penchant for hiding Easter eggs, he sees both the man and the teenager walking in the front door of their ranch-style home, grocery bags dangling from their wrists. Riley waves to them and the dad nods. The boy keeps his head down, headphones on his ears, his mouth moving, singing out lyrics to a privately-heard song.

When he gets inside his home, he locks the door and then removes his shoes before scouring each room in his house for some new surprise or note. He doesn't find anything but when he gets into his kitchen, he sees a half-full bottle of Maker's Mark on top of the refrigerator. Riley decides to treat himself and pulls the glass bottle down.

A shock of yellow catches his eye while he paces his house with the whisky in hand. He wanders over to the sliding glass door and notices the mannequin, his bizarre twin, is still sitting in the deck chair. He laughs at himself for thinking that it might have the power to move away from the chair. Guffaws for believing it could have followed him during his neighborhood outing. He takes a breath and slides open the door. He moves outside, pulling another chair in front of the seated dummy before sitting down himself.

"Well, I have no clue what to do with you," he says to it and unscrews the cap on the booze. He takes three healthy gulps of amber liquid and licks his lips. It warms his esophagus and his gut and he settles back into the chair. He brings up his good foot and nudges the mannequin until it tips to the side, the shaggy wig slipping a bit from the dummy's bald dome.

"Look at you. Yellow isn't even your color. You're more of an autumn," he says and laughs, taking another drink. "Ah, to be you. Nothing hurts. Nothing goes unsatisfied because you want for nothing. If we're supposed to be twins, then how come you got the looks *and* the Zen-like mind? That's bullshit."

Minutes later, when Riley can already feel the alcohol at work, he leans closer to the mannequin. He whispers at the dummy, right into its ear that cannot process sound waves. Reaching over, he plucks one of the straps of the tank top up off its plastic skin and then lets it slip away from his fingers. The taut strap impacts with a sharp thwack against the synthetic torso.

"I'm doing the right thing, aren't I? Warning these people? I didn't tell Soo Lim. I figure she'll be safe in the hospital. But Nicole is out there, somewhere, and I need to alert her. We have a past. I can be more direct with her than I was with the others. Maybe even tell her my theory. Not that we ever did much talking. More sex than conversing. Still, she deserves to know she might be in danger."

The mannequin doesn't respond. Riley offers it a sip of whisky then pulls the bottle back and finishes off the rest of the liquid. He pauses to thank his body for developing a stout tolerance to alcohol. The amount he's downed in short order could put another drinker in the ER.

"I hate a drinking buddy who refuses to drink. Makes me feel bad about myself. Well, worse, I guess."

Riley stays with the dummy until the sun disappears and the crickets begin rubbing their legs together. He waits for the sound of the bird, the owl that's accompanied his time in the backyard before, but it never comes. Riley wonders if it's scared off by the presence of two bodies instead of just one lonely, ineffectual soul.

Before he passes out, his head shuffles through a mess of confusing imagery: a shadowy representation of his stalker, Tate all grown up and angry, Mayra lounging in the embrace of her girlfriend. One realization occurs as he grapples with the onset of slumber. He takes one last stab at identifying the scent of the mannequin. His nostrils work at the mannequin and finally he realizes it's the smell of baby powder dallying with the smell of plastic. It reminds him of the way a particular doll smelled that belonged to one of his friends when he was young—a doll mythically born in a cabbage patch, a cherubic thing with fat, plastic cheeks.

It's both unsettling and comforting to Riley, this smell, as he slips away to sleep off his drunkenness.

THURSDAY, THE 11TH OF JUNE, 2015

51   PEACH

When she looks in her gift bag, this one decorated in
sparkly stars, she can see she has just enough supplies for one
last visit to the hospital. She prays her time there will be
sufficient to see her task to completion. She understand that if it
isn't, she'll be forced to revisit her teal, Moleskine book and her
days will be crunched, numbered in order for her to see to
another sacrifice. She can't chance other methods with the
bedridden woman. A knife slid past her ribs into her lungs would
cause issues Peach wasn't willing to face. She remembers this
kill was supposed to be easy. Then she remembers she started on
this path knowing some of her own blood must be spilt in order
to spill the blood of another. Yet, she is becoming less inclined
to accept such a taxing give and take.

Thursday afternoon proves to be a good time to visit the
respiratory ward of St. Luke's. The only nurses she sees on duty
she's not familiar with. She's happy about this, proud of herself
that she's spaced out her visitations in such a way to never be

recognizable to any of the staff. As long as she stays a passing specter to others, that's enough. For now, at least.

When she gets in the woman's room, she shuts the door and goes into the bathroom, pulling the blue, boxy scrub shirt over her golden t-shirt. The woman is unconscious, as she has been during each of Peach's visits. Luck has been on her side; she's never run into one of the friends or relatives of the woman there for a visitation.

She has her ritual down to a science, proceeding with focus and diligence. Typically, she finishes in less than ten minutes. She examines the woman briefly, sitting on the side of the hospital bed, her bag of supplies at her feet. Her cheeks are swollen and deep pink and the skin around her mouth is shedding in white, dry swatches. Sweat pricks up at the woman's brunette hairline. Peach believes these are all good signs, but she does not want to count her chicks before they hatch. Or rather, count such symptoms as signs of victory.

The woman has tubes in her nose. Peach bends down to get out her glass jar, the torch, and the mask and begins her work. As she pops back up, she's confronted with the open eyes of the woman. They roll about in the sockets, locking on to Peach's pupils. For a second the woman holds her gaze before her pupils drift up and to the side. Peach freezes, uncertain of how she should proceed until the intended sacrifice speaks.

"I'm having trouble seeing," she says and her voice is small, words coming out in pairs with each new gasp of air.

"I know," Peach says and smiles. "I'm a nurse. I'm here to give you something for your lungs, okay? It might even help with the vision."

"Which nurse are you?" the woman gasps. "I don't know you."

Peach looks to a flattened pillow nestled at the side of the woman and considers picking it up and smothering the woman before she can depress a call button. She's certain there are no cameras trained on the room. If there were, she would have been stopped and arrested long ago. While suffocation would be an acceptable death for the woman and for Peach, she focuses on the energetic core in the deepness of her pelvis. Its light grows dimmer and any pulsation there halts. That's enough of a sign to keep her from placing the pillow over the woman's face. Only then does she consider the mess she would be in if the woman flat-lined and Peach was found in her room with a bag full of strange items.

Instead of answering the woman's questions, she looks for the opiate drip running into the IV on top of the woman's hand. She finds the button to deliver a dosage and clicks it three times until a buzzer beeps. No more will enter the tubing and the circulatory system of her sacrifice.

"Your name," the lady presses, her eyes still rolling and wide.

Peach gets her supplies ready, lights the torch and by the time she starts the process, the woman is quieter, her eyelids drooping shut, her words slurring.

The woman mumbles. "Your eyes…scare me."

Peach keeps her focus on the lance of blue flame. It licks the base of the glass jar and flickers up its sides.

The woman asks who Peach is one last time and then she's gone, back into drug-induced oblivion. Perhaps, Peach thinks, the woman could be making a foray into what lies next: a preview of incorporeal life and a release from suffering.

The woman has three new vases of fresh flowers. Peach fixates on a spray of yellow irises. When she's done with her task and her items are packed away, she walks to the bouquet and sniffs deeply. They smell of grape Kool-Aid and remind her of the wild irises which grow around the ponds throughout the parks of Boise. She takes this as another sign, another omen that coincides nicely with a plan she's had in mind over the past few weeks. Now she knows the plan should be carried out.

Except this plan she won't pursue alone. She'll invite Linx to come along.

52   RILEY

Like always, Kristin doesn't sound happy to hear Riley's
voice. Especially his voice right now, asking a question on par
with ones such as, "how much, exactly, do you weigh?" or "do
you intend to do something with your life" or even, "seriously,
what were you thinking when you bought that dress?"

"Really, Kristin. I need Nicole's address if you have it. I
have something important to tell her."

Riley can hear Tate's high-pitched voice in the background.
He screams something about clay and then his voice fades away.
He can almost feel Kristin's loathing for him emanating from the
screen of his phone. It feels like a prickling on his earlobe.

"You're asking me if I will give you the address of my
former best friend who not only slept with you while we were
dating, but was still sleeping with you when you both found out I
was pregnant? Is that the one? I've always known you consider
your balls to be massive. But this is bad, even for you."

"Kristin, I wouldn't be bugging you if I could find it any other way."

"Did you try the internet, genius? Under www.backstabbingbitches.com?"

"I'm not going to get anything from you, am I?" Riley huffs into the phone.

Kristin yells. "Are you stupid? I have nothing to tell you! I don't know where she lives. We aren't best friends forever anymore. I flushed my half of the silver heart pendant long ago. Get a clue."

Then there is a silence on the phone followed by Kristin arguing with Tate. He whines about talking to Riley and his voice grows more insistent while Kristin tells him that they can talk another time. Riley can hear her pry the phone away from the protesting five-year-old and his cries taper off.

"Make the time to come visit your son sooner than later. Might be good for both of you. Give you something to do rather than expending energy hunting down your old hookups."

He's not surprised she hangs up after she has the last say. Kristin is always one for getting the last word in before slamming a door, walking away from a gathering or ending a phone call. For all her admonishments about Riley's behavior, the woman still struggles with growing up as well.

He puts the phone down on his leg and thinks of Tate, how it was irksome and wrong he had been labeled Riley's son. Riley and Kristin aren't certain that's a fact. He thinks of how the small boy's birthday is in late January and he's glad of it. He hopes that by winter, no, by the end of this month, there will be nothing to worry about—no daunting, bizarre messages to convey to the angry, bitter mother of Tate concerning the safety of *her* son.

Riley decides all he can do now is call Nicole's number. So he does. Over and over. He leaves a message after each call. And on the tenth dial, when he's ready to leave another notification to go unreturned, Nicole's voice sounds over his phone. Except this time she's live, not a recording. And she's pissed.

"Are you fucking crazy? Why do you keep calling me?" she asks.

"Nicole, finally. Where have you been?"

She goes quiet for a moment and then answers, the venomous tone of her voice barely contained. "What do you mean? Why is it any of your business where I've been? Have you been reminiscing about the past? When you ran into me at Mike's house, was that on purpose?"

Riley avoids the fair assumption that he's coming off as creepy, even if he has called Nicole over twenty times in the past few days. He keeps himself from shouting into the phone, aware he needs to keep an even head if he'll have any hope of getting her to listen to him.

"It was just a random encounter, Nicole. I'm not stalking you. I don't think stalkers say they're not stalking people. They're probably proud of it. Just relax."

"Hey now. You're the one bringing up stalking. I never said it."

"You implied it. We aren't communicating via text. There's no mistaking your tone."

"How's my tone now?" she asks, her voice ever firmer and louder. "You hear me?"

"Nicole, you picked up the phone because somewhere inside of you, you're curious about what I have to say. You weren't afraid of me in the past. Why do you think I'd be out to get you now?"

"That's the dumbest shit I've heard in a while, Riley. You've always been a hop, skip and a jump away from a full-blown fucktard. Besides, people change. Perhaps you've gotten worse than you were. What is it that you want? Spit it out."

And he can't find the words that won't make him sound off-kilter. He bites his tongue; now is not the time to remind her she was the one who initiated their physical relationship years ago. Yet he realizes Nicole is so annoyed at him anything he says will have little to no effect on changing her mind. So he regroups and switches tactics, hoping he can maneuver her into another opportunity to talk.

"Coffee," he says, "Meet me for coffee tomorrow. I have some news I'd like to give you in person. We can meet somewhere public so you're comfortable. Please, Nicole. Just meet me once and then I'll leave you alone."

"I'll bring mace and a stun gun. Maybe borrow my neighbor's German Shepherd. His name is Fang."

"Whatever you need to do. Thirty minutes, max. I'll bring a dog biscuit."

She sighs into the phone. "I'm really busy. This better be important."

"The most important," he says.

"Fine. Coffee at one tomorrow. I'll text you when I decide whether or not I want a cappuccino or a latte. That will affect where we meet. That's my deal."

She hangs up on him before he can finish saying, "I'll take it."

There is no more whisky in the house to toast making contact with the last of his targeted Geminis. He checks his wallet for cash but he's dry. Instead of going to the liquor store, he rereads the note left in the palms of the mannequin. That abomination still remains seated on his deck. He reads the line about immortality out loud and wonders who would want such a thing. But then he realizes if he had immortality, he would likely never want to give it away.

FRIDAY,
THE 12TH OF JUNE,
2015

53   PEACH

She waves down Linx. He's on the opposite end of the pond
at Julia Davis Park, a large and lush area near downtown Boise
that had once been a wide stretch of orchards. A plastic sleeve of
cut bread dangles from his hand and he shields his eyes from the
noontime sun, a smile on his lips for Peach. She winds her way
around the pond toward him as he moves toward her. People on
paddleboats with sides of hardened plastic shaped into the
profiles of swans and alligators cruise through the water,
propelled by the legs of the riders. When Linx and Peach meet,
he hugs her tightly and hands over the bread.

"I've got an hour lunch. This should show you how much I
like you. I'm skipping an actual meal to throw bread at water
birds with you. Except I'll need to save myself a slice. I'm
starving."

Peach undoes the twist-tie around the neck of the bread and
digs out a slice of brown wheat for Linx. He takes it, pulls off the

crust and eats that first before wadding the softer center into a moist ball and shoving it whole into his mouth.

She pulls another slice from the bag and leads Linx towards the backside of the pond—away from Myrtle Street and the flush of fast moving cars and the din of their motors and brakes. A mob of geese begins to trail them, the first one to see the bread sending out a squawk and enlisting the interest of ten more birds. Mixed in with the geese are a pair of Mallard ducks, the male with a shiny head of iridescent green feathers, the female with a back of mottled grays and browns.

Peach breaks the bread into tiny portions. She tosses it away from her onto the matted grass caked in little cylindrical goose shits. The geese flap about, hissing at one another over the best, biggest pieces. When they swallow, they elongate their necks and work the bread into the back of their throats, past the ridges that grow in place of teeth.

Linx points out a vacant picnic table and they walk to it, both of them leaving bread in their wake. They have a seat and Peach points to a white swan on the water, its face masked in black. It has no interest in the doling out of food.

"Did you ever study Greek mythology in school?"

"A little, I think," Linx says and scatters more bread chunks. The first goose to arrive to their new location claims it, keeping a shiny black eye on the couple. "Why?"

"One of my favorite stories was about Leda and the Swan. She is a beautiful maiden and this swan, who is actually the god Zeus, rapes her. Zeus was always doing that. Raping women while in some shapeshifted form. He even turned himself into a bull once, to rape."

"Good story, Peach. Not weird at all."

"Do you remember Hera?" she continues, "She was Zeus's wife. I remember all the stories I read about her made her out to be a villain—some ancient, ugly harpy who was jealous of all of Zeus's lovers. But primarily, they were just his rape victims.

And she was always the bad one, the bitch haranguing him. But it was Zeus who was going around terrorizing women. He was just this good old boy with a white beard and lightning bolts who had a taste for virgins. Not fair at all to Hera. I've always wondered why people chose to worship Zeus over Hera. Sure, he was a god who took what he wanted and ruled with vigor. But she had resolve, strength of character, and a laser focus on vengeance."

A mother goose along with six goslings approaches Linx and Peach and they throw bread in their direction. One of the yellow, gangly birds gets close to Peach's foot and she reaches down slowly to touch its back. It skirts her hand and hurries away, peeping loudly. Before Peach sees it coming, the mother lands a hard pinch with her bill on Peach's shin.

"Oww," she shouts and swats the bird away. Linx laughs and breaks up the last piece of bread in the bag.

"Maybe they don't like you calling them rapists," he says.

"I'm not calling them rapists," she defends herself. Peach rubs at the offended skin on her leg once the angry goose wanders off with her little flock. "It was a swan, not a goose. Or rather it was a swan who wasn't really a swan but a god."

"Explain that to them," Linx says.

They stand and walk along the pond until they reach a stand of cottonwoods, poplar and bushy, low-growing willow. Peach looks around the area, spying a couple picnicking in the distance and a paddleboat cruising away from the shaded, wooded area near the banks of the pond. She grabs Linx by his shirt and pulls him into the vegetation.

"What the hell, Peach?" he protests. He grabs his shirt, too, to keep the buttons from coming undone.

She pushes him down into the long grass and unbuttons his pants. When he feels her hands at work, he stretches his arms over his head and smiles up to the sky. This is how Peach uses the rest of her lunch break near the waterfowl and the water smelling of fish and algae. She revels in sensations: the approaching summer sun warm on the skin of her naked back, the caw of a passing crow, the feeling of being physically joined to a human.

54   RILEY

The coffee shop is in West Boise, near the large shopping
mall and roads congested with traffic and giant box stores. It's a
place he might expect to see in Europe, though he's never been.
He convinces himself it has a very French feel to it. Potted plants
are stuffed into every corner of the building and house music
blares loudly from the speakers stuck in the ceiling tiles. The
walls are decorated with prints of street scenes. Some appear to
be Parisian, others perhaps little cities in Italy or Spain. He sees
Nicole sitting at a small, circular bistro table in the back of the
room, a cappuccino already in front of her. She looks down at
her phone on the table, a frown on her face.

A barista welcomes him but he decides against coffee and
makes his way back to Nicole. When she looks up at him, her
face remains dour and humorless. He pulls out the other seat and
sits.

"I see you left Fang at home," he kids.

"I thought the switchblade in my purse would be sufficient," she answers. His eyes scan her tote bag. There could be anything inside. It could house a bowling ball and still have room for a hardcover novel and a water bottle.

"I could have gotten your drink. For meeting to talk to me."

"I don't feel like owing you for anything, Riley," she says and locks her phone, the screen going black. She keeps her eyes on it though, bending over the table slightly. Riley notes her low-cut, V-neck shirt. Her cleavage draws his eye but he forces himself to look up at her face.

"Sorry," she says, "I'm just moody. Life is really heavy right now. Plus, I just had a weird conversation with someone."

This gets Riley's attention. He sits up straighter in his metal chair. "Might I ask with whom?"

"Oh! 'With whom' is it? Are you going to drink a doppio with a raised pinkie as well? It's not important who," she says, "just that it was weird. This person is acting paranoid, different."

Nicole straightens out her spine as well and takes a sip of her cappuccino. "Never mind that," she shakes her head. "What was it you wanted to tell me so badly? And don't think I've relaxed my suspicions about you. Consider them on pause. I've pressed the pause button."

Riley looks over to the coffee counter and barista and considers getting some caffeine to bolster his nerve, but he figures he can't make Nicole wait forever for the odd news. So he smiles and gets to business.

"I hate to bring this up, since, as you say, your life is already feeling heavy right now. But there have been some really strange incidences occurring in my life lately, some of them potentially dangerous to people who know me in some way. And while we've never been friends, we do have a past. And I don't want to see you get hurt."

"And what? You need to get close to me to protect me from this phantom threat?"

"I'm not offering that. This isn't a bizarre plot for me to get you back in my bed."

"We never had sex in a bed. A chairlift, once. That summer up at Bogus Basin. That was an exhilarating challenge."

He stays his course so she knows he's not there to find out what color of panties she's wearing.

"There is a real threat, Nicole. Please."

Nicole turns the little white cup around on the saucer and looks into Riley's eyes. "Is someone hurting people. Is that what you're saying?"

Riley knows if he wants to share his theory with her, now is the time. But there is a look of tiredness, perhaps even pain in her eyes and in the way she holds her shoulders high. He can't bring himself to launch into a full discussion of possible murders based on the evidence he has. Sometimes his old lawyer self wins out. This is one of those times.

"I don't want to add another stressor to your life. I'm just saying you should be careful, at least for the next few weeks. Keep your guard up. Be wary of strangers. I don't think it's likely anything bad will happen to you, but if it did and I said nothing, I would feel horrible."

She takes another sip of her beverage and checks her phone before answering him. Her voice is cold. "So you're warning me so that *you* feel better if anything bad happens to me. So this is about your feelings. Am I right?"

"That's not what I meant. I don't want you to be caught unaware and get injured. That's my goal here."

"Right," she says and nods, her eyes reddening, watering. Riley thinks he's gone too far, upset her too much, but as he's about to apologize, a bell chimes on her phone and she lifts it up off the table and reads the incoming text.

"I have to go," she says to Riley and downs the rest of her cappuccino in a single swig. "Thanks for the warning, but I don't

believe in your nonsense. I don't have time for anything
so…unreal right now."

She pulls her purse from off the back of the chair and
clutches the strap tightly in her fingers. Riley stands and Nicole
dodges his personal bubble. She must be afraid he'll embrace her.

"Just promise me that you'll take care of yourself," is all he
says.

Tears begin to flow down her cheeks. They leave light trails
where the salty water runs through her foundation. She looks at
him briefly before passing him by, making her way toward the
door.

"I'm fine," she says. "I have no right to complain. Life is
grand."

"Nicole, you're not fine. Obviously. Do you want to stay
and talk about what's happening? Can I help?"

"Riley Wanner: playing at chivalry but only thinking of his
sword."

To this, he has no reply.

She leaves him alone in the shop. He sits back down for a
moment and listens to the music that would be more suitable in a
posh lounge instead of a coffee house. Looking at the pictures on
the wall, he wonders if he'll ever see much more of the world
than Boise, Idaho. The black and white towns with their
cobblestone streets and window boxes of gray-toned geraniums
taunt him. They are not scenes of what he may visit one day, but
rather visions of what is unattainable. They are examples of what
he may never experience— such as the hot breath of Mayra on
his cheek, such as income without work, such as freedom from a
mysterious lunatic.

55 PEACH

She comes back to Julia Davis Park just after sunset and watches Pollux rise in the western sky. She places a little, water-resistant mat on the grass laden with poop and cigarette butts. She kneels down, her eyes fixated on the star, and asks for help.

"Help me find the guise in which your father masqueraded," she says to the star. Then she curls up on the pad, hopeful a passing cop doesn't kick her out of the park for being there after sunset. She focuses on her belly, her point of energy, until she can feel the muscle and skin around her pelvis lift away from her spine. Then she stands, shakes out her blanket, rolls it up and tucks it under her arm.

Because she saw the swan during the day, she figures there must be a swan's nest somewhere near the pond. It's full night, and Peach traipses around the edges of the water. The headlamp that Lars wore in the mineshaft sits snuggly against her forehead as she peels back the leaves of irises and other water plants in search of a nest.

The pulsing in her belly guides her now. She pats the lump of agate in her pocket and keeps her light down, trained on the ground, not pointing up to the sky or the middle distance. She doesn't wish to attract attention. As she gets farther away from the main body of the pond—toward the concrete pad where they launch the paddleboats and approaching the perimeter of the Boise Zoo—her energy center beats wildly.

Taking her time to explore each clump of grass and vegetation in the area pays off. She finds the swan nest. Only one adult is present and she wonders if it is the bird she saw earlier—skimming across the water, ambivalent about the offering of food. The swan sleeps, undisturbed by the light on Peach's forehead. She clicks it off all the same, and waits for her eyes to adjust in the low light of a crescent moon.

When she can see well enough, she pulls on the pair of rubber gloves she wore while cleaning up the mess she made out of Lars and nudges the adult swan off the nest. It stumbles about, confused and sleepy before squatting over a patch of wet grass. Peach notes five cygnets, their bills tucked in their backs, their webbed feet pulled up to their chests. They look content hunkered down in the nest. She snatches two of the babies and leaves the nest immediately. They don't make a noise until they are far away from their parent. Once fully awake, they squeak in protest as Peach loads them into a clean, high-sided plastic trash can in the back of her Honda and heads home.

In her apartment, she fills up the bathtub in her master bedroom with a bit of water, leaving the backside that slopes upwards as a dry landing. She gently places the two cygnets in the bathtub and places a towel on the upslope, winding it around into a little circular nest.

In the light of the bathroom, she can get a good look at the baby waterfowl. One of the cygnets is bigger than the other. It has less fluff and more feathers than its sibling. Its coloring is a lighter heather gray. The smaller one has more down and its dark, webbed feet look too big for its petite body. Both cygnets squeak their displeasure and take to the small pool of water in the bathtub, leaving a smear of excrement on the porcelain surface.

Peach sits by the tub and watches how they paddle in the water, only to make for the blanket and call for their parents with sharp squeaks. The biggest one flaps its stubby wings and jumps up to the ledge running around the edge of the tub. It teeters about, placing one foot in front of another until it gets to what it must have spied from below.

A slight, almost unnoticeable smear of mud sits where the tiled walls come together. The cygnet pecks at the mud, aware of its scent and texture. It is the only thing in the tub similar to its native environment.

Peach gets on her knees and eyes the dirt. She figures it must be some of the mud she placed on her neck after her sacrifice in the mountains near Idaho City. It's a speck made of earth and her own lifeblood. The cygnet tastes the muck with its tongue and lets out an aspirated attempt at a hiss. Then it jumps back down to the basin of the tub and waddles up next to its sibling. They bump sides, the touch of one another a comfort in the strange setting of an urban bathroom. Once calmed, they lose interest in the water and shuffle under the blanket together and close their eyes to sleep.

She watches them an hour longer. They twitch as they sleep, smacking their black bills together. Peach says another prayer to Pollux before heading to bed herself. She prays once they serve their purpose, they'll somehow find their way back to the pond in the park, back to their siblings and their parents, both swans, both just animals.

SATURDAY, THE 13TH OF JUNE, 2015

56   RILEY

When he wakes the morning after his discussion with Nicole, he feels a sense of ease and satisfaction that's been missing in his life since he lost his toes at the metal shop. The past week, though stressful, has felt like a week of work and focused intent. For the first time in a long while, he gets up, eager for the day, unafraid of what might happen to him or the people in his life.

This doesn't negate the fact that the people he's connected to might be in mortal danger. But Riley is tired of thinking at any moment another person might die. So he lets his mind and nerves have a rest. He takes an extra long shower and gives his face a thorough, attentive shave. He pulls his hair back and ties it with a band, keeping his dishwater blond locks slicked close to his scalp. In the past, he would have thought to cut his hair, but he appraises himself in the mirror and decides, at least for the time being, he's good just as he is.

He makes waffles and tops them with fresh blueberries. He fries up five slices of thick bacon and washes it all down with a glass of fresh-squeezed grapefruit juice. He takes care in picking out his outfit for the day, finally deciding on a linen button-down in light green and a pair of distressed jeans. He squeezes his bad foot into a pair of leather dress shoes and nods when they don't aggravate the stitches or the mending flesh when he walks around his house.

At eleven, he grabs the keys to his Nissan and locks up his house. He has plans to meet Walker for an early lunch at a burger joint near Boise State University. His SUV is parked in the driveway and as he walks to it, he decides he needs to start parking it in his garage.

That's when he sees a peculiar sight on the hood of his vehicle.

He approaches slowly, his keys out in front of him like they are ample weapons, able to fight off danger or aid in warding off his own onslaught of fear. From what he can see, from where he creeps along on his walkway, he has a new present to contend with. A giant plastic egg sits on the hood of his car, shaded by the wide leaves of an ash tree.

He's cautious, remembering the time the bomb went off downtown and his hearing was impaired for hours. Afraid that the egg might be an explosive, he takes a felled branch from a dogwood in his front yard, snapping off the smaller branches until he has a sizable rod with which to poke at the egg. He's not certain of his plan, but he also doesn't want to call the police and tell them someone has left a big Easter egg on his car. Would they please come and save him from the vibrant yellow shell and the possible mother lode of jellybeans within it?

Reaching out with the branch, he gets close enough to tap the egg lightly. It reminds him of the large ovals which would house his mother's new pantyhose purchases. He hits it again, until it begins to roll off the hood of his car, toward the concrete of his driveway. Riley panics. Uncertain if the egg hitting the ground would be a good thing, he makes a split-second decision to toss away the stick and hustle to catch the egg.

When it lands in his hands he's happy he made the decision to save it from impact. Because the plastic the size of a small watermelon rocks around in his grasp and muffled noises sound from within. He balances it back on the hood of his car, keeping one hand on it while turning it around. On one side of the egg is the phrase he first read in Hamal's belated birthday card. Except this time it's written in the loopy, wispy hand of Pollux: *lucky number 8.*

He takes a deep breath and squeezes at the seam circling the middle of the plastic.

Two cygnets, one tiny swan older than the other, crouch in the split halves of the cracked egg. Their mouths are open and they pant readily, little useless wings out to their sides to keep their bodies cool. Riley scoops up the animals and carries them over to his garden hose. He turns it on to a trickle and uses his body to corral the cygnets between his legs and the foundation of his house. He runs the hose over their heads, bodies, and into their mouths. After a few minutes of this water treatment, they rally, begin to protest louder and muster up enough energy to try and bolt away from Riley.

He calls Walker and tells him he'll be a bit late. Riley dumps a car tote clean of rope, an empty gas can and other tools and places the birds inside. He loads them into his SUV and sits in the driver's seat, hands tight on the steering wheel.

Not sure what to do with the birds, he knows he can't keep them. They are the first living gifts his stalker has presented him with, and he's unwilling to raise two swans because of the odd actions of a crazy stranger. Perhaps he can drive them to a bird rescue operation. Then another option comes to mind and as soon as he thinks it, he's compelled to follow through.

It's a short drive. He hits all the green lights, the sound of the birds' fear and stress keeping him company on the journey. It plays out as mild hisses and insistent peeps. He parks his car and scoops the young waterfowl out of the tote. The larger one takes a nip at his hand but his bill is feeble and doesn't break Riley's skin.

He walks them to the edge of the pond in Julia Davis Park and notes a pair of adult swans, trailed by a handful of cygnets in the center of the murky water. When the youngest bird in Riley's grasp lets out a call, both of the adult swans begin to flap their wings. Riley watches as they run over the water like speedy magicians, not flying, not swimming, to their lost children. He puts them down on the waterlogged grass and backs away to watch the reunion. When the adults get a few feet away they stop, pursued by the cygnets they've left behind, rushed by the two cygnets Riley has returned. The adult swans wait in the middle for them all to coalesce and when they are once again together and whole, they act as if nothing has happened. The family paddles off toward a shadowy, reed-covered bend in a flowing neck of the pond.

This latest gift from Pollux has not shaken Riley. The why behind the two birds eludes him. He focuses instead on the reward for trusting his instinct and depositing the birds safely back to their family. It was a lucky win, but he'll take it. The day is just beginning. He knows he can come out ahead. Instead of getting stuck, he found a solution. Instead of retreating back inside his home, his action has made him feel adamant that there might be a way out of his situation. Riley has felt something today he hasn't felt in a long while.

Hope.

57   PEACH

She stays in bed until mid-afternoon on Saturday. She sniffs at her sheets and they smell musty and sweat-soaked. When she finally commands herself to get up, she strips the bed and places the dark blue cotton sheets in a pile near the door out of her bedroom. She puts on a pair of tattered workout pants and a plain t-shirt and busies herself with gathering up all the soiled towels and washcloths and clothes around her apartment. As focused as she is on the audacious and ambitious path ahead of her, sometimes the basic chores of life win out.

As she's about to place all the dirty items in a laundry basket, the remembrance of the hospitalized woman's rolling, dilated eyes hits Peach. She was unable to focus and it was unlikely she got a good look at Peach. But still, even if she noted some general characteristics and Peach's visits didn't result in her death, Peach might have something to worry about.

But more worrisome than the woman telling someone about Peach is the fear the woman will not die.

If the woman doesn't die, Peach will miss the sacrifice for the Gemini cycle. Going into the hospital and killing her in another, more direct manner is out of the question. It would be in direct defiance of all the messages she's received and lead to heat from the police. She doesn't want attention like that. Not so soon into her maturation. Yet if she misses her opportunity, she misses the whole gambit, and the end game dissipates like drops of water on a hot pan. There will never be another time that fits so well with Peach's aims. And the universe is currently on her side. But Peach is clever enough to know that once blessed doesn't mean eternal favoritism. The stars and masters of fate could choose another path for her or her sacrifices. Or they could even side with Riley.

That thought alone makes her determined to ensure a sacrifice before the end of the Gemini cycle.

So instead of taking her laundry down to the three sets of washers and dryers open to residents of her apartment building, she digs her teal notebook out of her green duffel bag. It has been hidden there since she took her trip out to the Owyhee Mountains. She wipes off the cover caked in dust from the steppe and looks for the pink-tipped parrot budgie feather. Only then does she remember she gave it away to Air out on the open expanse, full of sagebrush and cattle and lightning.

She opens up the journal as she sits on the edge of her unmade bed. She looks at the name of the woman in the hospital, remembers the way the gust of wind lifted the page containing the inked words. Her mark, her sacrifice still feels right to her. But she must prepare for a luckless result from her hospital visitations. If the woman does not die, she needs a backup plan. Or rather, a backup kill.

As she looks at the other potential sacrifices, she recalls when she had to work with the spontaneity of her very first kill. Nell would have been easier than the tattooist Roman, but she hadn't planned for her omnipresent, paranoid boyfriend Sev to always be around. And when Riley became part of the contest to gain Nell's attention—much to Peach's surprise—she had to decide if Nell as a sacrifice was really worth it, especially when Roman was so open and available. She is glad she did not claim Nell. There would have been too much baggage and regret encapsulated in that action. But Peach knows she got lucky with Roman. If he'd seen her attack coming, he likely could have fought her off. And she was even luckier with Lars.

She touches the wound on her neck, covered with a fresh Band-Aid, and can't recall the pain of the jagged rock ripping her flesh. Her adrenaline had kept her focused on her sacrifice. But she'd been hurt, all the same. She knows the risk of tackling another sacrifice, unprepared and unplanned.

Peach could be seriously injured or imprisoned. She could be killed. But she knows the risk is worth it. For the end game. For Perfect Peach.

She flips through the pages of names she has written in her little notebook. She closes her eyes and puts her finger down on an unseen sheet. When she pries open her eyes, she acknowledges who she has chosen. The name is written in bright blue ink; the ballpoint had skittered over the last few letters.

Newt Parnwell.

SUMMER, 1988

58 RILEY

They are lying in her bed together. Riley remembers his short, chubby legs entangled in his mother's long, smooth limbs. She has a picture book propped up on her chest and it rides her like a buoy bobbing about in an ocean harbor. He watches it move up and down. She smells like orange-scented hand cream. Her wavy hair is piled on the top of her head and pinned there. Her glasses are large, the plastic holding the glass cut into a shape with many sides.

Riley thinks she is the most beautiful human he has ever seen.

"Pay attention to the story, Riley," she says to him and pats a place on the mattress closer to her chest and the book.

He shuffles his upper body up next to hers, his head propped up against a pillow. He leans over her and takes a look at the picture in the book. It is of a boy, older than Riley, who gazes up the length of a green vine shooting straight up into the sky.

"What just happened with Jack?" his mother asks and Riley
has to think about where the tale began.

"He put a bean in the ground and a plant came out and he
wants to climb it!"

"That's right," his mother says and then turns the page.
Riley looks at the bright wash of colors and shapes on the paper.
Now the boy climbs the vine into the sky. A blackbird flies past
his legs. A dark cloud lets out bolts of lightning in the far
distance.

"Is Jack going to die?" Riley asks.

His mother turns her head to Riley and closes the book for a
moment, keeping a finger in the binding fold to mark her place.

"Why would you ask that, Riley?"

"Because," Riley says, his lips quivering, his eyes wide,
"he's up so high. And I don't think he is supposed to be doing
what he's doing."

"So you think he'll fall off the beanstalk back to earth? And
that's how he'll die?"

"Maybe," Riley says and pauses to think. "But what if
someone doesn't want him to climb it? What if they get angry
with him?"

His mother opens the book back up and flips through the
pages. She raises her eyebrows and shifts her body so that she's
leaning on her side, facing Riley.

"Have I read this book to you before? I thought this was a
new story."

Riley answers with the earnest innocence of his four years
of life. "No, I don't know this story, Mom. But something bad is
going to happen to the boy. I know."

"Has your dad said anything to you lately? Has he been
talking to you about death? If so, you can ask me questions. We
can talk about scary things together, Riley."

Riley tries to think of what his father has talked to him
about. But all he can remember about his father is the way they

watch cartoons together, snuggled up on their couch or how they wake up early in the morning on Sundays to go into the backyard and turn over earth and pluck up fat, pink nightcrawlers from the soil.

"Maybe?" Riley guesses but doesn't know. He tries to get his mother to understand. "That isn't it. The boy Jack is going to get in trouble for going up so high. You'll see, Mom."

Then Riley pulls the book away from his mother and flips through the pages until he finds the same illustration of the boy on the vine and the ominous bird and cloud and hands it back into his mother's grasp.

"Keep reading," he tells her. "You'll see."

FALL,
1992

59 PEACH

Peach is the first to leave the household. Rather, she is the first innocent child to leave the household. Her foster sister doesn't toddle out from their shared bedroom to see her go. Peach—already trying to be a big girl at age eight—tells herself that her foster sister is just a child, that she's scared, that she doesn't understand. Perhaps the two-year-old thinks Peach will be back or she will simply forget Peach—just as she quits her crying when a balloon once tied around her wrist is removed from sight.

Her few personal belongings are packed into cardboard boxes behind her. Her foster parents, the ones she's come to call Mom and Dad, stand in front of her, between her and the door. The social worker who has come to take Peach to another foster home is waiting outside on the porch. She's a woman with black hair and a happy smile and after she talked with Peach's foster parents for a good, long while, she left to wait outside. Now they can say their goodbyes to Peach in private.

"I don't want to go," Peach says, her eyes on the wood of the entranceway floor. It's pitted and aged but she's grown to like it in the time she's spent with these people who have become her trusted guardians. She knows where the grooves and snags are deepest, the places that will cut your toes if you shuffle over them. She knows how to run deftly past them all. And she knows now she will never see this floor again.

"Can't you adopt me? Can't you keep me somehow?"

Her foster mother, a woman she used to call Janice until she started calling her Mom, bends down and cups her hands around Peach's feet, like she is trying to use some type of prayer to anchor Peach to the floor of the house. Her face is red, her eyes puffy. Peach knows she's been crying for over a week. She cries at the dinner table. She cries when she's getting Peach's little foster sister dressed in the mornings. It is her most defining action now. Crying.

"I would take you in a heartbeat, Peach Blossom. But they won't let us keep you. And your sister will be leaving us in two days as well. I've asked that they place you two together in a new foster home. Let's hope that happens, okay?"

It hurts Peach to look at her mother and the pain playing out on her face, so she turns her eyes up to her father, the man she once called Owen. Except he's crying as well, silent tears, no wailing or choking on his sadness. Peach tells herself that she can't cry. Someone needs to stay in control.

Her father bends down next to her mother and acts to touch Peach but then he pulls away his hands.

"You know that you've done nothing wrong, right? You know that none of this is your fault. What happened was an accident. And the people from the state office are just following the rules and doing their job. Please tell us that you know all this."

"I know," Peach says.

But she doesn't say everything she wants to say because she doesn't want to keep upsetting her foster parents. She knows what happened wasn't an accident. It was deliberate. It might have been planned. She knows because she was there. She saw it all.

Because she knows what truly happened, Peach decides that what's happening to her and the family, the ripping apart of their home, is her fault. If she'd been able to stop it, she might have been able to stay with her foster mom and dad.

Peach does tell them something she feels deep within her heart. "I'm tired of losing people. I don't want to lose you guys, too."

Then her father embraces her, her mother too, and they squeeze Peach so tightly that she loses the air in her lungs. But she doesn't pull away from them. It's the most joyous pain she has ever felt.

"Don't worry about your brother," her father whispers in her ear. "He's going to be okay, too. Just like you. Just like your sister. They'll see that it was an accident. And maybe one day we can get you all back."

Her mother hears what her father has whispered. She releases Peach and gives her husband a look of disbelief and shame. Peach knows then that she will never come back. No matter what her father has told her. She is now on her own. Again.

The social worker with the happy smile knocks on the front door before pushing it open. Her teeth show behind her parted lips and she rubs her hands along the lengths of her arms as if she's chilled and can't warm up. Peach can feel her watching. She plants a kiss on the cheeks of her father and mother before they stand and each hoist a box into their arms, ready to move Peach's belongings outside.

"You ready, Peach Blossom?" her mother asks and gives her a wink, her eyelashes laden with water.

Peach doesn't answer and stares at the woman who has come to take her away. Whatever her mother did to her feet, it's working. If she could see through her shoes, she might see little silver nails bolting her feet to the wood. The woman doesn't talk to Peach. Instead she rotates her beaming smile to her mother and then her father.

"I promise she'll be fine, Mr. and Mrs. Barrow. I promise Peach will have a great life."

SUNDAY,
THE 14TH OF JUNE,
2015

60   RILEY

When he was late to lunch with Walker, his friend had
grilled him about what was going on with the letters from the
stalker. But Riley kept mum about the mannequin and the
cygnets. And when Walker asked if Riley had ever completed
his master list, a grilled onion from a burger hanging out the side
of Walker's mouth, Riley reported he had. He told his best friend
his work was done for this short while and he felt good about
things, better, in fact, than he'd felt in a long while. And because
Walker didn't press for more details, Riley figured he'd had
enough of his strange theories and stubbornness about not
notifying the police. They ate their burgers and tater tots, talked
about the law firm, talked about a woman with big, brown
areolas that Walker was screwing, talked about the coming
summer and floating the Boise River, camping, getting drunk at
Lucky Peak, stargazing.

Today, he's still high on his altered perspective. His change in attitude keeps him up. But he's not prepared for the phone call from Nicole. Her voice is tremulous and quiet.

"I need to talk with you. Again," she says and Riley asks her what's wrong, what's happened. Like that, the positive wave he's been riding falls flat and he's back in the stew of his contrived, panicked, stalker-centric obsession.

"Did someone hurt you? Are you in trouble?" he presses.

"I'll be okay. It's just…something spooky happened last night. And I need someone to talk to. And strangely enough, I feel like talking to you. Since you, you know. You claim to be focused on my well-being."

"Come to my house," he pushes.

"No," she says, "you come to mine."

She gives him the address and he tells her he'll be there in fifteen minutes. He pushes the dial on his speedometer as he drives, flying past a cop car idling in the parking lot of a grocery store. Riley swears, slows down, but the officer doesn't give chase.

He comes to a stop outside a sprawling apartment complex near Boise's North End as it changes into the higher class, suburbanite community of Eagle, Idaho. He walks the grounds, counting the building numbers until he finds building number five. He gazes up the three flights of concrete steps and gets to business. He uses the railing to his left to keep some of the pressure of climbing off his foot.

He moves to knock on the apartment door but Nicole is already there, pulling it back, motioning him inside. A dog barks from next door and he envisions a strapping beast with ropey saliva on his lips. Riley scans the apartment. It's decorated in a sort of French Country aesthetic. A small dining table is painted white, stripped and notched to look weathered. A fake, bushy ivy rests in a wire stand in the living room. The mantle above a gas fireplace is decorated with pictures. Riley doesn't know any of the people in the pictures but he notes Nicole's face in a few of them.

"You have a nice place," he says and smiles at Nicole.

She greets him with a frown and shakes her head. "It's not mine. I was staying with my asshole boyfriend. I'm watching this apartment for a bit."

"Well, you've made it cozy very quickly," he says and Nicole lifts her eyebrows at the compliment. "Thank you, by the way. For letting down your guard a bit and trusting I have decent intentions."

"Trust me, I'm guarded," she says. "But hopeful."

He nods. "I'll take it."

"I have beer. Do you want?" she offers and Riley accepts. She pulls a few long-necked Coronas from the fridge and hands one to Riley. Then she curls up her legs on an overstuffed couch and pats the cushion next to her.

Riley takes a seat and uses his calloused hands to twist the cap from the beer. Soon they will become soft from lack of manual labor. Nicole holds her beer out to him as well and he does the same for her. They each take a drink in silence, a ticking grandfather clock interjecting a click every second.

"So what happened?" Riley says. "You said you wanted to talk about something spooky."

Nicole drains away half her beer and then places the bottle down on the white carpet next to the couch. She rolls her shoulders around, loosening the muscles and chews on her lower lip.

"It was a conversation I had with someone. It was bizarre. Talk about demons and murder. I don't really know where to start, even," and then her voice trails off and she turns her head toward the sound of the ticking clock.

"Demons and murder? Amen on the weird. I can see why you'd get scared. But I was the right one to call. I consider myself close to being un-shockable at this point in my life."

Nicole swivels her face back to Riley and smiles. "It's just I've been under so much stress. I need to relieve it somehow. Nothing I've been doing helps. Fuck yoga. And mediation puts me to sleep if I don't stand up from the cushion after three minutes and chuck it across the room."

Riley laughs and polishes off his beer in one final, long pull. He places the bottle next to Nicole's on the carpet: empty twins.

"Come on, Nicole. Tell me more about your conversation. Who were you talking to? Where were you?"

She smiles at Riley and takes up rolling her shoulders again. "You know," she says, "we never talked in the past. Honestly, I'm not sure I want to start now."

When she lunges at Riley, he brings his hands up to block her body and hits her sharply in the chin. She pulls away from him, swearing, her mouth ajar.

"You fucker. I bit my tongue!"

Riley scoots closer to check on her bleeding mouth. He realizes he was on edge, defensive, and he doesn't want to admit to himself that he thought Nicole was moving in to attack.

"Sorry, but you've been doing nothing but threatening me in our conversations. You could have had a kitchen knife up your sleeve for all I know."

"I'm wearing a sleeveless top, fucker. I was trying to get friendly with you," she says, holding her tongue out of her mouth so her words are garbled. "Bad on me for trying."

He kisses her then, hard, unconcerned about the blood that flows from the bite on her tongue. She kisses back, their lips mashing together in crazy, wild need. Their tongues join in and he can taste the iron sweetness of her blood in his own mouth.

Nicole is in a pair of Capri pants and she struggles to unzip them and pull them down off her legs. Riley watches, pulling his shirt over his head before pulling her body towards him on the couch. She straddles his pelvis and grinds against his engorged penis. Her small breasts dance before his face and he arches up to lick at her nipples.

"You know," he says, "the first time we fucked around was on a couch."

She grabs his head and mashes his face into her chest before using her free hand to guide him home. She sighs when he enters her and throws her head back.

"No talking," she chides.

Then, she yells.

61   PEACH

Just so she can see what she's potentially up against, Peach drives by the address listed for Newt Parnwell. It's a part of town she rarely frequents, a section of Boise in the south of the valley, on the side of the interstate where the vast majority of Boiseans do not live. The road she travels down is pitted with potholes and the lines of paint delineating lanes have long since worn away.

The address itself turns out to be in a trailer park. Before Peach figures out which trailer in particular belongs to Newt, she parks down the main road and gets a ball cap out of her glove box with the embroidered phrase *I Heart Oregon* on the front. She puts it on, adopts a look of confusion on her face, and wanders into the park. The trailers create a promenade, their sides tilted in toward the next trailers in the row. It looks a bit like they bow at something unseen.

As she walks, she replays her story over in her head. She's looking for a particular subdivision in Boise, but she thinks she might have gotten turned around. Could someone point her in the right direction? But no one comes out of their doublewides to ask her what she's doing wandering around their small neighborhood.

She locates the man's house. His trailer is at the very back of the park and its siding is dilapidated and sloughing off. A *No Trespassing* sign hangs on the front door, orange font on a black background. All the windows are shaded with closed curtains made of orange burlap and wooden dowels. A chain link fence runs around the perimeter of the trailer's plot. Attached to the gate is a hand bell, brass and wood, the kind one of Peach's teachers would ring to call in kids from recess. It hangs from a piece of string looped around its wooden handle. Peach thinks it an odd doorbell, but it must get the job done.

Peach already feels uneasy about the situation. The trailer conveys a measure of coldness, isolation, and plucky self-reliance. She figures Newt Parnwell might be a very difficult mark. And she considers that she has one week, perhaps less to plot out her plan of attack. She ponders the option of killing him in his trailer. But the idea is immediately out of the question. It doesn't fit the requirements of a sacrificial site suitable for Air. That means she'd have to transport him or lure him somewhere else. One of the reasons the woman in the respiratory ward of the hospital is such an alluring and appropriate candidate for sacrifice is because of her location.

Because she's there, she decides to walk around the edge of the chain link, to see if any windows might be ajar or if there might be any good cover that could hide her body from sight. When she gets toward the back of the trailer, a massive Rottweiler lunges at her from behind the fence. She moves away, stunned, surprised she didn't hear him coming at her. She finds some relief when she sees his collar is linked to a chain bolted into the earth via a heavy length of piping.

Peach raises her hands over her head, a demonstration of her passiveness, but the large, black and tan beast continues to bark, saliva dripping from his sharp teeth.

"Nice dog," Peach says and takes a few steps farther back from the fence. She's aware the barking dog will surely draw attention to her poking around the park. She walks quickly down the main lane through the trailers, her chin tucked to her neck, the bill of her hat pulled down over her eyes. Not a soul steps out to question her or say hello, but she can feel eyes on her. How many pairs, she cannot say.

When she gets back to her car, she pauses to catch her breath. Newt Parnwell doesn't seem like the easiest of sacrificial options. She visualizes the woman in the hospital bed as she lays her forehead on her steering wheel. Peach prays to Pollux, to the agate in her pocket, to the other elements and entities who impact this time of Gemini.

"Please," she pleads. "Please, please make her die."

MONDAY, THE 15TH OF JUNE, 2015

62   RILEY

As he leaves the hospital, he flexes the muscles in his
toeless foot and enjoys the way his skin doesn't catch on stiff,
sharp stitches. They'd come out easily enough. It had taken a
nurse fifteen minutes to clean his foot and pull out the stitching.
She'd looked at his chart and laughed before letting him go,
sending him away with the warning not to play any soccer
anytime soon. He thinks of Sev Ross's head as an inflated ball
just begging to be kicked.

Riley considers going back inside the hospital and talking to
Soo Lim, to give her an actual warning about the danger she
could be in. But he decides he can't do it today. He'll do it
tomorrow. A day won't win the war. Today, he'll enjoy the way
his foot feels. It's nothing like it used to be, but with the fishing-
line-esque stitches out of his skin, he can now adapt to a new
sense of normal for his amputated stump.

He starts his car, thinks of Nicole and the way it felt to be
inside her again. When they'd finished, she refused to tell him

more about what had made her freak out and call him. He was beginning to think there had never been a scary occurrence. Perhaps she'd just wanted an excuse to get laid in order to de-stress a bit. Or despite all her protesting about Riley's aims, once she'd had coffee with him she gave in to the dance of pheromones which made him so attractive to her.

Riley knew he felt better after the sex. He'd only thought of Mayra twice while he was inside Nicole. He considered two thoughts to be better than an intense fixation. Nicole's face hadn't morphed into the rounder curve of Mayra's soft cheeks. Her hair hadn't shimmered like a shifting mirage from brown to black. For the most part, he had been with Nicole and that gave him hope he could soon detangle himself from his attachment to Mayra.

Instead of driving home, Riley decides to go through a drive-thru near St. Luke's and order a large boat of curly fries and two containers of fry sauce. He balances the salty treat on his lap and scrolls through the calendar on his phone with a greasy finger.

"It's the fifteenth," he says to himself. "Just a few more days, less than a week and if no one dies, my theory will be proven wrong. I can go back to just having a stalker that gives me gifts and might be terrorizing Boise with odd bombs and livestock. I think I can live with that. Until I can't and then I'll figure out how to make it stop."

He places a conjoined fry that looks like a spiral of DNA into his open mouth and squeezes a bit of the ketchup-mayonnaise mixture in after it. He watches people order hamburgers and shakes at the walk-up window. Cars pass through the drive-thru, shouting into the speaker near an outdoor menu for what their bellies desire.

Riley is envious of their lives. He knows most of them have shitty jobs or high-interest mortgages. Some of them might have cancer or cheating spouses. But he doubts any of them have a Hamal, an Aldebaran, or a Pollux.

He doubts any of them are taxed with keeping a potential murder victim alive. He looks back down at the calendar and shakes his head. But his whole body shakes along with him, pitching the basket of curly fries onto his gear shift. He doesn't react to the spill. His nerves are still addled even after the release that comes with recent coitus. Instead he counts the days over and over until the end of the Gemini cycle which ends right around the time of the summer solstice.

"I've never cared so much about the longest day of the year in my life," he says, picking out fries from his cup holder and placing them in his mouth.

TUESDAY, THE 16TH OF JUNE, 2015

63 PEACH

Before Peach leaves for work, she packs up her dark green duffel bag. She places it in the trunk of her Honda and covers it with a wool blanket she keeps in the back for picnics or emergencies. She's undecided on whether or not she'll use it today. Part of her wants to be more proactive, to go out to Newt Parnwell's trailer, wait for him to get home from work and attack. But only injure him enough so he's incapacitated. Only enough so he'll survive being moved somewhere more amiable and sufficient for sacrificial rites to Gemini.

There are no weapons in her duffel. Instead Peach plans on using knives found within the trailer. She's not picky about it. For this cycle, there is no particular weapon she needs to use in her ritual. She'll make do with a paring knife, a chef's blade or a long, thin serrated piece of metal meant for cutting ripe, red tomatoes. She has no doubt there will be some sort of knife in the trailer. All she really needs is one. And if a knife is not to be readily had, she will use another weapon. This entire step, this jumping for Newt Parnwell, is an exercise in flexibility.

Nor does she have anything to use in order to knock the man out or smother him to a point of unconsciousness. She figures these things will also be on site: the base of a lamp or a heavy ashtray, an arm cushion plucked off a sofa, a plastic bag with a warning to keep away from children printed in white on its clear body.

It's the dog that truly stymies her. Peach needs to get around the animal somehow, but she's not about to kill it to get at Newt. Hinder it in some way, even wound it, yes. Humans, at least the ones she needs for her sacrifices, are different. But Peach has a kinship with animals. She believes them to be pure in their instincts and actions. She looks up to them. The Rottweiler will need to be dealt with, but she's adamant the dog will not die.

Her mind is a mess of ideas, "what ifs" and potentialities as she places her work satchel full of client case notes on the passenger side seat of her car. She tells herself to focus, to be calm. Peach puts her hands on her chest and feels the way her torso lifts when it takes in air and compresses with each exhalation. She thinks of her lungs, how they're ruled by Gemini. She thinks of all the parts of the body that are ruled by Gemini. The lungs aren't the only part of the human form dominated by the twins.

"Arms, fingers, collarbone and nerves. Arms, fingers, collarbone and nerves," she chants the names out loud. She repeats them again and again, setting them to a jaunty tune. It's reminiscent of "head, shoulders, knees and toes," a verse of a childhood song she would sing in class, all the pupils alighting the tips of their fingers on the appropriate body part mentioned in the ditty.

She tries this out now. She brushes her arms, clasps one hand to the other for fingers, runs her index finger on the sharp ridge of her collarbone. For her nerves, there is no need to seek them out. She feels them everywhere.

She's glad of this. And emboldened by her song and gestures. A knife would work best once he's driven to an allowable and sanctified site. The many parts of Gemini, outside of the lungs, they give her options. Choices on how she might go about sacrificing Mr. Newt Parnwell.

64   RILEY

He's back at St. Luke's, fulfilling the promise he made to himself the day before. Whether he wants to or not, he must speak with Soo Lim and cover all his bases. He owes it to the girl who made him macaroni and cheese and let him stay up late to watch Jay Leno when his parents were out at cocktail parties that ran past three am.

Riley stands in the foyer of the hospital. There are giant planters with tropical foliage of white and chartreuse leaves. Miniature waterfalls and pools scattered around the staircase that leads to an information desk lend a soothing sound of rushing water to the space. A coffee shop and a florist shop no bigger than a walk-in closet provide opportunities to snatch a gift. Outside the florist is a handcart, painted white, with stuffed bears sitting on its frame, shiny balloons tied to its handles.

Last time he came to see Soo Lim, he forgot a gift. He decides this time he'll go up prepared. He slowly climbs the short staircase that leads to the flower shop and gift cart, his eyes on a particularly fuzzy looking stuffed animal. An elderly woman with an apron in red and white pinstripes —a throwback to the old candy striper uniforms young women used to wear around the hospital—smiles at him and asks if he needs any help. He tells her no; he says he's just picking up a gift for a woman he wants to save from a homicidal maniac.

When he gets the electric yellow teddy bear in his hands, he runs his fingers over the black eyes and threaded mouth of the toy. He wonders if the gift is too juvenile; perhaps he should take her up some flowers. The lady purses her lips and folds her arms. Maybe she thinks of his flippant remark about murder and weighs her responsibility in the matter.

"What do you mean, a homicidal maniac?"

"I thought the term was cliché enough for there to be no confusion."

She frowns and he decides to backpedal.

"It's an in-joke. Don't worry. 'Homicidal Maniac' is a code name for her brother-in-law who talks incessantly and aims for squirrels when he drives. A real winner."

That's when he feels a hand on his shoulder.

Still clutching the bear, he turns to see Nicole Trey. She seems to wilt while standing in front of him. Her fingers have a steely grip around her phone, tears coursing their way down the frown lines around her mouth.

Riley puts the bear down on the cart and opens his arms. Nicole hesitates for a moment before stepping into his embrace. Her shoulders collapse against his and sobs erupt out of her parted lips. The elderly woman gives Riley a pitying look and reorients the bear he'd handled, placing it just so, fluffing up its fur. After a minute of intense crying, Riley attempts to guide Nicole toward a padded bench near one of the heavily-foliaged planters. But when he tries to direct her, she resists, shakes her head, and looks into Riley's eyes.

"What are you doing here?" she asks but she doesn't wait for him to answer. Instead, he can see her mind working by the way her eyes dance. She grabs Riley's arms with her hands, mashing her phone into his left bicep.

"Will you come with me? I just got a horrible call. And I'm scared. Please, you're already here. I don't need to you to do anything else but be with me."

He doesn't know what to think so he goes with what he feels. He nods at the elevators to the patient wings of the hospital. Nicole releases his arms and takes one of his hands in hers, pulling him in that direction. The touch of her skin is arousing to Riley, but he shakes away the desire. Only then does he realize that when they had sex, he never took off his shoes. Nicole doesn't know about his missing toes. This odd realization sticks in his mind. Would he be thought of as odd for keeping on his casual loafers during sex? Will his lack of toes be off-putting to future conquests, perhaps even Mayra?

At the elevators Nicole presses the call button with her thumb seven times. Riley gets his mind in order. This isn't the time to be concerned over the relationship of shoes, a toeless foot, and getting laid. He watches her bite her lip and she lets go of his hand, apparently secure in the belief that he won't desert her now.

"Do you want to tell me what's going on? Does this have to do with what spooked you the other day?" he asks.

"You'll see in a minute," she answers. Then the tears start again. "You'll see her soon."

And the word *soon* reminds him of the name Soo. Yesterday, he had made the cocky assumption he could focus on his own physical heartiness for a day and she wouldn't be in any danger.

He reaches over and presses the elevator button three more times. With each depression, the red light behind the little square button flickers. It's as if it acknowledges his need, but does not deliver. His toeless foot begins to throb, the pulsation beating out a simple and direct admonishment: *stupid Riley, stupid Riley, stupid Riley.*

65   PEACH

Instead of taking a lunch break, Peach gets a Coke from a
vending machine in the foyer of her office building. Aside from
the counseling agency, the other suites contain a Reiki
practitioner, a CPA, and a non-profit organization aiding blind
adults. Rooms on the floors above are rented by entrepreneurs
and the self-employed. Some sit empty, inhabited by spiders and
dust. She pops the tab on the canned soft drink and passes
Camille on her way out the door.

"Hey," Camille says. "I'm going to get some teriyaki
chicken. It's holding a sit-in in my mind. If I don't placate it, it'll
protest during the rest of my day. You want to come?"

Peach looks down at her Coke and her stomach gurgles. The
antsy uncertainty over what she should do about Newt Parnwell
has her feeling queasy and absent an appetite.

"No thanks, but I'll walk you out to your car," Peach says
and falls in next to Camille. She pushes the door open for her

coworker and Camille frowns at Peach, all too cognizant of her friend's level of stress.

"You know you have a tell, don't you?" Camille says as they walk slowly through the parking lot.

"No. What do you mean?"

"When you're significantly stressed or upset by something, you drink something with sugar in it. No food for you. Just liquid. And you drink it like it's the last sip of anything you'll ever have. Like you're going to the grave as soon as you polish off the can."

Peach keeps her Coke lowered to her side, decides not to bring it up to drink again in front of Camille. If her co-worker easily attaches meaning to this habit, what else is she astute enough to see?

Instead of worrying about Camille picking up on some of Peach's less desirable qualities, she decides to test out a theory that's been percolating over the past weeks. As someone who deals deftly with more clients than Peach and has worked with special needs patients for years, Peach trusts her keen ability to perceive. Camille is the type of woman who revels in helping "borderlines," some of the most direly afflicted personality disorder patients imaginable. Peach decides if anyone besides herself could put some stock in her wild idea, it would be Camille.

"Before you head out, can I ask you something?" Peach starts, the Coke still pressed against her hip.

"I've got a client in forty-five minutes and the rice bowl is calling. You sure you don't want to just come with?"

"No, but this will take just a minute," Peach takes a gulp of air and exhales slowly. "Do you think people transfer energy from one person to another?"

Camille doesn't pause to consider her answer. "Of course. That's interaction, communication, relationship. You name it, it's energy exchange."

"Right," Peach smiles, "that's what I think, too. Now, with that in mind, do you think it's possible for people to transfer, not exactly powers, but perhaps traits, or talents to one another?"

Camille and Peach end their stroll next to the bumper of Camille's midsize, American sedan. "You don't mean like teaching, do you?" Then Camille laughs. "Wow, I just got a funny visual. Are you old enough to remember the show that came on in the late eighties or early nineties called *Highlander*? There were movies, too. What was the catch-phrase...yes, 'there can be only one'."

Peach knows what her co-worker is talking about. But she's not speaking of decapitation, or leading her into a cloaked conversation about her sacrifices. Peach remembers the few episodes she's seen. After a head was sliced from a body, all the elements seemed to converge, and imbue the Highlander with strength and immortality.

If only she could swing a sword once and get back what was taken from her. But she has chosen a plodding, patient path. Though she starves, she doesn't sprint for the loaf of bread. Instead, she picks up every single crumb she finds while moving toward her ultimate goal.

"Think more along the lines of superheroes. Like maybe if one dies, another one gains one of the dead superhero's powers. That sort of thing."

"I think," Camille says, "there are no such things as superheroes and direct power transfers and stealing another's talents or traits. I believe in simple things, like chicken teriyaki and long lunches."

Peach smirks at Camille and waves her away. "I completely understand. Get out of here and enjoy your food."

Camille hits the key fob for her car, unlocking it, before looking back at Peach.

"Do you think you've taken someone's power? Are you the Highlander? Should I be concerned that there can only be one?" She laughs again and winks at Peach.

Peach turns and walks away, desperate to get the Coke can back up to her lips. But she refuses to let Camille see her display of unease. Instead, she lifts her empty hand up to her face and slices at the air, downward, diagonally, her approximation of a cutting great sword. She can hear Camille's laugh grow louder until she shuts her car door and lights up the ignition.

66 RILEY

Riley's chest tightens when he and Nicole step out of the elevator at St. Luke's Hospital. They're on the same floor, in the same ward his old babysitter Soo Lim is on, the same place he came to visit her weeks before. There is a slight spinning of his perception and then the vertigo kicks in completely. His breathing becomes shallow and he drags his feet and anchors them. Nicole clings to his arm, looking at him with her bottom lip still clamped tightly with her front teeth.

"What's wrong?" she asks. "Shouldn't I be the one having a breakdown?"

He leans over and places his forearms on his thighs and does his best to regulate his lungs. He focuses on the doorknob on a janitorial closet ahead of him. It helps calm the rocking and spinning of his vision. Riley tells himself he can't afford to fall apart now. Even if he did miscalculate, even if he should have warned her, he didn't. Now all he can do is accept the consequences and bear witness to Soo Lim's pain, or perhaps, death.

Standing up, he keeps his eyes on the doorknob until his dizziness settles. He allows Nicole to lead him down the same hallway he traversed the only time he came to the hospital with the intent to talk with Soo Lim. As fast as the tease of a panic attack hits Riley, it dissipates and a sense of calm and acceptance pervades his mind and body. At least, Riley thinks, he was right in his theory. And if he couldn't save Soo Lim, he now understands the basics of the game. The next cycle will be different. The cycle of Cancer will present another chance for him to get the upper hand before anyone else dies. This stalker will not get the better of him. He will come out on top. No other outcome is acceptable.

But then, there is the death of Soo Lim here, now.

As they walk toward one of the pods of hospital rooms, nurses and a solitary doctor in a long, white surgical coat mill about the area. Riley looks at Nicole's face. Her lower lip is bleeding from her continual gnawing on it. Her tears build up, making her eyes look like they are coated in a glassy sheen before the water falls down her cheekbones and chin.

"I didn't know you two were friends," Riley says, referring to Nicole and Soo Lim.

Nicole pulls him into the room full of other nurses and beeping monitors. The shades on the window are drawn and the overhead lights are turned up, creating an aura of falsified sun that permeates the room.

It's then that Riley takes a look around and realizes he's not in the same room Soo Lim convalesced in before. He looks to the hospital bed and notes the woman in it is not his old babysitter. Instead, it is another young woman with brunette hair.

And this woman looks identical to Nicole Trey.

Nicole clings to Riley and he looks from the bed to the woman pinching the skin of his arms. A nurse approaches them.

"If you're family and on the list, you stay. If not, you need to get out. Now."

"Am I family? Am *I*?" Nicole asks, her voice shrill. "Take a look at my fucking face, lady. Then ask me the question again. Go right ahead."

Other nurses and an orderly weave around the couple. The bold nurse disappears. They stand frozen together, gaping at the woman in the bed for entirely different reasons. Riley realizes he's staring at Nicole's identical twin, but he doesn't know what to say in encouragement. Nicole finally releases her clutch on Riley's arm and goes to her sister.

"Nicole," Nicole says to her sister.

Riley knows he's heard her correctly. Nicole calls her bedridden sister by her own name. He pushes away the confusion, knows he can ask what's going on later. For now, he stands perfectly still, as if his motion, his very breathing, has caused all this chaos and calamity. Perhaps in some way, it has.

At the sound of Nicole's voice, the woman in the bed opens her eyes. Thin gaps, slivers of dark nestle between her eyelids. Nicole, at least the one who Riley knows, puts her face close to her sister's puffy cheeks. Riley can see, even through the pallor and illness of the bedridden twin, that they are not just identical twins. They are uncannily similar, nearly perfect reflections of one another. Except one is healthy and one is very ill.

Nicole is whispering something to her sister and the sister in the bed whispers something back. Then, the eyes of the bedridden Nicole become visible. Riley notes how they roll about, unable to focus on much in the room. Until, that is, they land on Riley.

The woman lets out a weak wail as if she is a colicky infant low on energy. It builds in strength and volume until it becomes a proper scream, her mouth pulling back violently, her teeth bared. She begins to choke and as she does so, she nods towards Riley. There is foam at her mouth and her body begins to shake so hard that the bed, its wheels locked into place, inches towards Riley across the smooth, laminate floor.

One of the nurses sneers at Riley. The doctor rushes back into the room, flying past Riley who is still anchored to his chosen spot. Nicole looks at Riley and her eyes widen, too. Then she buries her face in her sister's hair, a ratty halo around the crown of her skull. Riley feels a warm, large palm pressed against his upper back.

He turns to find a man six inches taller than him, dressed in a hospital security uniform. He looks down on Riley.

"Get the hell out," is all the man says and this is enough to get Riley moving.

67   PEACH

By two o'clock in the afternoon, Peach is done with her
sessions for the day. She tucks her paperwork into a drawer in
her work desk and stares at the empty Coke can in her garbage.
She plucks it out and sets it on her desktop, reminding herself
that she should recycle. Peach doesn't believe in things going to
waste. This extends to missing opportunities.

So.

So Newt Parnwell will have to die.

She doesn't say goodbye to Camille before leaving the
office, figuring the woman might already be concerned about her.
She doesn't want to give Camille an opening in which Peach
might be nabbed and sat down for a talk or a lecture. Peach has
little time to do what needs to be done. The why of it and her
friend's perceptions of energy, sanity and right and wrong can
wait until another day.

The drive to the trailer park takes a half hour from Peach's
office building. This time, she parks a half-mile down the road

287

so her car won't be visible to any residents on the premises. She wonders how she'll get Newt Parnwell in her Honda, but she doesn't worry about that now. She figures if she incapacitates him well and soundly, she'll have time to figure out a way to smuggle him out of his trailer.

While Peach doesn't have a plan, she does have faith. Not just in the stars, or the elements or the signs. She has faith in Perfect Peach, the one she's becoming: her future. Perfect Peach will accept nothing but success. And the Peach who sits in her parked car, anxiously weighing options and exits and ideas, is still terrified of letting her down. It's the same resolve which led her to moving ahead in the time of Aries. And it's here, now, pushing her forward into an unknown, risky situation.

But it is enough. It is enough to force her out of the car and to her hatchback trunk. It is enough for her to take up her dark green duffel bag and start the walk toward the trailer park.

She spies a small hawk perched on a tar-stained telephone pole. Unlike the ones she saw on her way out to the desert for her stone and her metal, this one does not peel off feathers and flesh. It clutches the top of the wood with its small talons and regards Peach with a transfixing gaze. She meets its stare for a moment, hopes she can harness even a fraction of that hunter's keen skill to kill. It parts its beak slightly and aspirates with its tongue sliding forward and back before it lifts into the air and becomes a dark mote against a cluster of clouds. Their billowiness reminds her of the creamy crown of an ice cream sundae.

She tries to stay present as she walks, but her mind tugs her about. She thinks of having talons capable of ripping sinew into translucent tatters. She wonders if the hawk ever has a thought for its defenseless meal. Does it know what its prey feels in the moments leading to death? Can it taste the terror and desire for escape in the rich swallows of blood and flesh?

Peach thinks of that singular moment of passing through the veil, of stepping from the messiness of living into the transformative awesomeness of death. She will surely experience it, just as all must. Just not today, she decides.

Instead, another will face the ephemeral leap. From everything she's ever read, from everything she's ever been told, the transition is not done alone. Visions flank the soul on its journey. This is the moment when those still trapped in earthly bodies become the specters. This is the moment when ancestors may come to usher one home or darker, dangerous shadows materialize to beckon one onward, downward.

68   RILEY

He paces the hall outside Nicole's sister's room for fifteen minutes, waiting for some news of what's happening inside. Eventually he gets fed up with the back and forth of his feet and he wanders away from the mess of hospital staff to find Soo Lim's room. He locates the correct cluster of rooms, checks the number on the plaque against a note he'd made on his phone and faces a closed door. He asks a female nurse filling small, plastic cups with a red liquid if Soo Lim is doing all right.

"She's gone," the nurse replies.

His chest constricts. A metal cart laden with spent food trays sways in Riley's peripheral vision. He blinks hard, touches his stomach.

"She was released last week. No indication of pneumonia so we sent her home. She had a great smile when she learned she was getting out of the hospital. Such a nice woman. If all our patients could be a Soo Lim."

Water wells in his eyes and he's quick to wipe it away before he could be mistaken for crying. The touch of dizziness dissipates.

"So she's okay? She's fine, my Soo Lim?"

"I don't know about *yours*, Casanova. I think another man came and took her home."

Riley walks back to the room housing Nicole and her sister. He knows there are more days left in the Gemini cycle, and that his theory isn't completely vetted yet. As happy as he is that Soo Lim is fine, he doesn't consider her out of danger. He doesn't think any of the five Geminis on his list are free from potential harm. Not yet.

Then he thinks he might have another Gemini on his list. Nicole's sister, even if their link is only via Nicole. Such a tenuous connection shouldn't make his pared down list, but he's willing to make an exception.

Before he can formulate the questions he wants answered, about why Nicole's sister is in the hospital, and what is wrong with her, Nicole, the healthy, angry Nicole, bursts into the hallway and marches straight to Riley. Her face is mess of smeared makeup and her lip still bleeds.

"We hadn't been good to one another. We'd been so cruel. Do you know we didn't celebrate our birthday together last year? And this year we didn't, either? Even with her in the hospital, I didn't come. I could have brought her a damn cupcake or a card. But I went out with my friends and got plastered instead."

"Nicole," Riley says. "Nicole, you can't blame yourself for living."

"Nicole," Nicole repeats. "Do you know what it's like to hear your name used against you your whole childhood?"

She smirks and wipes at the tears on her face. A run of black mascara drips from her lower lid like a pen illustration of icicles.

"My parents thought they were so cute. They named me Nicole Beth Trey. And they named her Beth Nicole Trey. And do you know what they would tell us when we fought? They would say that we were the same, separate physically, but together, forever. And when we hated one another, when we fought or were spiteful, we had to remember we shared the same face and the same genes. We had to stop our fighting and remember we had the same name. Different, but the same."

"Different, but the same," Nicole repeats and then cradles her head in her arms.

She folds into herself, until she's crouching on the ground, her forearms pressed over her ears. Riley doesn't know what to do, so he stands over her, witnessing her suffering. After a minute, she looks up at him, snot escaping her nose.

"We even had a twin language. It's not a mythical thing. It's real. And it was ours alone. It was born with us, there since we floated around in the same amniotic sack."

Then Nicole looks back down at the ground and mumbles something through her wailing. Nurses pass by her, the door of her sister's room now open. And Riley looks. He can see the lights have been dimmed and he knows then for certain Beth Nicole Trey has passed away.

He crouches down next to Nicole and takes her arms away from her head. He holds her hands in his because if she were Mayra or his mother, that is what he would do. She continues to mumble so he puts his face closer to hers, so he can make out what she's saying.

She explodes then, her voice piercing and raw so close to his ears. She raises her face to the ceiling of the hospital hallway and vocalizes her commandment. Nicole speaks to someone on high, but Riley can't be sure if it's God, angels, or her own haze of anger hovering over her bent form like a menacing swarm of flies.

"She wasn't that sick. She wasn't supposed to die. I want

tests. I want an autopsy. My sister was killed. I swear it. My Nicole was murdered."

69   PEACH

The dog isn't in the gated yard outside Newt Parnwell's trailer. Peach approaches the area from a hedge of tall, ratty cypress trees running along the perimeter of the park. She brushes dry, sharp needles from her yellow shirt and stops to assess the situation.

She whistles and the dog does not appear. So she walks around the gate, keeping quiet as she approaches the area where she'd encountered the giant Rottweiler. But she finds no metal pipe in the ground, no length of chain, and no canine in sight.

Peach can't decide if this is a good thing, or a bad thing. Perhaps the man has taken the dog somewhere for the day. Or perhaps the dog is inside the trailer. Maybe Newt Parnwell is inside the trailer with his guard dog. Maybe they stand watch together, camaraderie in their defensive vigil. Maybe. Her head spins with this maybe and several other variations of maybes.

This is a complication that gives Peach enough cause to stop, close her eyes, and think.

She hears a sound somewhere behind her: a rattle and a sliding of glass. Peach turns to find a face staring at her from a window in the next trailer over. It's the face of a young girl, no more than nine or ten. There is a red stain on the skin around her mouth, likely from a huge, cherry lollipop or too much fruit punch. Her face is pressed against a torn screen that keeps the elements and Peach from getting to her.

"What you doing?" the girl asks.

Peach smiles and steps toward the trailer, but the girl holds up a bright orange water pistol to the screen and closes one eye.

"I'm a good shot," the child says and Peach stays where she is. Now that she's been seen, she can't bring herself to deal with Newt Parnwell. Not today. With the missing dog and now the child, she gets the feeling the fates are not with her.

"I'm sure you are," Peach replies. "Aren't you supposed to be in school?"

"Yep," the girl says and squirts a tiny stream of water from the gun into her mouth. "But I'm on guard right now. Newty's orders."

Peach takes a cautious shuffle forward, so she can be certain she hasn't misheard the girl.

"What did you say, about Newt?" Peach presses.

"I'm on guard. Told me to watch his house. And I take my job serious, lady."

"Sure you do," Peach says.

She's about to ask the girl why Newt Parnwell knew he needed a sentry posted on his trailer while he's absent. But she doesn't get a chance.

Peach's body goes stiff and the hairs on her skin prickle upward. A flow of energy hits her pelvic center, making her core pulsate with a new sense of power and life. And seconds later, it's gone, leaving her limbs feeling wobbly and weak.

"You feel sick?" the girl asks, her mouth pressed up against the screen.

The sensation accompanying the energy transfer is markedly different than what Peach felt when she killed Roman and Lars. She's certain the woman in the hospital is dead and likely due to her work, since she obtained some energetic charge from her passing. But she also knows something is not quite right. What she expected to get from the woman should have been substantial, greater in impact. She was expecting a deluge of energy, not a just a few drops. A walloping that would have brought Peach to her knees.

Though she can't see her friend Pollux, she looks to the sky and takes direction that comes to her: get to the hospital.

She turns away from the girl and heads toward the row of cypress trees. Peach can feel a weak spurt of warm water hit her square on the back. It soaks into her shirt the color of sunshine, right onto the skin covering her lungs.

70   RILEY

Because Nicole insists he wait for her, Riley stays put on a hard, wooden bench outside the hospital administration office. There is a rattle in his chest each time he inhales. His shirt feels constrictive, as if it morphed into a corset. He tugs at his collar and counts his inhales up to five before exhaling with the same, paced intention. A cough or three and his chest finally relaxes.

He can hear clearly what Nicole is shouting at a hospital representative. Her voice carries through the sterile, non-descript wing of the hospital. She tells them to run tests. She tells them to open up her twin sister and look at her insides. She swears it will all be paid for, out of pocket, at her wealthy family's expense.

When she pushes open the door ten minutes later, her face is no longer a mask of grief. Instead, she's huffing loudly and pulling her hair away from her scalp, wadding it into a tight bun, before letting it all fall through her fingers.

"They keep telling me it was the throat cancer. But I know it wasn't. She's been acting odd for weeks now. Symptoms and mutterings, things that can't be explained by the cancer. All the doctors said they caught it in time. It had been inching into her lungs, but they stopped its advance. She was stage two, cruising to remission. How could she have been on the mend and now, gone?"

Nicole looks to the elevator and wordlessly moves toward it.

Riley follows and presses the button. They ride in silence back down to the foyer. The sound of running water and the smell of the plants mask the din of anxious visitors and the scent of cleaning solvents. She walks ahead of him and Riley wonders if she's done with him, wants him to leave. After all, as they both admit, they aren't friends. Together, they are good at sex and destroying the feelings of others. It isn't a union in which there can be any sort of pride.

Yet he follows her outside anyway, to a wide, concrete sidewalk where the street runs into an underground parking structure next to the emergency room. Nicole stops short of walking her thighs into a trashcan and turns her anger and confusion on Riley.

"Do you know what she said to me? Right after she saw you and the security guard made you leave the room? She said that you looked like the demon. Something about your eyes but I couldn't understand the rest of it."

He runs his fingers over his head and down his neck. The weariness is seeping into his muscles: the weeks of living on edge, the confusion over strange occurrences, the bizarre letters. Riley's body is finally telling him it needs a break. If the panic attacks are his body's attempt to get Riley to take it easy, he knows now that if he doesn't take care of himself, he's liable to crack. And now, to add to his misery, he's being called a demon.

"That I look like a demon?" Riley mutters, the annoyance clear in his voice. "Nicole, sometimes people see things that aren't there. Before, you know. They go."

"No," Nicole shouts. "Not *a* demon, *the* demon."

"I'm at a loss," he says. "I don't know what that means."

"I don't either, Riley. But my sister was tough. She was a fighter, literally. State champion boxer, a quick featherweight in high school. She owned her own Krav Maga studio. And she smoked two packs of cigarettes a day. Iron fucking strong."

"So tell me why," Nicole gets in Riley's face. He watches as her screaming causes a blood vessel to pop in the white of her eye. A line of red snakes towards her iris, like the feeler of a climbing vine. "Tell me why she was terrified of you! Fuck what they say about the cancer, my sister was meant to be immortal. And you made her scream like she was broken."

Riley can't stand the verbal accosting. His first thought is to lash out at her, push her away, but he decides to move his body backward a step and play at being a gentlemen. When he does, he steps awkwardly on his left foot, causing him to kick up his calf in pain and shock.

"What the hell is wrong with you?" she pushes, stepping to close the distance between them.

He yells back, the pain in his foot firing his attack.

"She was dying! She was probably seeing all sorts of shit on her deathbed. You're mad your twin sister is dead. I get it. But I'm not going to accept the blame for her death. I have enough guilt and worry balanced square on my shoulders. You're reeling after what just happened. Going off the rails even. But don't vilify me, Nicole."

Riley waits for Nicole to fire back. She rubs her eye where the blood vessel burst. Instead of going on the offense, she takes measured breaths. While she does, Riley puts his foot back down on the concrete and is satisfied when the stabbing pain he felt at the misstep doesn't flare up again.

He lowers his voice, adopts a calm tone and touches Nicole on the shoulder.

"Listen. I have a theory, about what might have happened to your sister. If it wasn't the cancer, I mean. Please, just let me talk to you about it. Let's sit down somewhere, away from here, and I'll tell you what I think."

Nicole brushes his touch off with a shrug of her shoulders. "I have family to call. Besides, I remember now why I never wanted to talk to you. Still don't."

Riley licks his lips and shakes his head. "Why is that?"

"Because even though you fuck well, the conversation is always about you. And really Riley, I can't stand to listen to countless reasons why your shit is golden while my sister takes her last elevator ride to the basement of the hospital."

Before he can think, he speaks.

"You're a bitch, Nicole."

"Yeah," she responds, still glaring into his face. "Well, maybe the good twin died."

71   PEACH

With her moist back pressed up against her seat, Peach speeds toward downtown Boise. With the interstate Connector, she makes the trip in good time and pulls into the underground parking structure outside the main tower of St. Luke's.

She locks her car and forces herself to walk slowly up the stairs leading from the dank, concrete underground to the sun of a Tuesday, June afternoon. She doesn't know what she'll say once she's up in the respiratory ward. She'll have to ask someone about the woman and whether or not she is dead. She will be tasked with coming up with a deft way of finding out if they know whether it was the illness that quashed her life or if it was something else. She thinks of the glass jar she has at home, residing in a gift bag with the mini torch and the respirator. Muddy brown granules remain in the container: unprocessed and unpolished bits of gold.

Once she's back above ground, she dodges a car zipping under the portico over the automatic doors opening into the ER.

She watches as a man in his sixties puts the car in park, gets out and dashes to the back door of the vehicle. He flings it open and scoops up a child; he's a small, frail-limbed boy. The boy's eyes are shut, but Peach notices he's not in an unconscious state. He squeezes his eyelids together so tightly, Peach can almost make out the lines around his eyes on his young, flawless skin. It's not a sign of sleep or loss of mind. It's a sign of pain.

And then there is Riley.

Peach sees him, standing outside the main door of the hospital's giant foyer, shouting in the face of a brunette woman. Peach is completely exposed on the expansive sidewalk surrounding the hospital. Instead of running and calling attention to herself while she tries to find somewhere to duck or hide, she stays where she is. She watches. And when the woman turns her face in Peach's direction, Peach gasps.

It's the face of the woman Peach has worked so diligently to kill. And the energy that flowed into Peach, all the way from the respiratory ward of this place to her location, in a trailer park on the outskirts of Boise proper, should have belonged to this woman. It should have been akin to warm blood caught in a sacramental chalice, offered up to Peach upon the woman's death. The energy was the direct reward for a sacrifice done well. But what Peach got wasn't the energy of Nicole Trey.

It must have been the energy of her twin.

Peach curses herself for being so stupid, for not knowing her intended sacrifice was a twin. And judging from the way Riley yells at the woman yards away from Peach, this twin was the one she was gunning for. She thinks back to her research and can immediately see the flaws in her work. But she'd been so insistent on an easier kill, she didn't make certain the hospitalized woman was her intended offering.

If only she'd killed the former babysitter instead.

Peach stands in the sun, the heat of it bouncing up from the concrete and cooking her skin. She wonders why, how the names of two twins could be so close. She feels like she's been set up, somehow, someway. Though she killed the wrong twin, she wonders if it's enough of an impact on Riley. Though the incoming energy was weaker, more dilute in power, she got something all the same. She just hopes it's enough to allow her to take what she needs, in the end. For now, she won't question why she got any energy at all. The masters of Gemini must be pleased enough. Perhaps they have machinations set in motion Peach can't fathom. She must trust and stand resolutely at the helm.

The shouting between Riley and Nicole comes to an end. The woman, her intended mark, walks away quickly, her hands at her sides, her face angled to the ground. Riley stays where he is and rubs his head and his eyes.

Peach watches him, watches his pain and considers the fouled, but finished sacrifice might be good enough. When he pulls his hands away from his eyes, he looks around the area and his gaze falls on Peach.

Exposed, present, all she can do is smile at him.

And she smiles bigger, until the corners of her mouth feel like they will split. It's a grin for a rendezvous with a friend assumed lost, the first day of sun after an arctic winter, the feel of silk on the skin, chocolate on the tongue, of a lover's ardor, warm and hard, between her legs.

For Riley stares straight through her, and knows her not at all.

Secret Chapters

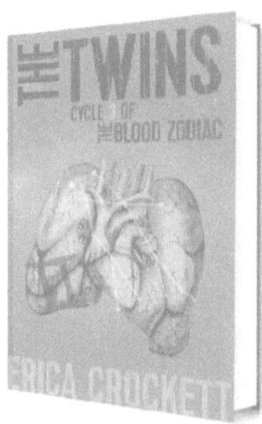

There are more than two
sides to the story!

Get exclusive chapters
from the perspectives of
other characters in
Series!

ACKNOWLEDGMENTS

To the humans who have always looked to the stars and seen stories written there, I am proud to carry on your work and share your myths. To my family, friends and support team that cheered me on and worked with me to bring the third book in *The Blood Zodiac* series to life, I cannot thank you all enough. And lastly, but in no way least, I am indebted to my guides. Another one bites the dust. Literally *and* metaphorically.

THE BLOOD ZODIAC CONTINUES...

BECAUSE

HIDE & SEEK

IS A LETHAL GAME.

Cycle 4: THE CRAB

THE CRAB: CYCLE 4 OF *THE BLOOD ZODIAC*

AVAILABLE SOON!

www.ingramcontent.com/pod-product-compliance
Lightning Source LLC
Chambersburg PA
CBHW020406260626
47156CB00007B/2259